Alex stretched out on the ground with his head against his saddle. Who was his companion?

The attractive musical voice was not that of a servant. Unless his companion was a legal offspring of Sir James! A daughter who resented her stepmother and had raised the lady's wrath by saying her father had been murdered. When threatened, the slightly crazed Mistress Appleby had fled and headed for Lathom House, only to encounter himself on the way.

It was now that Alex's imagination stalled. His young companion had not behaved as if crazed, but that was women for you. Illogical. They were too often ruled by their emotions.

For one in fear of her life, who did not trust him, he reckoned she showed a foolish faith in her disguise. Alex made up his mind that for now he would play her game. But sooner or later he was going to have to inform her about what was needful to impersonate a man…

June Francis's interest in old wives' tales and folk customs led her into a writing career. History has always fascinated her, and her first five novels were set in Medieval times. She has also written fourteen sagas based in Liverpool and Chester. Married with three grown-up sons, she lives on Merseyside. On a clear day she can see the sea and the distant Welsh hills from her house. She enjoys swimming, fell-walking, music, lunching with friends and smoochie dancing with her husband. More information about June can be found at her website: www.junefrancis.co.uk

Previous novels by this author:

ROWAN'S REVENGE
TAMED BY THE BARBARIAN
REBEL LADY, CONVENIENT WIFE

HIS RUNAWAY MAIDEN

June Francis

First published in Great Britain 2009
Large Print edition 2010
Harlequin Mills & Boon Limited,
Eton House, 18-24 Paradise Road, Richmond, Surrey TW9 1SR

© June Francis 2009

ISBN: 978 0 263 21141 2

Harlequin Mills & Boon policy is to use papers that are natural,
renewable and recyclable products and made from wood grown in
sustainable forests. The logging and manufacturing process conform
to the legal environmental regulations of the country of origin.

Printed and bound in Great Britain
by CPI Antony Rowe, Chippenham, Wiltshire

HIS RUNAWAY MAIDEN

Prologue

January 1502

Alex steadied his restless horse with a firm hand but, just like his steed, he was impatient to be on his way.

'You understand what I want you to do?' growled the Earl of Douglas.

'Aye,' said Alex, meeting the Scotsman's gaze. 'You want me to act as your spy.'

'I'm led to believe that you have a particular talent for gathering information and you will be well rewarded for your troubles. I had a particular fondness for your mother and propose to give you the house and land that she loved in recognition of you as my son.'

Alex thanked him in a dry voice, thinking that a house on the east coast of Scotland, close to the border with England, could prove useful, but such 'recognition' from his natural father was a little late in arriving. But the journey had not been a waste of time—the earl had provided him with information about the McDonalds that had shed a light on a matter that had vexed him during his investigations in London six months ago.

'You have memorised the password?' asked the earl.

'Aye. I'm not a fool.'

'Nay, you just showed a bad lack of judgement in the woman you chose to lavish your attentions on,' growled the earl. 'You're not the first man to do so, and neither will you be the last.'

Alex's jaw clenched and he wished his beloved grandmother had not been so frank in her missive to the earl about Ingrid. His romantic attachments were certainly none of his father's business and, looking at the man before him, he wondered what it was that had attracted his own mother to him. However, it had been his grandmother's dying wish that he make himself known to his father. Perhaps to make amends for the falsehood she had told him as a small boy, something that he had believed to be true until the day she died.

'Well?' demanded the earl.

'I am to make myself known to the elderly Lady Elizabeth Stanley and she will see to it that I am enlisted in her troupe of performers for the proxy wedding of the Princess Margaret to your King James of Scotland at Richmond Palace. You trust this woman?' There was a touch of irony in Alex's voice.

The earl frowned. 'She is kin by marriage to the wife of one of my allies, and both are related to King Henry's stepfather, the Earl of Derby.'

'Aye, so you have already said, but even those closest to us can prove false,' said Alex.

'According to your grandmother, she was also a highly regarded customer of your grandfather for several years.'

A vague memory stirred in Alex's mind. 'Where will I find her? If she is the person I remember, she was fond of travel.'

'She is spending the twelve days of Christmas at Lathom House in the Palatine of Lancaster.' Alex stiffened, but remained silent as his father continued. 'If the weather worsens or you lose your way and find that she has already left by the time you arrive there, then make all speed to her mansion in London.' The earl gazed at the shadowy, powerfully built figure beneath the dark, leafless branches of the trees. 'If my enemies were to learn of your relationship to me, then your life could be in danger, so take care. We must stop the piracy in the northern seas so the peace pact can go ahead.'

Alex agreed, but his expression remained impassive. He had lived with danger for years, risking his life on several occasions during his travels gathering information for his Swedish grandfather and his country; but it was in London that Alex had come closest to losing his life.

'Hopefully, I'll find that all is as you say,' he murmured.

'Aye. Fare thee well, then, laddie.' The earl clapped him on the shoulder. 'Trust no one. A man can so easily be persuaded to reveal secrets when between the sheets.'

Alex ignored this sally and bid his father '*Adjö*!'

As he set off on the road south, his thoughts were not of his mission, but of the beautiful Ingrid and Harry, whom he had cared for like a younger brother, but whom he suspected had betrayed him for love and money.

His grandmother had told Alex not to pursue revenge. She had called Harry that *crazy English boy*, but did not believe him duplicitous. *You must seek the truth*, she had said with her dying breath. Part of him had wanted to yell at her, *But you deceived me, just as they did, and this day you have taken something precious from me that was lodged in my heart and helped to make me the man I am.* But instead, he had quashed his hurt and anger and gathered her emaciated body in his arms and wept, for she had cared for him since he was a babe and had loved him unconditionally.

Despite her words, the desire for revenge still burned in Alex's heart and he decided to seek out Sir James Appleby, who had a manor in the Palatine of Lancaster, and see if he could help him find the treacherous couple.

Chapter One

They were coming!

With a rising panic, Rosamund Appleby gazed about her, searching for a place to hide. Her eyes alighted on the oak chest, carved with field mice and conies and curling tendrils of woodbine, and she hurried over to it. Bundling her faded brown homespun skirts about her thighs, she climbed inside the chest and hastily closed the lid. The slap, slap, slap of their leather-soled shoes on stone came nearer and nearer. Their voices grew louder. She buried herself amongst the garments in the chest and, scarcely breathing, prayed they would not find her.

'Where in the devil's name has she gone now?' demanded Rosamund's stepmother, Lady Monica Appleby. 'I checked her bedchamber and she was not there.'

'You frightened her, Mama. She fled like a rabbit with a ferret on its heels and has probably left the house.' William giggled. 'Edward said six months ago that she should be locked away. I know you agreed with him, so why did you wait until today?'

'Because her death, so close to her father's, could have roused suspicion. Whilst Sir James lived, I had to pretend to care about her well-being.'

Rosamund's eyes filled with tears when she thought of her father and her fists clenched at the memory of her stepmother's cruel duplicity. She wished she could spring out of the chest and tell her exactly what she thought of her—but that would be foolish.

'Now time has passed since his *very timely* death, I must deal with her,' muttered Lady Monica. 'Especially since *that woman*'s servant called here yesterday. I cannot risk Rosamund voicing her suspicions to her.'

'Who is this woman?' asked William.

'Lady Elizabeth Stanley. I knew her when I was a girl and I hated her even then. She's been staying at Lathom House after spending years going backwards and forwards between England and Europe, but hopefully she should be leaving for London soon. I told her messenger that her goddaughter was sick abed and could see no one. Her taking notice of Rosamund right now is extremely inconvenient. I can see her proving a nuisance.'

Rosamund stuffed a handful of linen into her mouth to stifle a gasp. She had been a child last time she had seen Lady Elizabeth and her memories of that period in her life were hazy. She had believed that her godmother had died of the same disease that had killed Rosamund's mother. If only she could speak to Lady Elizabeth, perhaps she could help her out of the terrible situation she was in.

'You should have sent her a message asking her to call and given her one of your potions,' said William with another of his irritating giggles.

Rosamund heard the sound of a slap and memories of past punishments caused her to shudder.

'That would not have served us, dolt,' snapped Lady Monica, sitting on the lid of the chest, so causing the wood to creak with the force of her weight. 'I'd have the whole of the Stanley family down on my head. Oh, why couldn't you have been born with your brother's wits?'

'That hurt!' wailed William.

'Well, think before you speak. At least I'll be able to mould the wife I have chosen for you into shape.'

'A wife for me!' babbled William. 'What's her name?'

'Bridget,' replied his mother. 'She is sixteen and the niece of a close kinsman of mine. You'll be meeting them soon.'

'You won't leave me alone with her, Mama?' William's voice was sharp with anxiety.

'Of course not,' she said in a soothing voice. 'There are questions her uncle and I need answers to from her. She'll need a close watch kept on her, but first we need to find Rosamund. If only Edward was here instead of in London. He would have been able to deal with this troublesome girl. As it is, he is obsessed with his campaign to be the next Lord Mayor of London and that will need a fortune to fund it. But enough of this talk—we must get on with our search.'

William said, 'Perhaps Rosamund has gone to the woodcutter's hut. You know how friendly she was with Joshua Wood.'

'If she has fled there in the hope of gaining his help, then she will be disappointed. He has gone, never to return. But you could be right about her visiting that hovel. We'll hasten in that direction. If we find her, then…' Lady Monica made a sound that sent a chill through her stepdaughter.

Rosamund waited until their footsteps had died away before pushing up the lid and casting aside the garments in the chest and climbing out. She felt heartsick, knowing that, with Joshua gone, she was utterly friendless. Tears trickled down her cheeks as she remembered two boys at swordplay. One of them was Joshua and the other her brother, Harry, who had drowned round about the same time as their mother's death. His clothes had been found by a river where he used to swim. Sometimes in her sleep, she had dark dreams of her mother crying out to save her and of Harry, warning her to run for her life as he was carried away before he was silenced. She would wake up, filled with fear and drenched in perspiration. Perhaps, once she was away from this place, the dreams would fade.

She dried her eyes on her sleeve and considered her situation. If she were to make her escape in her present guise, she would be too easily recognised. She picked up the white shirt that she had thrown to one side and remembered the time when she had dressed as a boy. Delving into the chest, she found a pair of hose, a russet doublet and a boy's hat with a feather in it. She gnawed on her nether lip. Did she dare? Last time she had donned these garments her stepmother had whipped her until she could scarcely stand. Rosamund's father had been away at the time and Lady Monica had warned her that if she dared to speak of it to her father then she would be punished more severely. She needed the devil beaten out of her for such sinful behaviour.

Rosamund wished she'd had the courage to talk to her father about wanting to have been born a boy, then he might have cared for her as much as he had for Harry. Instead, fear had guaranteed her silence. But what was she thinking of standing here, wasting time? She had to escape. She must change her clothes. There was naught so comfortable as a youth's nether garments for sitting astride a horse and riding hell for leather. Not that she'd had the opportunity to ride out alone since her father's death. There was only one problem about pretending to be a youth now. She gazed down at her breasts and attempted to flatten them with both hands and knew she would need binding.

Fortunately there was no one in sight as she passed, like a shadow, to the turret where her bedchamber was situated. It was the work of moments to find the binding she used for her monthly courses. She removed her clothes and bound her breasts before donning the shirt, padded brown hose and a green woollen doublet. Slipping off her shoes, she shoved her feet into a pair of stout boots before pulling on the feathered hat over the linen cap that confined her dark hair. Removing her winter cloak from a hook on the back of the door, she swung it round her shoulders and fastened its strings. Her heart was beating fast and, in her haste, she almost forgot Harry's short-sword that she had found hidden away in a chest several years ago. Although England was more settled and peaceful than in those early years after Henry VII had defeated Richard III at Bosworth Field, it still did not do to go out unarmed.

She picked up her gloves and hurried down-stairs, relieved that she could hear no sounds of activity coming from the kitchen. She left by the door that led into the yard and made her way to the stables. Her lips moved in silent prayer, hoping that the groom and stable boys were busy else-where.

To her relief the building was empty, but there was only one horse in the stalls and that was the oldest nag on the manor. Her spirits sank at the sight of Betsy, but she knew that she had no option but to saddle her up. She did so with hands that trembled.

Away from the house she found pleasure in the bite of the wind that whipped colour into her cheeks as she set out across the fields in the direction of Lathom House. Twenty-two years old and penniless, she could only pray that her godmother would help her. Fear and apprehension was a cold knot in her belly. Yet surely when she explained her situation, her godmother would understand her need for such a disguise?

Rosamund was still fretting about whether she would be turned away from Lathom's gates when a hedge loomed up. She groaned and had to back up Betsy. Taking a deep breath, she urged the horse towards the jump. They barely cleared the thicket of hazel. As they landed Rosamund sensed that the nag had caught a hoof on something. The beast landed awkwardly and one of Rosamund's feet came loose from the stirrup. The force of the jolt caused her to slip sideways. For several moments she dangled with her hands brushing the ground and then she managed to free her other foot. She fell into a patch of half-frozen muddy turf.

Pushing herself up, she spat out dirt before wiping her face with the back of her glove. Then she glanced back towards the hedge and saw a man stretched out on the ground. Her heart jerked inside her breast and, with knees that shook, she walked towards him.

His hat lay a few feet away and Rosamund picked it up before hunkering down beside him. She stared into the stranger's handsomely rugged face and with a sinking heart observed a swelling and an abrasion on his jaw where Betsy's hoof must have caught him a blow. To her relief his golden lashes lifted and a pair of penetrating tawny-brown eyes gazed into hers. She experienced the oddest sensation. Then his arm shot up and seized her by the throat and in one swift movement he rose to his feet, carrying her with him.

'Who are you?' he growled.

The hat fell from her fingers and, terrified, she clawed at that hand that threatened to cut off her breathing. She wanted to say, *Are you mad? I can scarcely breathe, never mind speak.*

As if he had read her thoughts, his fingers slackened a fraction. 'Answer my question!' he demanded.

But Rosamund could not get a word out, for fear still held her in its grip. She felt him fumble beneath her homespun cloak and a strangled gasp escaped her lips. Instinctively she kicked out at him. He swore in an unfamiliar tongue as he disarmed her. Her short-sword was thrust in his belt before he seized her dainty booted foot.

'I would not try that again if I were you,' he warned.

Alex was not in the best of moods. Not only had he failed to meet Lady Elizabeth at Lathom House, but he had also lost himself in the back lanes in his search for Appleby Manor. He had asked for directions from one of the guards, but obviously they had not been clear enough.

'Come, lad, speak!' he ordered, loosening his grip a fraction more.

Rosamund was not about to admit to being a woman to this barbaric stranger, whose voice held an inflection that, despite her fear of him, she found attractive. He was obviously a foreigner and perhaps that was the reason for his aggression. She blurted out the first name that came to mind. 'Joshua Wood!'

Alex flicked back a lock of flaxen hair and brought the youth's filthy face closer to his and rasped, 'I deem you deliberately rode me down, Master Wood.'

'No! You were out of sight behind the hedge so I could not see you,' she croaked, struggling to free her foot. 'If I was as suspicious of folk as you are, then I would want to know if you were hiding there to waylay me.'

'You flatter yourself that I should consider you important enough to wish to pounce on you.' His hand moved disturbingly from her foot to her knee and he hoisted her higher against him.

'That is true,' she stammered. 'I—I am b-but a simple woodcutter.'

Alex scrutinised the frightened face with its uncommon blue-violet eyes and long black lashes and he had the strangest feeling of familiarity. Abruptly he released his captive. 'You lie!'

'You brute,' she gasped, slumping on the ground and rubbing her throat.

'You will come with me,' he said, going over to his horse.

'What!' She sat up straight. 'Why should you believe I would want to go anywhere with you?' she said hoarsely. 'Your intention might be to kill me.'

'Aye, you could be right. Keep that in mind, my fine lad, if you wish to see the end of this day. You deal honestly with me and I will free you when I have finished with you.' Alex took a coil of thin rope from his horse and strode over to her. 'I am looking for Appleby Manor. You will take me there.'

His words filled her with dismay. It would be disastrous for her to do what he said. Yet if she didn't, perhaps he would slit her throat. A squeak of fear escaped her. What could he want at Appleby Manor? Did he have aught to do with her stepmother's schemes? Surely he could not be the close kinsman she was expecting? He did not speak like a Scotsman. What was she to do? Suddenly she realised that there was only one thing she could do and that was to lead him astray.

'Why do you hesitate? Is it that you are not frightened enough?' growled Alex. He had met some effeminate young men in his time, but there was something different about this one. Perhaps Master Wood felt a need to prove to himself that he was a real man and that was why he had lied about being a woodcutter. To wield an axe, to chop down trees and slice trunks into planks needed strength.

'I would be mad not to be frightened of you,' said Rosamund, trying to control the tremor in her voice. Slowly she rose to her feet. 'But return my weapon to me and I will prove my courage by fighting with you.'

Alex's smile was grim. 'You are a brave but foolish young man to challenge me. Who are you really? I reckon your weapon is too good to belong to a woodcutter. It would fetch a goodly sum if placed on the market. No doubt you stole it. You could be part of a gang of ruffians out to act as a decoy and lead me into a trap.'

'I am no thief,' she said indignantly. 'Nor do I belong to a gang.'

'I have only your word for that,' said Alex calmly, unwinding the cord. 'We will be roped together so you cannot gallop off and warn the others that there's rich pickings on the way.'

Rosamund was aghast and backed away from him, only to slip in a patch of mud. He dragged her to her feet and, despite her struggles, he managed to tie one end of the cord to her wrist and the other he looped about his hand.

'You are quite mad,' she said in a shaken voice.

'If I am, then I have been driven mad.'

She had spoken those very words to her father once and he had sunk his head in his hands. She had stared in anguish, watching his shoulders shake before he had waved a hand at her in dismissal. She, too, had wept as she had left the room. She could not believe this stranger could have descended to the depths that she had and that caused her to spit out at him.

'You mock me! I do not like having my word

doubted. It is you who are the thief. Return that short-sword to me at once. It belonged to my dead brother and it is all I have of him.'

The lad sounded so sincere that Alex almost believed him. But then he reminded himself that he had heard many a word spoken in so-called sincerity. 'I will return it at my convenience,' he said coldly.

Rosamund felt a familiar helplessness creep over her. She told herself that she must not give in to the lowness of spirits that had gripped her so often in the past. She remembered how she had managed to overcome those dark moods by riding out on her beautiful horse. The one that Edward, her elder stepbrother, had removed from the stable after her father's death. She had not been allowed beyond the gardens after that and there had been times when life was so utterly unbearable that she had given vent to her anger by smashing many a jar. Then they had locked her in her bedchamber and she had resorted to the submissive behaviour that had served her well in the past. But she was in no mood to act so at the moment. After all, she was supposed to be a brave youth, not a fearful girl.

'I should have left you lying on the ground and ridden over you,' she seethed. 'Instead, I behaved like a Christian, and what thanks do I receive? You treat me like a cur.' She glowered at him, thinking that she would have her revenge when they reached Lathom. She would call on the guards to take this foreigner prisoner.

'If you wish for better treatment, Master Wood, I suggest you only speak when spoken to,' said Alex.

He tugged on the rope and she went flying into him. He picked her up as if she weighed no more than a bundle of rags and threw her into the saddle. As Rosamund grappled for the reins, Old Betsy let out a deep sigh and seemed to sag in the middle. The next moment Rosamund was almost dragged off her horse as Alex swung up on to his own mount.

'This is intolerable!' Her voice shook. 'What is your reason for wishing to go to Appleby Manor, anyway?'

'That is none of your business, lad,' said Alex, giving her some slack. 'Take me there and I might even reward you.'

She wanted to give him a hot answer, but her sense of desolation was suddenly such that she knew if she spoke she would burst into tears and that would never do. She felt another jerk on the rope.

'You are supposed to be leading the way,' he said.

Rosamund darted him a poisonous look.

'Forgive me if I appear overly cautious, Master Wood, but one has difficulty these days even trusting one's friends,' said Alex. That slight inflection was evident in his voice and once again Rosamund was oddly affected by it. 'Now tell your horse to walk on,' he added.

Rosamund did so. Then she spent several seconds imagining the moment when he would get his comeuppance. Then the reality of her situation struck her and the corners of her mouth drooped. A mournful sigh escaped her.

Alex gave her a sidelong glance and felt a stir of pity at the sight of such abject misery. Then he hardened his heart. Pity could have no place in his armoury. The youth had lied to him. He could be all that he had accused him of being, but Alex was prepared to risk that to discover if Harry and Ingrid were at Appleby Manor.

They rode on in silence between high, bare hedgerows until they reached an open aspect. Suddenly Alex had a growing conviction that he had passed this way before. When he recognised the walls of Lathom ahead, he turned on his companion and pulled on the cord, causing Rosamund to almost tumble from the horse.

'Do you take me for a fool, Master Wood?'

roared Alex. 'This is not Appleby Manor, but Lathom House!'

Rosamund managed to grab the pommel and heave herself back into the saddle. 'You could have killed me!' she cried.

'But I didn't,' snapped Alex. 'What jape is this you play? I left this place only a couple of hours ago.'

His words took Rosamund utterly by surprise. 'What were you doing at the Earl of Derby's mansion?'

'That is none of your business.' His eyes flashed golden fire 'Answer my question or I'll cut your throat. Why have you brought me here?'

'I—I have no w-wish to return to A-Appleby Manor,' she stuttered. 'They would kill me.'

Alex gazed into the delicate features and his anger abated. 'Why? What wrong have you done?'

Rosamund felt her ire rising again. 'Why do you believe it is I who am in the wrong when I am fleeing for my life?'

Alex frowned. 'Because, Master Wood, I deem you are no woodcutter, which means you lied to me.'

She felt sick with fear. 'Wh-what evidence do you have to make such an accusation?'

Alex smiled humourlessly. 'Your stature is

enough. It takes strength to chop down trees, Master Wood—you look more suited to needlepoint. Tell me, who is it you fear at Appleby Manor?'

Rosamund had no intention of telling him. After all, he could be in the pay of her stepbrother, Edward Fustian, who had dealings in London with foreigners.

'Why should I answer your question when you will not answer mine?' she muttered.

'Because I am the stronger, little bantam.'

'You mean you would bully me like you have already done in order to have your own way,' she said sullenly.

He raised his tawny eyebrows. 'I beg pardon if I have hurt you,' he said in a mocking voice. 'But if you do not wish to take me to Appleby Manor, then answer my questions.'

'Will you let me go if I do?'

'If I judge you are telling me the truth. Who dwells there?'

Rosamund could see no harm in answering him. 'The family is small and consists of Lady Monica Appleby and her son William. She has another son who lives in London.'

This news was not what Alex had hoped to hear. 'What of Sir James?'

'Dead!'

The news came as something of a shock.

Rosamund saw that he paled beneath his tanned skin. 'You knew Sir James?' she asked.

Alex pulled himself together. 'I met him only the once.'

'You seem very shocked by the news, sir.'

'Indeed, I am. I had hoped to gain information from him. When did he die?'

'Six months ago.' Her expression was bleak.

That news was a further shock. 'I met him shortly before he died,' said Alex. 'He made no mention that he had two sons.'

'That is because they are *not* his sons, but belong to his second wife, Lady Monica.' Rosamund watched his expression alter and wondered what this information was that he had wanted from her father, but she did not see how she could be of help to him on that score. 'Did you meet him in London?'

'Aye, and that is where I must go now. I will risk showing you some trust. Are you able to guide me out of this palatine and set me on the road to that city? I will pay you to act as my guide.'

She shook her head. 'No! I can't come with you. I have business at Lathom House.'

Alex scowled. 'So that is why you brought me

here. I don't care what your business is, you will guide me out of this backwater or you will be sorry.'

Alarmed, she said, 'I will do what you say if you answer me one question. Did you speak to Lady Elizabeth Stanley whilst you were at Lathom?'

Alex's suspicions were immediately roused. 'Why do you ask, lad? What business do you have with the lady?'

Rosamund knew if she told him the truth, then he would know for certain that she had deceived him. 'It is a private matter.'

'I wager it is,' said Alex silkily. 'Well, I will not keep secret from you that the lady and her entourage left yesterday afternoon for London.'

Rosamund's spirits plummeted. Her hope in coming here was all in vain. What was she to do now?

Watching the dismay cloud Master Wood's face, Alex had the strangest feeling that he was right to be suspicious of this slender youth and determined to discover more about him. 'If you still wish to speak to the lady, then I suggest you accompany me to London.'

Rosamund knew that she should not agree to his suggestion. Yet, he was giving her a second chance to gain the help of her godmother. Would it be a bigger mistake not to agree? On the other hand, was it crazy to even consider going with him? He was a foreigner who had almost choked the life out of her. This should have told her, if aught else didn't, that he was a dangerous man. No, it would be sheer folly to fall in with his plan.

She tilted her chin. 'I do not wish to go with you! In fact, I refuse to do so!' She dug her heels into Betsy's flanks. The horse jerked forward and then collapsed.

Chapter Two

Rosamund's shock was intense. She barely had time to kick her feet free of the stirrups before she felt a tug on her wrist as Alex bent over and lifted her from the saddle. He lowered her to the ground before dismounting and hunkering down beside the horse. He placed his hand on the beast's neck and held it there for several moments before looking up at her.

'I'm sorry, Master Wood, but your horse is dead.'

Rosamund fell on her knees besides the horse and a sob burst from her. She stroked the horse's head before burying her face against its shaggy coat to hide her tears. 'Poor Betsy,' she whispered.

Alex gazed down at the bent head and the exposed slender neck. Had he imagined that sob? What conclusions could he draw from it? He could recall having difficulty holding back tears when his first pony had died. Grieving for a beloved horse was natural. Perhaps he was mistaken to have considered even for a moment that this uncommon youth was a thief.

'We are presented with a problem, Master Wood,' he said. 'I am short of time, but you are without a mount. What do you want to do?'

Rosamund turned a tearstained face towards him. 'You are giving me a choice?'

Alex wondered if he was being overly sympathetic, but told himself that it was important that he discovered what Master Wood's business was with her ladyship. 'I need to go to London. You wish to speak with Lady Elizabeth, who is on her way there. Someone is bound to pass this way and they will find your horse and do what is necessary.'

Rosamund wiped her face with the back of her hand and rose to her feet. 'I will walk to London,' she said in a small voice.

Alex frowned. His suspicions, his common sense and his sympathy for a fellow human being in such a situation were at war with each other. 'You will not catch up with the lady on the road, Master Wood. I doubt I will do so on horseback. Besides, it will take you a long time to walk to

London. If your strength does not fail you and you are not attacked by robbers and you manage to reach your destination, it is even possible that you might find the lady not at home. What would you do then?'

'I had not thought so far ahead.' She heaved a deep sigh.

'You must make a decision.'

Rosamund lifted her head and saw a look in his eyes that surprised her. 'Are you suggesting that I share your horse?' she asked.

'I do not have all day, Master Wood,' said Alex, untying the cord at her wrist. 'If I were in your situation, I wouldn't accept my offer. But of course, it would depend on how desperate I was to speak to Lady Elizabeth.'

Rosamund was extremely desperate. If she stayed here, who was to say that her stepmother and her men would not find her as soon as he left? Of course, in London there was the risk of being seen by Edward.

'If you are going to decide to come with me, we must make a move now,' rasped Alex. 'The horse will not be able to travel swiftly carrying the two of us and I need to be in London by the twenty-second of this month.'

'Why are you so keen to help me?' asked Rosamund suspiciously.

He shrugged. 'You are a fellow traveller and did not our Lord say we should help one another?'

'You have not particularly behaved like a Christian so far,' Rosamund dared to say. 'But what choice do I have? I pray that you will prove to be the better of my options.'

'I am truly honoured by your confidence in me,' said Alex drily.

Rosamund flushed and could only hope that he did not guess her secret. So far he appeared not to have penetrated her disguise and God willing he would never do so.

'But any wrong moves, such as trying to remove your weapon from my belt, Master Wood, and you're in trouble. I'm not so naïve as to believe you might not try.'

The thought had not occurred to her. 'I give you my word!'

'The word of a liar!' His gold-brown eyes flashed fire. 'I will be on my guard. I have not forgotten waking up with such a headache that I could not remember where I was or who I was and had a knife wound in my shoulder that almost killed me.'

Rosamund's curiosity was roused. 'Who was the person that did this to you? Perhaps you gave them such a dislike of your boorish behaviour that they feared what you might do next.'

Alex growled, 'Watch your mouth, lad. Ingrid knew I trusted her and that was why she was able to betray me.' He pulled himself up short. What was he thinking of, speaking of a matter that had cut him to the heart to this—this—? He bent over her. His nose twitched as the feather in Master Wood's hat tickled his nostrils and he sneezed, then swore. 'I hope you are not going to make me regret my offer, but you will come to no harm, unless you give me real cause to slit your throat.'

Rosamund went as white as a sheet beneath her dirt. 'I will do exactly as you say,' she said in a trembling voice. 'I like my throat as it is.'

I must be mad, thought Alex. Gaining information from this one could cause me more trouble than it is worth. Yet he felt a monster for frightening this slender youth. Yet his brush with death six months ago had proved to him the dangers of allowing anyone to get too close to him.

Taking a blanket from a saddlebag, he formed it into a kind of cushion. Then he told Master Wood he would give him a leg up. Rosamund placed a foot in his laced hands and gripped his shoulder. She felt his muscles bunch and thought with a man as strong as him on her side, she would not need to fear her stepfamily again. Then she asked herself what was she thinking of even to consider he could be an ally?

As soon as she was up on the horse, Alex climbed into the saddle. 'Now which direction do we take to reach the London road?' he asked, thinking he would not be in this situation now if he had asked for a guide before leaving Lathom House, instead of just directions.

'Take the left-hand turn,' replied Rosamund.

As he took the turning, she was jerked against him and needed to clutch his cloak if she was not to slide from the horse. Suddenly she felt far removed from her previous existence and excitement stirred inside her. Even so, after a while, she began to feel apprehensive and questioned whether she had made the right decision. They would be on the road for days and that meant spending nights with this man.

'I want information,' said Alex, aware of those small hands on his back and the soft breath on his neck. 'Tell me—how did Sir James die?'

'It happened when he was in London. Lady

Monica told me that it was an apoplexy, but I did not believe her. Far—' Rosamund clamped her mouth shut on the word and recalled how often she had been told *to watch her tongue* or *keep silent* and *no one is going to believe what a mad girl has to say.*

'Why do you not believe her?'

'If I say what I think, you might accuse me of being mad,' she said in a toneless voice.

'Why should I believe you mad?' he asked.

She did not answer him immediately, remembering vividly Edward accusing her of being possessed by demons. In her loneliness, she had created an imaginary companion to whom she talked. He had overheard her and taunted her. She had screamed her denial and flew at him. He had knocked her to the ground and then dragged her by her hair to his mother. Lady Monica had locked Rosamund in her bedchamber for three days and nights and fed her solely on dry bread and water. Rosamund had threatened that she would tell her father what they had done to her when he returned home. But her stepmother had said that Sir James would agree with their actions because he knew his daughter was mad, but pretended not to notice her strange behaviour because he was ashamed of her. So again, she had kept her mouth shut, wanting her father to love her and hoping that the next time he went away they would remember her silence and she would suffer less at their hands.

'Answer me!' demanded Alex.

'If I told you that I believed he was murdered, then you might agree with them that it was a figment of my fevered imagination,' she said in a fierce voice.

'Murdered! By "them" I presume you mean those that live at Appleby Manor?'

'Perhaps, but I will say no more and you cannot make me do so. Even if you were to dismount and drag me from this horse and beat me.'

What a strange mixture was this youth, thought Alex. One moment he is frightened of me and prepared to do what I say, but the next he speaks out bravely and it is obvious that he can be stubborn. He seriously considered the possibility that the youth had been beaten before in an attempt to gain information from him or for punishment. Another thought struck him. A father might beat an effeminate son, or—even a daughter who dressed as a youth. But the thought that bothered him most was that his travelling companion suspected Sir James of having been murdered in London. Was it possible? And if so—why?

He thought of Harry and recalled how when he had rescued him that he had been unable to remember whether he had once had siblings. Harry's earliest memory was of the cupboard-like space on the ship, where he had woken with a sore head and a frightening loss of identity.

Alex's thoughts were interrupted by his sudden awareness that Master Wood must have dozed off. His head was going bump, bump, bump against his shoulder. Alex reached behind him and seized the front of the youth's doublet and bellowed at him to rouse himself.

Rosamund started awake and at first could not think where she was and then the motion of the horse and the scent of the man filled her nostrils. She realised that her face was squashed against his shoulder and she found herself breathing in the smell of sandalwood and his maleness with an unfamiliar pleasure. Then she realised he was holding on to the material at her chest. Feeling hot all over, she tugged herself free. What if he had felt her breast despite the binding? Her secret would be out.

'Stay awake, Master Wood,' ordered Alex. 'What good is a sleeping guide to me?'

Rosamund said gruffly, 'It will not happen again.'

'It had better not.'

* * *

After that incident Rosamund made certain that she stayed awake. It amazed her that she had managed to fall asleep in such a precarious position and in the company of this foreigner who had threatened her. She forced herself to concentrate on anything but him. She gazed at the frosty landscape and recalled the only time she had travelled to London.

It had been in the company of her father, stepmother and William. Edward was getting married and Rosamund could not help but pity his future wife, Marion. She remembered how besotted the new Mistress Fustian had been with her husband. Such adoration had not survived. Last time Marion had visited Appleby Manor with their two daughters, Rosamund had noticed the bruising on her neck and wrists. Edward wanted a son and his wife suffered for what he called her lack of success.

It was that kind of behaviour that caused Rosamund to consider spinsterhood preferable to marrying a man such as her stepbrother, although her stepmother had once suggested such a possibility. A long-suppressed memory reared its dragon-like head and she quickly quashed it.

There were some things it was better not to dwell upon and fortunately her father had been against such a match.

The temperature had dropped by the time they crossed the border into the Palatine of Chester and the sun had disappeared below the horizon. Soon it would be dark and Rosamund was worried. Surely they should have reached an inn by now, but the road stretched ahead of them with no sign of a building.

Alex's thoughts were running in a similar direction and he twisted in the saddle to speak to his travelling companion. He had difficulty in making out the slender features beneath the brim of the hat. 'Have you any idea where the nearest inn is, Master Wood?'

'It is some time since I passed this way,' answered Rosamund. 'I was certain we should have reached the one I had in mind by now, but I must be mistaken. Still, I am certain if we continue along this road then we will come to another sooner or later.'

'If this is the main London road, then that is likely,' said Alex, exacerbated. 'I would know how far we have to go.'

'I cannot help you with exact distances.' She felt irritated by the tone of his voice. 'We must just travel on.'

'So be it,' he growled. 'Let us hope we don't have to sleep in the open.'

The idea alarmed her, but she remained silent, not wishing to annoy him further by complaining. Visions of mulled wine, hot broth and a warm bed began to float before her eyes and she was tempted to snuggle into his back to keep warm. She resisted and somehow managed to remain upright.

They continued along the road, watching the silhouettes of trees and hedges merge into the darkness and stars prick the sky. To their dismay, when they finally reached the dark outline of a building Alex had spotted some distance away, it was to discover that it was just a burnt-out shell with charred beams criss-crossed against the sky.

Alex dismounted and wandered about the ruins before returning to his horse. 'There is nowhere to take shelter here. We must ride on,' he said brusquely.

He half-expected his companion to complain, but despite being near to tears with disappointment, hunger and weariness, Rosamund remained silent. She pulled her hood over her hat and huddled inside her cloak and prayed that they would soon come to another inn.

The wind rose and she was glad of the bulwark his body provided. Frantically, she tried to remember whether there were any other places where they could take shelter. For a while nothing occurred to her and no inns hovered into view. At least she could be thankful that the moon had risen. By its light she noticed an odd-shaped escarpment ahead. Suddenly she remembered her father mentioning to William that there were old mine workings in the sandstone that formed the roots of this area.

'Master…' She paused remembering that the stranger had still not introduced himself, and then added, 'No Name, I believe there are caves somewhere around here.' Her voice sounded loud in the eerie silence. 'If I remember rightly, copper used to be mined in this area hundreds of years ago.'

Alex, who had been keeping his eyes peeled for even a hovel, hoped his companion was right. His horse would be too exhausted to travel the following day if they persisted on riding through the night. 'Can you remember exactly where these caves are, Master Wood?'

Rosamund looked up at the hill in the moonlight.

'I did not see them myself, but I remember William being told to follow a stream and that there was a shelf of rock a little way up that hill.'

'We'll walk and give the horse a rest,' said Alex, dismounting and holding up a hand. 'Come, let's not delay.'

Rosamund placed her small hand in his and slid down from the horse and almost into his arms. Their bodies collided and she withdrew her hand hastily and stepped away from him. At least a walk would warm her up.

'Stay close,' murmured Alex, considering not for the first time the smallness of that hand. He seized his horse's bridle and suggested Master Wood hold on to his cloak so they would not lose each other. Following the sound of running water, he ended up finding the stream by walking into it. He swore in his own tongue and added in English, 'Step back if you do not want to get your feet wet.'

'Perhaps I should have kept my mouth shut about caves,' muttered Rosamund, certain he would be in a bad mood after getting his boot wet.

'Too late now,' growled Alex, shaking his foot. 'Let us not give up. At least there is some moonlight to help us see the way ahead, although perhaps it is best you stay here with the horse whilst I see what I can discover.'

Rosamund did not want to be left behind, but decided as he seemed to be trusting her with his horse, that she would do as he said.

It was not long before he called down to her. 'I have found a shelf of rock. Let us hope that it is the one you mentioned. Bring my horse and help me search for the caves.'

Rosamund did not need telling twice and was soon standing next to him. They began to search, dislodging small rocks and punctuating the air with the sound of snapping twigs as they looked for an opening. She realised that she was finding a peculiar enjoyment in sharing in the search with him. She wondered what country he came from and whether he had a family waiting for him at home, worrying about him. She recalled his mention of a woman called Ingrid and deduced that, from the way he had spoken about her, that he had once been in love with her, but something had gone wrong, so it was unlikely that he had married her. Perhaps he had married someone else. If so, what was he doing in England, far away from his own country?

* * *

It took some searching, but at last Alex found an opening and called her over. He soon discovered that he had to bend himself almost in half to get inside. The cave was pitch-black, but at least it was out of the wind; as his hands searched the rock face, he realised that the wall was gaining in height and soon he was able to stand upright. When he turned and looked towards the opening, he could see a faint light.

'Shall I come inside?' called Rosamund.

'No, wait there. I will need to come out.' His voice seemed to bounce off the walls, causing an echo.

He felt his way to the outside and stretched. 'We need a fire,' he said.

'You have flint and steel?'

'Aye. And tinder. But we will need more kindling and twigs,' he said.

'There are plenty of them around,' said Rosamund. 'I will gather some up.'

'Good man,' he said, squeezing her shoulder and thinking how slender were the bones. 'This cave will do us for the night.'

She was warmed by his praise—she'd had little of that in her life—and set about gathering twigs. In the meantime he unfastened his saddlebags before removing his saddle and throwing a blanket over his horse. He carried both saddle and saddle-bags into the cave and dumped them there before going back outside and helping gather firewood.

When they had collected great armfuls, he told her to take her bundle inside. She obeyed him and was glad to be out of the wind despite the intense velvet blackness inside the cave. She looked towards the faint strip of light and waited for him to follow her. Feeling close to exhaustion, she sank to the ground.

Rosamund did not have long to wait before she heard the sound of flint against steel. She saw sparks and then a flicker of light in the cave close to the entrance. Tiny flames began to curl about the tinder and she could smell burning. Then the flames grew and eventually there came the crackling of wood. Not long after, it was light enough in the cave for her to see the rosy colour of the sandstone.

'You've done it,' she said, relieved.

He darted her a glance. 'Come closer to the fire. I have a pot here and a flagon of ale that I can heat up.'

'I don't suppose you have any nutmeg and honey?' she asked wistfully, pushing back her hood, the better to keep an eye on him. Now she could see more clearly his expression and the attractive planes and angles of his face by the light of the fire.

'Then you suppose wrong,' he said. 'I once worked for a spice merchant and he paid me in cinnamon and nutmeg. You can have no idea how that pleased my grandmother.' He took several items from one of the saddlebags.

So he had a grandmother. 'You say you once worked for a spice merchant—what do you do now to earn a living?' she asked.

'You could say that I am a jack of all trades. I enjoy travelling and turn my hand to any task to support myself,' said Alex smoothly. 'Are you hungry?'

'Extremely so. But I had resigned myself to go hungry and thirsty this night.'

'I have a little salted pork, a couple of apples and a hunk of wheaten bread and cheese.' He smiled good humouredly. 'A meal fit for a king if one is hungry.'

His smile took her by surprise and she found herself returning his with one of her own and agreeing with him. He seemed less frightening, more approachable than he had done earlier. 'If I had some money, I would buy some food from you,' she said. 'As it is, I left home in some haste, as I told you.'

'I deem you have well earned a meal, so let us not talk of payment. We would still be out in that freezing wind if you had not remembered about this cave.'

Rosamund flushed with pleasure at this second dose of praise. 'We have both contributed to the comfortable place we now find ourselves in,' she said shyly.

The hand holding an apple in mid-air hovered there. 'You consider this comfortable?' He could not conceal his surprise.

'We are warm and dry, are we not?' Her tone was a little on the defensive now. 'You have built the fire so that hopefully most of the smoke will find its way outside.'

Alex said drily, 'You are easily pleased, but I doubt we will be able to keep the fire burning all night.'

'But the cave will hold some heat and we have our cloaks,' said Rosamund, flinging back her own now the heat from the fire was beginning to pene-trate the woollen fabric. She wanted it to get to that part of her that still felt chilled.

Alex's growing conviction that this youth was a

woman in disguise intensified due to the delight-
ful music in the voice that echoed around the cave.
He took the knife strapped to his leg and cut an
apple and offered half to his companion.

Rosamund thanked him and bit into the fruit.
Her imagination took wing and she thought about
Adam and Eve in the Garden of Eden. She
grimaced. What nonsense was this? She and this
foreigner were not the only man and woman in the
world. And probably even if he knew that she was
a woman, he would not be tempted to lie with her.
Her stepmother and stepbrothers had told her
often enough that she was ugly and no man would
want her without an enormous dowry—and that
was not forthcoming because her father believed
she was mad. Tears itched the back of her eyes and
she blinked them away.

'What is it?' asked Alex.

She started. 'What do you mean?'

'Is some smoke getting in your eyes?'

She was amazed that he had noticed that tiny
movement and realised that there was little that
this man missed. 'Aye, it is,' she said gruffly.

'Obviously it is also affecting your throat.' His
penetrating gaze met hers through the flames.

Rosamund lowered her eyes and was silent.

Having finished his half of the apple and aware that he had unnerved his companion, Alex set about preparing the spiced ale. After grating nutmeg into the liquid and adding half a stick of cinnamon, he stirred it with his knife. Then he poured the ale into a small iron pot before placing it on the fire. He then divided the bread and meat and gave some to her.

She thanked him and bit into the food as if half-starved. She was not only grateful for his provision, but surprised by his generosity and capacity for caring for his own needs. It was difficult to imagine her stepbrothers doing what he had done. They had never shared what was theirs with her, but had always expected to be waited on hand and foot. Edward, in particular, had found a perverse pleasure in forcing her to her knees and insisting she remove his boots. She had done so with loathing in her heart, dwelling on the thought that one day she would see him grovel at her feet. Thank God, she had managed to escape from being humiliated in such a way again.

No sooner had she finished eating than Alex offered her a leather cup of steaming ale. 'I have but the one cup, so we will have to share,' he said.

'My thanks,' she said, adding awkwardly, 'I did

not think that when we met you would willingly share what was yours with me.'

She felt a need to talk to someone of her suspicions, but although this foreigner might now be showing kindness to her, somehow the words stuck in her throat. She drew her cloak tightly about her and rested her back against a wall before closing her eyes.

Alex drained the cup and drew his own cloak about him and stretched out on the ground with his head against his saddle. Who was his companion? Possibly Sir James had bedded a serving wench who worked at the manor. Yet the attractive musical voice was not that of a servant, so it was possible that Sir James had been as fond of her mother as Alex's natural father claimed to have been of his mother and seen to it that he was treated like a son or daughter of the house. Unless—his companion was a legal offspring of Sir James! A daughter who resented her stepmother and had raised the lady's wrath by saying her father had been murdered. When threatened, the slightly crazed Mistress Appleby had fled and headed for Lathom House, only to encounter Alex on the way.

It was now that Alex's imagination stalled. His

young companion had not behaved as if crazed, although if she were seeking help to prove that her father had been murdered, it would have made more sense to speak to the Lord of Lathom House, the Earl of Derby, and not Lady Elizabeth, but that was women for you. Illogical. They were too often ruled by their emotions. He thought of Ingrid and how she had played him and Harry off against each other as the mood took her. No! He would not torture himself with painful memories.

He decided he would leave his musings there for the moment and catch up on some sleep. From beneath drooping eyelids, he watched his companion, aware of every movement as she sought the most comfortable position on the sandy floor of the cave. Eventually, she fell asleep. For one in fear of her life, who did not trust him, he reckoned she showed a foolish faith in her disguise. Alex made up his mind that, for now, he would play her game, but sooner or later he was going to have to inform her about what was needful to impersonate a man.

Rosamund woke the following morning to a cold and crisp sunny day. She ached all over, but had slept surprisingly well, considering the discomfort of sleeping on the ground. She glanced across to where Master No Name, as she was beginning to think of him, sat in the shaft of sunlight that flooded through the low opening. Their eyes met and an awareness of his maleness almost over-whelmed her. She wanted to shrink into a corner away from his muscular strength and that penetrat-ing gaze. It made her feel small and vulnerable and intensely feminine. No doubt if he were to discover the truth about her, he would turn away in disgust and abandon her to her fate. Her safety lay in his never knowing what or who she was, so she must keep that constantly in her mind and strut like a youth.

'You have slept well, Master Wood,' said Alex, casting aside the folds of his cloak and getting to his feet. 'But the sun is up and it is time we were on our way.'

She remembered to deepen her voice when she opened her mouth to ask him a question. 'Do you think there is any chance of us catching up with Lady Elizabeth this day?'

He gave her an odd look and shrugged before lifting his saddle and asking her to carry out his saddlebags. She nodded, but did not immediately follow him, instead relieving herself in a distant corner of the cave. She determined that she would not be lured into telling him anything about herself. She still did not know in what circumstances he had met her father and what information he had wanted from him.

this because, although they switched horses periodically, he did not know in what direction, since the sun that rose and shone in their faces in the early mornings was at their backs.

Chapter Three

Rosamund washed her face in the stream outside and then resumed her position on the horse with a determined tilt to her chin.

Alex soon realised that any hope he had of gaining information about Sir James and his stepson in London was firmly quashed. There was little he could do about it without bringing force to bear on his companion and he was reluctant to rekindle the fear in the blue-violet eyes. So he held his peace and prayed that his patience would eventually pay off. His conviction concerning his companion's femininity made it almost impossible for him to give his full attention to the passing landmarks. He had planned on committing them to memory, so that if he needed to travel to the north-west of

England again, he would find his way without too much difficulty. The scent of the slender figure and the feel of that small hand against his back triggered his imagination.

He tried not to dwell on there being feminine curves beneath the male garb by forcing himself to concentrate on what part Lady Elizabeth would expect him to play in her troupe of performers. It would not be the first time he had donned the disguise of a player and part of him looked forward to doing so. Hopefully the disguise would serve its purpose in having him accepted by those attending the proxy wedding of Princess Margaret to James of Scotland at Richmond Palace and would not suspect his real aim in being there. He had committed to memory the names of those whom his father regarded as not only his personal enemies, but those of the proposed peace pact between England and Scotland. Peace between the two countries was essential if the piracy in the northern seas was to be brought to an end. Ships from his own country had discovered to their cost that the buccaneering Scots and English did not always differentiate between ally and enemy. But his task lay more than a sennight ahead and, right now, he would be glad when they came to a town. He was hungry and no doubt his travelling companion was, too.

They had travelled twelve leagues or more that day, stopping only once in Congleton to eat and drink and stretch their legs. As dusk fell they came to a village with but one inn. Alex dismounted and went inside, calling to Rosamund that he would see what were the sleeping arrangements.

Hastily, she slid from the horse and followed him inside and was just in time to hear the inn-keeper say that there was only one sleeping chamber available. As they were his only guests, they would have it to themselves and sleeping pallets were included in the charge for the night. Alex had no choice but to accept what was on offer. On hearing the sounds of men roistering in the tap room and being told there was no private parlour available, he said they would eat their supper upstairs.

Rosamund assured herself that sharing a chamber with Master No Name was no different from sleeping in the cave, but she soon realised that she was deceiving herself. Conscious of several pairs of eyes upon them, she squirmed with embarrassment at having to be dependent on this man to see that she had a roof over her head and food in her stomach.

The innkeeper lit a lantern from a burning candle and handed it to Alex and gave him directions to the stables. He thanked him and went over to Rosamund. He gazed down into her sullen face, noticing the dark rings of weariness beneath the violet eyes. 'You're weary. Why don't you go upstairs and take your ease? I'll tend to the horse.'

Rosamund shook her head. 'I am no weakling. I will help you.' She did not want to be left alone in the inn. She went out into the freezing night and took hold of the horse's bridle and led it towards a huddle of outbuildings that showed up against the darkening sky.

Alex gazed after her, looking for those signs common to her sex. Was he right in believing her to be Sir James's daughter? He noted the swing of her hips and the way she held her head. He considered the possibility of training her as one of his accomplices if he could prove her trustworthy. She certainly seemed to possess some of the traits needed to be a spy by being prepared to set aside the mores of the day by disguising herself as a member of the opposite sex. Something Ingrid would never do; she much preferred donning a nun's outfit or the silken skirts of a lady. Mistress Appleby was obviously desperate and in need of money—and if she really turned out to be a little crazy after all, perhaps that was necessary when playing such dangerous games as spying. But he was running ahead of himself; she had not yet proved herself trustworthy and he must never forget that he had mistakenly trusted Ingrid to his cost.

Alex set the lantern down on a bench and glanced about the stable. His companion was struggling to unsaddle his horse, but it was obvious she was not accustomed to tending such a large animal, and was finding it difficult. Without a by your leave, he seized her by the elbows and lifted her out of the way. 'Leave this to me, Master Wood. You fetch some water,' he ordered.

Rosamund bit back a retort and looked about her for a bucket. She picked one up and went outside to where she had noticed a water trough. She scooped up as much water as she could, only to stagger beneath its weight when she lifted it up. She entered the stable, carrying the bucket with both hands.

Alex moved swiftly to relieve her of her burden. 'Allow me,' he said in a voice that brooked no argument.

Rosamund had no choice but to hand it over to him, though could not resist saying, 'I know you are the stronger man, but I could have managed it, you know.'

Alex realised his mistake in rushing to her aid and instantly tried to rectify it. 'Why must you be on the defensive, young Master Wood? We have both had a long day and are weary. Get inside and leave me to finish tending my own horse.'

Rosamund did not move, remembering the noise of the men drinking in the tap room. What if one were to come out and pick a fight with her? 'I would rather wait here,' she said.

Alex shrugged. 'Please yourself. I am not your keeper.'

Are you not? she almost said.

Alex decided to test her. 'Do you have a mother?'

'She is dead. Died when I was just a child. What about you?'

Alex decided that it should do no harm telling her a little about himself—it might encourage her to talk more. 'My mother died shortly after I was born.'

'So who looked after you?'

'A wet nurse and my grandparents.' Alex recalled his grandmother telling him that his mother, Maria Nilsson, had gone to Scotland in the train of Princess Margaret of Denmark on the occasion of her marriage to Scotland's then king. She was a widow and the Earl Douglas already married when they met. Apparently the affair had lasted several years. Maria had given birth to him in Scotland and he had been named Alexander Christian. His mother had died a week later.

'What about your father?'

The muscles of Alex's face stiffened, remembering as a boy asking his grandparents about his father. They had told him that Christian Nilsson had been a mighty soldier, killed in a battle with the Danes before Alex was born. He had grown up, believing himself to be the son of a Swedish soldier hero, and was proud of the fact. He had been devastated when he had discovered that he was Earl Douglas's bastard instead of the son of the Swedish hero.

'You don't have to tell me,' said Rosamund softly. She had been watching his expression and hazarded that his thoughts were not happy ones.

'My father had naught to do with my upbringing,' he said tersely. 'I was reared by my grandparents in Sweden.'

'So you are Swedish,' said Rosamund, satisfied

that she now knew where he came from. 'I have heard that the sun scarcely rises there in the winter.'

Alex made no comment, only saying, 'You can go inside now. I'll only be a moment here. Perhaps you can carry the saddlebags.'

She was disappointed that he was not prepared to tell her more about his country. She hastened to pick up the saddlebags and managed to sling them over her shoulder in what she deemed a manly fashion.

Alex rolled his eyes and picked up the saddle. 'I don't know about you, but I'm famished, Master Wood.'

She agreed that she was hungry and followed him out and remained hard on his heels as they crossed the darkened stable yard. Alex had a word with the innkeeper before leading the way upstairs.

The sleeping chamber was not as large as she had imagined and the air was exceeding chilly. She soon discovered that the pallet and blanket were damp, but did not comment, unlike Alex. 'This will not do,' he muttered, bundling pallets and blankets beneath his arm and leaving her alone in the darkened bedchamber. She would have followed him, but the thought of facing the raucous crowd downstairs was enough for her to stay put. She perched on his saddle and hoped he would not be too long.

Rosamund had no idea how long she was there before she heard someone coming upstairs. Instantly, she rose to her feet and went to open the door. A buxom woman stood there, carrying a lantern in one hand and a pitcher in the other. 'Here you are, young master.'

'Thank you,' said Rosamund gruffly, taking both from her.

The woman entered the sleeping chamber. 'Your mate is making a right fuss downstairs. Yer'd think he owned the bloody place. A furriner, too. He wants to watch his step.'

'The pallets and blankets were damp,' said Rosamund, placing the lantern and pitcher on the floor. 'He paid good money for hiring this chamber.'

The woman sniggered and brushed against her. 'There's more than one way of keeping warm, young master.' She placed a hand on Rosamund's thigh.

Shocked, Rosamund reacted by pushing her away. 'Get out of here,' she said roughly.

'Oh, we've a haughty one here, have we? Or are yer one of them?' She placed a hand on her hip and swayed about the room.

Rosamund watched her uneasily. 'I don't know what you mean. Will you leave!'

The woman ignored her and went over to the saddlebags on the floor. 'What have we in here?'

Rosamund rushed over to her. 'Leave them alone! They're not your property.'

'What is going on here?' said Alex.

Rosamund felt a rush of relief as she whirled round to see him standing in the doorway. She noticed that he had slung the bedding over his shoulder and carried a tray. 'This woman is being offensive,' she said stiffly.

He thrust the tray at Rosamund, but before he could lay a hand on the woman she scuttled past him and out of the door. Alex slammed it behind her and locked it. He dropped the bedding on the floor and stared at Rosamund. 'What did she do?'

Her cheeks reddened. 'I'd rather not say.' She breathed in the appetising smell of the broth and placed the tray on the floor. 'Now you're here, she'll not come back.'

Alex had some idea of what the serving wench might have said to her and thought that must have given *Master Wood* a fright. 'I had the innkeeper's wife air the bedding in front of her fire. She was willing to do so for an extra penny.'

'I am not surprised,' said Rosamund. 'One can buy a lot for a penny.'

Alex realised he had made a mistake by revealing he was not short of money. 'I deemed it worth it and we did not have to pay for our shelter last night. As for that wench, she was no one of importance, so you can forget aught that she said.' He took off his hat and his fair hair seemed to glow in the lantern light.

Her breath caught in her throat and for a moment she could only stare at that handsome leonine head. Then she pulled herself together and went over to the pallets and rolled them out several feet from each other on each side of the tray.

Alex picked up the lantern and pitcher and put them close by so they could see what they were eating and removed his gloves. 'The broth smells good,' he said.

She agreed and removed her own gloves, but decided against taking off her hat. She lowered herself on to the pallet and eased off her boots before reaching for one of the bowls. She placed it at her side on the wooden floor.

Alex glanced her way and noticed that the lantern cast light on her weary face with its delicate nose and generously curved lips. He considered how not a word of complaint had escaped her that day and could not help but admire her stamina. He reached for the jug of mulled wine and poured her a drink and decided to test her further.

'Have you ever paid court to a woman, Master Wood?' he asked casually.

Rosamund was in the act of tearing bread from the loaf and almost dropped it. She paused. 'No. I do not have the means to support a wife…and besides, I doubt a woman would find me to her taste.'

'Why? You've a handsome face,' said Alex, pushing the cup across the floor to her.

Rosamund looked at him in astonishment before picking up the cup and taking a thirsty gulp of the warm liquid. 'My stepbrothers told me I was ugly. I confess I am not in the habit of gazing at myself in a looking glass.'

'You are an extremely modest young man if you can resist preening in front of a mirror. Most youths of your age are obsessed by the growth on their faces.' He dipped his spoon into the bowl of barley broth and waited for her reaction.

Rosamund's stomach clenched. She had given no thought to the male need to shave. 'I am not most youths,' she muttered.

'I would agree,' said Alex smoothly. 'How old are you?'

She hesitated and decided it would serve her best to not give her proper age. 'I have seen eighteen summers.'

'Then you are young to know much about women or to have a beard.'

'I know enough about them to know what they want from a man,' she retorted without thinking.

Her reply amused him and he gave one of his rare smiles. 'Your confidence amazes me. I am twenty-eight years old and I reckon I will find women difficult to understand till the day I die.'

Rosamund realised her mistake in giving such a confident answer. She picked up her spoon with unsteady fingers. 'You don't have a wife?'

'No. I enjoy travelling too much to give much thought to marriage. Although, one day I will need to settle down, for I would like to have children. But not yet.'

'Tell me, do you consider women greatly inferior to men and good for nought but keeping house and bearing babies?'

Alex wondered who had said that to her. 'Is it not a woman's role to keep house and give her husband children? Even my grandmother believed that was only right. She was an intelligent woman who organised the family business when both my grandfather and I were away from home. She was wont to say that it was in her blood, for it was what the womenfolk of the Vikings of old had to do when their men were away for months—even years, sometimes. Unfortunately, except for my mother, all her children died in infancy.'

'How sad,' murmured Rosamund, dunking bread in her soup. 'I was told that the Vikings were bloodthirsty warriors who raided our coast.' She shot him a challenging look.

'Ach! The Danes and Norsemen might have been warriors, but according to my grandmother, who has Danish blood, they were also farmers, fishermen and traders. Their womenfolk had to be strong, not knowing if their husbands or sons would ever return. They had to be both mother and father to their children. Our folklore speaks of many a mythical heroine who bested the men.'

'The men must not have liked that,' said Rosamund, encouraged by hearing of such brave women.

'The men transformed some women into monsters when they told their tales round their fires in the great halls. I remember hearing of the

Valkyries, or Odin's Maids as they are also named.' His eyes darkened as he remembered Ingrid referring to herself as one such maid—that was when she was not boasting of being a descendent of Lady Ingeborg Knutsdotter.

Rosamund smiled. 'I would hear more of them. I know of Odin. My brother used to tell me tales of the old gods when I was a child. Of Thor and his hammer and how he—' She stopped abruptly and looked confused. 'I had forgotten about that until you reminded me. How strange.'

'The mind has a habit of throwing up the unexpected,' he said softly. 'Do not let it disturb you. It has happened to me often since I received that blow on the head that rendered me unconscious. Do you remember aught else about your brother?'

'I was told that he had drowned.' She hesitated. 'For years I had dreams in which I saw him being carried away, but my stepmother said I was hallucinating and quite mad. There have been times when I wished that I had died like my mother and brother.'

Alex frowned. 'You should never wish death upon yourself. Life is for living, however painful it might be.'

She flushed. 'I know such thoughts are sinful, but my life was difficult after their deaths. I have long believed Lady Monica hated me because of my mother.'

Alex reflected on the selfishness of parents and the vulnerability of children. Had Sir James been aware of Lady Monica's treatment of his daughter? He remembered her mention of step-brothers.

'What about Lady Monica's sons?' he asked.

Suddenly Rosamund realised that she had been talking too much and wondered if the question was meant to trick her. She knew so little about this foreigner, not even his name. 'I have said enough,' she murmured, wondering what it was about this man that had so loosened her tongue—or perhaps it was the wine that had done that?

Alex would have liked to have continued the conversation, but decided that tomorrow would be soon enough to resume their conversation. So he ate his supper; when she had finished eating, he removed the tray. He returned to discover that she had fallen asleep curled up in her cloak, and seeing her so vulnerable, his instincts were to protect her. Then he told himself he must not allow his feelings to soften too much towards her. He already knew her to be a liar. Yet he found himself picking up the blanket folded at the foot of her pallet and covering her with it. Then he placed his saddlebags between them, settled himself on his own pallet and almost immediately fell asleep.

Rosamund woke, feeling snug and comfortable until she realised that she was using the Swedish man's saddlebags as a pillow. There was also a weight on her chest and a heaviness on her hip. She started up in fright and attempted to move her sleeping companion's hand without waking him.

Alex was having a nightmare and surfaced from fathoms deep, believing himself under attack. His hand curled on a slender hose-clad thigh and he struggled to free his other one that was being held. He dragged his hand free and the next moment had drawn his dagger and was astride his assailant with the blade against his throat.

Rosamund squealed and dug her fingernails into the back of his hand. 'I beg you don't kill me! I have no weapon!'

Alex paused, blinked and stared down into the panic-stricken face. Now he was aware of the curve of a very feminine hip against his thigh and felt a stirring in his loins. He watched the soft lips part and the tip of her tongue dart nervously along her upper lip and felt an overwhelming urge to plunder her mouth with lips and tongue. A long moment passed and he could feel the pulse in her neck racing against his fingers. The blue-violet eyes appeared larger than usual as they entreated him not to hurt her. He loosened his grip and backed away. Deeply disturbed by the feelings she had roused in him, he moved away from her over to the window.

A stupefied Rosamund could scarcely believe that from being convinced he might kill her, several heart-thudding moments later, she was persuaded that he had been about to kiss her. What madness was that? Surely if she had betrayed herself and he knew her to be a woman, then he would have turned away in disgust? She told herself that it might yet happen.

Warily, she gazed at his back and then her scrutiny lowered to his tapering waist and then even lower. She stared at the length of his long, muscular legs in the tightly fitting hose as he stood there, unmoving for several moments. Then he shook his head, yawned and stretched. Transfixed, she watched the hem of his shirt ride up over his thighs to reveal the swell of his buttocks beneath the hose. Blushing fiercely, she turned her back on him.

When face to face with him once more, it was to see that he had donned doublet and boots. 'We've slept too long,' he said, averting his eyes from her flushed face. 'Get yourself up, Master Wood.'

Rosamund wasted no time in doing so. 'Does the late hour and such haste mean that we do not have time to break our fast?' she asked gruffly.

'We'll eat in the saddle,' he replied. 'I'll speak to the innkeeper about food and then fetch the horse.'

She nodded, wondering what it would have felt like to be kissed by him. Immediately she felt ashamed of herself for thinking such thoughts. He believed her to be a youth and she was wicked to even consider it. Besides, the only kisses she had experienced were those forced upon her by Edward and he had crushed her teeth against her inner lip so that it bled. Kissing was no fun and she still knew so little about this Swede.

Rosamund locked the door so she could tend to a desperate need in the chamber pot before hurrying downstairs, thinking how much easier attending certain bodily needs were for men. She was on her way to the stables when she saw her travelling companion coming towards her. He was leading his horse and carrying what appeared to

be a pillion seat in the other hand. 'I have pur-
chased this from the innkeeper,' he said. 'I will fix
it on to my horse and it will be more comfortable
for you. We will stop to eat after we have a good
few miles behind us.'

Her brow puckered, and reluctantly she said,
'We will not make much speed sharing the same
horse. You'll reach London the swifter without
me. Why do you not go on ahead without me?'

Alex was annoyed by her suggestion and thought
he knew what had caused it. 'No,' he said tersely.
'You scarcely managed to cope with that woman
last night. What if you were set upon by thieves? I
reckon we will still arrive in the city in time for the
business I have to tend to there. Besides, I deem
you could be of use to me when we reach London.'

She was surprised. 'In what way can I be of
use to you?'

'I will tell you when I know you better.'

'You know more about me than I do you,' she
retorted. 'Do you not think it is time I have a name
by which to call you?'

Alex studied her features. 'Why?'

'You address me as Master Wood as is polite,
but you are Master No Name and that does not
seem right to me.'

He hesitated. 'My name is Master Nilsson and my home is in Gotland, Sweden.'

Rosamund smiled. 'I recognise the name of the place. My father imported furs, amber and silver goods from your northern climes, although he complained about having trouble with Scottish pirates, as well as the Hanseatic League due to the latter's monopoly of trade in the Baltic.'

'Aye. I have experienced trouble with pirates myself,' he said drily.

'You have?' She would like to know more.

He looked thoughtful as he busied himself attaching the pillion seat to his horse. Then he seized her by the waist, causing her to squeal as he lifted her up on to the pillion seat.

She clung to the wooden arms. 'Why could you not have allowed me to climb into the seat myself?' she asked in a breathless voice, aware of a pleasurable tremor that she could only believe was the result of his actions.

'It was quicker my way,' said Alex. 'What of your stepbrother who lives in London?'

'Oh, he never complains of being troubled with pirates,' she said blandly.

'How fortunate.' And how suspicious, thought Alex.

Rosamund thought Master Nilsson's mouth tightened as he dragged himself into the saddle and guessed she was not going to discover any more about pirates from him. Which was vexatious—there were conversations she had overheard that could have interested him.

Chapter Four

Now Rosamund had the security of the pillion seat, she no longer needed to cling to Master Nilsson for safety and would be able to keep her distance from him.

Alex was also thinking that the pillion seat was money well spent. No longer would he be disturbed by thoughts of the wench's soft body brushing his back and those small hands holding on to him so she would not fall. Which meant he could concentrate on considering why her stepbrother had no trouble with pirates. This caused him to consider with which countries he traded. It was possible that he had no interest in his stepfather's markets and instead did business with southern Europe and Africa, so his ships did not risk crossing the northern seas.

Having come to that conclusion, Alex let his

mind drift to thoughts of the blonde and beautiful Ingrid Wrangel and the message she had
brought him from Harry the morning after Sir
James had asked about Harry, saying that the
young man reminded him of someone he had
known in the past. If Alex had not been distracted
just then, he would have asked Sir James for more
information. As it was, Alex had not seen him or
Harry again that evening. Then had come the
message and he had hastened to Cheapside,
where the Royal Company of Mercers had their
headquarters, in response to its summons.
Apparently Harry had information concerning a
stolen cargo belonging to Alex. There he was
attacked in a cowardly fashion so that he did not
even catch sight of his attacker. The only proof
he had that his erstwhile friend had been there
was a silver amulet of Thor's hammer reworked
into the shape of a cross that he had bent down to
pick up.

Fortunately a member of the Royal Company of
Mercers had found the unconscious Alex with the
amulet still clenched in his hand. He'd had him
carried to the monastic hospital that was part of the
building. There the monks had nursed him back to
health until he was well enough to return to

Sweden, having received a missive informing him that his grandmother was dying.

His thoughts were interrupted by a question from his companion. 'Do you visit London often, Master Nilsson?'

'Whenever it is necessary,' he replied, wondering what was behind her question.

'Have you ever met the Lord Mayor?'

'Why do you ask?'

'Because I am interested in your answer.'

'No, I have not.'

'A pity. I would have liked to have known your opinion on what kind of man makes a good Lord Mayor of London. Perhaps you have heard of Richard Whittington, who was a member of the Royal Company of Mercers and filled the position several times?'

'I can't say that I have.' Despite his denial, Alex was alert to any information to do with the Royal Company of Mercers. 'What is your interest?'

'It is my stepbrother's ambition to be Lord Mayor of London and he is a member of that exalted company. From what I have heard, it takes a plentiful supply of funds to become Lord Mayor,' said Rosamund.

'What are you suggesting?'

'I am not suggesting anything,' she answered in a colourless voice.

Alex guessed that she was doing exactly that, but showing caution. She wanted him to ponder on her words and come to a conclusion that might match her own. 'What is your step-brother's name?'

'I would rather not say at this moment. If you have met Sir James, then perhaps you can work that out for yourself, too.'

'I suspect, Master Wood, you are playing games with me.'

'I would not dare, Master Nilsson,' she said, sounding horrified that he should consider such a thought. 'But there is always the possibility,' she could not resist adding mischievously.

'Do not push my patience too far, Master Wood,' warned Alex.

'I hear you and obey. I will not plague you any more,' said Rosamund meekly. 'I feel a megrim coming on so I will be silent.'

Alex was not sure if he believed in her megrim, but he hoped that she would keep her word and leave him to his thoughts that now concerned a stepbrother whose stepfather was Sir James Appleby and who was a member of the Royal

Company of Mercers and was in need of lots of money to fund his ambitions. He was not bothered by pirates, unlike his stepfather, and *Master Wood* suspected Sir James had been murdered. Was she saying that the prime suspect for his murder was her stepbrother? It seemed extremely likely. Well, it shouldn't be too difficult for him to discover the identity of Sir James's stepson once he reached London. But did any of this have aught to do with Harry and Sir James's words about a likeness to someone he had known in the past?

As the day wore on, the pain in Rosamund's head increased and her whole body ached. She worried in case Master Nilsson thought she was quite mad, playing games with him instead of giving him straight answers. She did not really believe that he was in the pay of her stepbrother, but how was she to know for certain?

The miles fell behind them until, just before dusk, they stopped at an inn a short distance south of Stafford. By then Rosamund's head was thumping and she had stomach cramps. As she dismounted, her knees buckled and she would have fallen if Alex had not been there to lift her upright. For a moment she rested her weary body against the strong line of his and was glad of his arm about her. Then with a start of fright, she realised she was behaving like a woman and drew away from him.

By means of clinging on to the horse's bridle, she managed to remain on her feet, but her gait was unsteady and she felt sick. Yet she insisted on leading the horse to the stable.

Once again Alex watched her with admiration. They had spent hours on horseback and there had been no word of complaint from her. He was not surprised she was exhausted. He wasted no time going inside the inn. It was a finer one than that in which they had stayed last night and he was able to obtain a private bedchamber with a proper bed. He asked for a fire to be lit and supper prepared for them. Then, carrying a lantern, he headed for the stables where he found Rosamund resting against a stall with her eyes closed. He took one look at her face, which appeared to have lost all colour and was damp with perspiration, and told her to get to the inn and rest.

'But I have not…' she began.

'Never mind that. Tell the innkeeper to show you up to our bedchamber.' His tone was harsh.

'You're angry with me because you believe I am

playing games with you. Perhaps you believe I am mad,' cried Rosamund in dismay.

'Not now,' said Alex sharply.

She made to continue, but he roared, 'Get yourself inside and to bed before you collapse!'

Rosamund shrank away from him and stumbled outside and threw up behind some bushes. She felt a little better after that and, despite being near to tears and aching all over, she managed to reach their bedchamber without falling. She peeled off her outer clothes and, with a sense of doom and horror, discovered blood on her nether male undergarment. She must have miscounted the days to when her next monthly courses were due. What was she going to do now? She had never been in such a dilemma before and, for a moment, was at a loss how to deal with the situation. Then common sense asserted itself and she locked the door.

Hastily she took off her shirt and began to remove the binding that constrained her breasts. Tearing a length of the material, she made it into a pad and placed it inside the nether garment. Then she put on her shirt and hose before ripping up more of the binding and placing them with her cloak and doublet before climbing into bed. She curled up on one side of it and fell into an exhausted sleep.

* * *

When Alex arrived outside the bedchamber it was to discover that the door was locked. He knocked at the wooden panel gently, but there came no sound from within. Had he frightened her so much by roaring at her earlier that she was scared he would hurt her? He tapped again and called, 'Master Wood, of your courtesy, open the door?'

But still there was no response and, due to the utter silence, he concluded that his travelling companion had fallen asleep. He went downstairs and told the innkeeper that he had changed his mind and would have supper in the parlour. As for Master Wood, he had fallen asleep and perhaps it was best not to disturb him.

Rosamund woke hours later. The candle had guttered out and the fire was but dead embers. She remembered locking the door and guessed that most likely Master Nilsson had remained downstairs to spend the night in discomfort. A groan escaped her. She had not intended keeping him from his bed. Had he decided that she had deliberately locked him out for losing his temper with her? But why had he not banged on the door to waken her?

Perhaps he had done so and she had not heard him. No doubt he was furious with her. Was it time she parted company with him? What had he thought of her suggestions? What interests did a so-called Swedish jack of all trades have in London after having visited Lathom House and seeking out her father? A man whom he had told her that he had only met once. And what was happening on the twenty-second of the month that he needed to be in London?

The cramps in her stomach had eased a little and she replaced the pad, anguishing over this evidence of her femininity. Despite the soreness beneath and her aching back, she managed to pull on her boots and buttoned up her doublet. She put on her hat and fastened her cloak and, picking up her pitifully few bindings, as well as the soiled one, she let herself out of the bedchamber and crept downstairs.

All was quiet as she drew back the bolts and peered outside. There was a pearly light in the sky towards the east, which meant it would soon be dawn. She went and dug a hole in the soil near the stable with a stick and buried the soiled cloth. Then she washed her hands in the horse trough before returning to the inn. She found her way to the kitchen and went over to the larder and took a hunk of bread and cut slices of ham from the joint there. Then she let herself outside again.

The freezing air seemed determined to take bites out of her face. Nevertheless, she pulled up her hood before hurrying across the yard to the stable.

She was in the act of trying to saddle up Alex's horse when a voice from behind said, 'And where are you going so early in the morning, Master Wood, and in such haste?' Her heart seemed to somersault as she turned to face the man silhouetted in the doorway.

'Have you no answer for me, little thief?' asked Alex coldly.

Rosamund took a deep breath in an attempt to calm herself. 'I am not a thief. I was just trying to have everything ready for when you came out. I thought you would be tired after my accidentally locking you out of the bedchamber. I beg pardon for doing so.' She swallowed nervously. 'I also knew that you would want to make an early start, knowing that my presence on your horse has lengthened the time of your journey.'

Alex was confounded. 'Are you being honest with me?'

'Why should I speak falsely?'

'Because you are scared,' he said bluntly. 'You ask much of me. I want to believe that you did not intend to steal my horse and escape, but give me a further reason why I should do so?'

'I will be honest with you and admit that I have deceived you.'

Alex's heart began to thud. Was she about to tell him that she was a woman? 'What is the manner of your deception?'

Rosamund's lips parted, but the words would not come and she despised herself for being a coward. Moments passed and Alex reached out and drew her towards him. 'What is wrong? Is the truth so terrible that you do not have the courage to reveal it?'

She nodded wordlessly, conscious that her breasts were crushed against his chest. Perhaps she would not need to speak because surely he could not be unaware of them and would guess her secret.

Alex was indeed aware that her breasts appeared to have sprouted overnight and to his astonishment his arousal was instant and he wanted to take her there and then in the straw. He imagined her expression if he should do so and instantly released her. He did not want such a complication in his life. 'I am disappointed that you still cannot be honest with me. I see you consider me no friend?'

She found her voice. 'How can I consider you a friend when I know so little about you?'

'I have given you a name and told you where I come from. You know that I like travelling and am a jack of all trades.'

'That is still not a lot of information when it comes to giving someone your trust,' said Rosamund.

Alex could not prevent a smile. 'You're not so crazed as your stepfamily seemed to want you to believe, Master Appleby.'

Rosamund started and a tiny laugh escaped her. 'How clever of you to guess my secret.'

Alex's smile deepened. Perhaps he should not blame her for wanting to continue to conceal her true identity from him. 'You gave yourself away on several occasions.'

'I would not make a very good conspirator, would I?'

'I disagree. You have deduced that it is not always safe to tell strangers your secrets and to answer a question with a question.'

Rosamund agreed.

'But of course, in providing me with the information that you have, I have come to the conclusion that you believe your stepbrother murdered your father.'

She hesitated. 'Would you say that is a sensible conclusion to draw?'

He nodded. 'But I would add that if you are Sir James's son, then surely you should be in charge of Appleby Manor and his business in London, not your stepfamily.'

Rosamund was silent.

Alex said abruptly, 'We will leave this for now. It is time we were on our way.'

Rosamund lifted her head and stared at him. 'I have some food I have taken from the kitchen as I missed supper—shall we eat it later?'

He nodded. 'Let us put some miles behind us.'

Whilst he was saddling up his horse, she went and fetched the pillion seat. They had travelled a few miles when Rosamund said, 'What was your opinion of my father?'

He glanced over his shoulder at her sombre face. 'As I told you, I met him but the once.'

'Where?'

'Down at the quayside,' answered Alex carefully. 'We were watching ships being unloaded. It was then he spotted the young captain of the *Thor's Hammer*. He said he reminded him of someone he had known in a past life.'

Rosamund said, 'What a strange comment to

make. Did he say whom this captain reminded him of?'

'No. And I have not seen either of them since then.'

'Perhaps your young captain is dead.'

Her words gave him a shock. 'That I have not considered.'

'Why? If he is a seafarer, then it is a possibility, is it not?'

Alex could not deny it. 'I sense he is alive,' he said abruptly.

'Why, if you have not seen him? Would you have expected to have seen him during the time that has passed since you last did so?'

'In the circumstances, no.'

'What circumstances are these?'

He gave her an exasperated look. 'It is I who ask the questions.'

'I have already answered several of yours,' she said.

'Then answer me this one,' said Alex. 'Give me the name of your stepbrother in London.'

She sighed. 'I cannot understand your interest if you are but a travelling jack of all trades. I deem, Master Nilsson, that you are not being honest with me.'

'I admit it, but I still want an answer to my question,' he said in a steely voice.

'Can't it wait until we reach London?'

'No! I have much to do when I arrive there,' he said, hanging on to his patience.

'Then if I must, I must. I just pray to our Lady and all the saints that I can trust you, Master Nilsson. His name is Edward Fustian.'

Fustian! Alex had met the man and considered him a smarmy, arrogant, insular fellow. He had a certain attraction for the ladies, which irritated Alex exceedingly. He had heard it from Ingrid that he beat his wife and treated her like dirt beneath his feet. Yet he had not thought to include him in the names on the list of those he suspected might be guilty of passing on information about cargoes and times of departure of ships sailing from the port of London.

'I have met him, but do not know him well,' said Alex. 'I have heard he is not kind to his wife.'

Rosamund nodded and said in a seething voice, 'She had several bruises last time I saw her. She was a cowed little woman and so were her daughters. I felt so sorry for her because I understood what she was going through.'

'Could you not have helped her?'

'I would have liked to, but you have not met my stepmother, Master Nilsson, or grown up with Edward.'

'Tell me about it.'

Rosamund took a deep breath. 'I thought at first that Edward might prove to be another brother to me. He is some five years older and at first he showed me some kindness, but it was not long before he revealed his true colours.' Her voice quivered. 'Overbearing, arrogant and swift to lash out at me with his tongue and fist.' The memory she had buried burst forth and she remembered, when first she had shown signs of early woman-hood, how Edward had whispered lewd sugges-tions in her ear and pulled up her skirts. She took a shuddering breath. 'I wish I'd had the courage to kill him.'

Aware that she was deeply disturbed, Alex said, 'You do not have to continue if you find speaking of it upsetting.'

'No. I deem there is a purpose in your question-ing. If somehow you could bring Edward to his knees, then I would do anything to help you.'

'Is that a promise?'

'In as much as I will be able to keep it.'

'Was he never chided?' he rasped.

'He was always careful not to misbehave when my father was there. Fortunately there came a day when he was caught out and despatched to serve his apprenticeship in Father's business. I was never so glad of anything in my life. Although that was not the end of it. My stepmother was furious because she was in favour of a match between us, but she could not persuade Father into her way of thinking. That made her even angrier with me, but I pretended to be a fool and allowed her to treat me like one. I discovered a long time ago that, if I remained quietly in a corner, people would forget I was there and carry on all kinds of conversations with no thought to whom might be listening.'

Alex was impressed by her perception, even as he was aware that she had let two nuggets of information slip. She had touched on a match between herself and Edward and mentioned that she had thought he would be like another brother to her. Had she realised she had just revealed to him that she was a woman? Also, that was twice she had referred to a brother. How long was it since she had lost her brother? How and when had he died? Why should her stepmother wish for a match between her son and the stepdaughter she believed crazy? Was it that she had persuaded her husband that he should not leave his property to his daughter and instead make her son his heir? Was it possible that she believed her son's position precarious and that was why she had suggested a match between the two? Obviously she had overplayed her hand. He wished that he could have met the lady so as to draw his own conclusions.

'What else have you learnt by your eavesdropping?' he asked.

She replied promptly, 'That the Hanseatic League's monopoly of trade in the Baltic infuriates Edward.'

That did not surprise Alex, for it angered most merchants who wanted to buy into such markets themselves. He asked her no more questions, deciding that a little silence would give them both time for reflection. He would like to know about her brother and how he had died, but that information could wait. They were still many leagues from London.

When they came to the next inn, Rosamund was too weary to attempt to converse with Master Nilsson. Indeed, she decided she had given him enough information about her stepfamily. Fortunately, he seemed in no mood to talk further; as it happened that night they were not alone in a sleeping chamber, but shared it with other travellers.

The next day she expected him to ask her more questions about Edward or Harry, but to her surprise he enquired instead about her other stepbrother.

The question startled her. 'William! You want to know about William?'

'Why not? Surely you have something to tell me about him?'

Rosamund's hands tightened on the pillion seat as she considered what he would make of her answer. She decided that it should be safe enough to speak honestly of William. 'He is a lack-wit, but one wonders if that is the fault of his mother. She is for ever hitting him across the head and comparing him to his elder brother. Yet he will do anything for her and his brother, which is a big mistake.'

'Why is that?'

'They are bad examples of how a decent man should behave. I feel sorry for the poor girl who is destined to marry him.'

'Who is this maiden?'

'I know only that her name is Bridget and that she is a niece to a close kinsman of my stepmother.'

'Your younger stepbrother takes no interest in your stepbrother's business?'

Rosamund shook her head. 'He does not have the wit.'

'Then who oversees Appleby Manor?'

'My stepmother,' she said bitterly. 'She persuaded my father I was incapable of doing so.'

'That must have infuriated you.'

'Indeed it did, but Father had no faith in my abilities. He believed my stepmother's estimation of my character.'

'Does your anger extend to him?'

Rosamund did not answer.

Alex did not press her. It was obvious that Mistress Appleby had been sorely treated by not only her stepfamily, but also her father. He recalled Sir James Appleby gazing up at Harry and the words he had spoken. Was the loss of his son reason enough for a father to treat his daughter so thoughtlessly? He set out to entertain her for the rest of the journey.

During the day he talked about the countries he had visited and told her about the ways he had kept body and soul together. He spoke of playing in a troupe of entertainers and made her laugh by telling her jests and describing some of the japes and dances they performed. He found himself enjoying sharing such tales with her. He spoke of Sweden and the beauty of its countryside and the splendour of its cities. Yet he never mentioned his title or wealth or the task his father had set him. He was only prepared to trust Mistress Appleby so far.

As for Rosamund, she was made only more wary by the change in him. Why was he trying to charm her? It was quite a struggle to resist him. Sometimes on wakening there was a moment when they turned over and their faces were but a foot away and they caught the other's eye. Then she thought she saw an expression in his face that melted her insides, but she fought against such feelings.

Chapter Five

By the time they arrived at St Albans, a town where two great battles had been fought between the Houses of Lancaster and York, she was feeling the strain of pretending that she was a man and she knew that she had to get away from Master Nilsson. This despite the promise she had voiced to bring Edward to his knees. For the last time on that journey, she went inside an inn and upstairs to the bedchamber that once again he arranged for them. The room was cold and she thought how often she would have liked to snuggle up to him and share his warmth and feel his strong arms holding her secure, but she told herself that this was confused thinking.

A sigh escaped her. Tomorrow they would arrive in London and she would need to find her god-mother's house. The thought lifted her heart. She might be uncertain of its whereabouts, but she could ask for directions; surely if her godmother had sent a servant to enquire about her, then she should be pleased to see her. The trouble was that after being on the road for so many days, wearing the same garments, she was travel-stained and smelly. The worry of it all quite made her lose her appetite and imbibe more wine than usual.

'Ach! Master Appleby, you haven't eaten enough to keep a sparrow alive,' said Alex, staring across the table at the slender face made rosy by wind and wintry sun. 'You have proved your stamina equal to mine in the last few days, so what is it that has ruined your taste for food now we are nearing journey's end?'

'Would you say I have proved myself as good as many a man?' The words were slurred as she swirled the mulled wine in her cup.

Alex's eyes narrowed. 'There is no need for you to prove yourself to me. Although I suppose in the circumstances it is natural for you to do so.'

'What circumstances?' she muttered, staring at him from beneath drooping eyelids as she reached for the wine.

He did not answer her question, but moved the

pitcher beyond her reach. 'You will want a clear head when you reach London,' he said.

'London,' she uttered drowsily. 'There all will change between us.' She yawned and closed her eyes and her head nodded.

Alex reached forward and cupped her chin before her face could land in the bowl of soup. He stood up, eased himself around the table and managed to place an arm beneath her knees. He lifted her and carried her over to the bed. There he drew back the bedcovers and laid her down before tucking them in round her. Then he went and sat in a chair and brooded on their situation and what to do when they arrived in London. Would she volunteer the truth at last?

He reached for his cloak and wrapped it round him and prepared himself for a long night.

At some point he must have dozed off, because he was roused by the sound of a woman sobbing. Forcing his eyelids open, he pushed himself out of the chair and went over to the bed.

'What is troubling you?' he asked gently.

She did not respond, but continued to weep. By the dying light of the fire he could see that her eyes were still closed. Suddenly, she ceased crying and, instead, started to speak. He lowered his head in an attempt to catch the words.

'Harry, where are you, Harry? Where are they taking you? Don't leave me alone with her!' Her voice dropped and he had to bring his head even closer to hers. 'Papa, listen to me. It was not my fault! I wanted to save Mama, but she would not let me near her. She would force that vile potion down my throat and Edward stood watching and laughing.' She fell silent a moment and then she spoke again. 'Edward, keep away from me! Do not touch me! It is wrong!' she cried. 'Papa, listen to me. I am telling the truth. I am not mad. Oh, why don't you believe me? Why can't you love me like you did Harry and Mama?' Suddenly she sat up and Alex had to draw away from her. Her hat fell off, along with her cap, and her dark hair tumbled about her shoulders. A small hand shot out and seized hold of Alex. 'You must find Harry!' she cried.

Alex was deeply disturbed by her distress. 'You need not fear. I will find him,' he assured her.

'Good,' she murmured, subsiding.

Only when he thought she had fallen asleep again did Alex make a move to remove the hand that rested on his thigh. Her fingers tightened about his and she rolled over and rested her head against his leg. He could not resist stroking her hair or brushing her lips with his own. She let out a wine-scented breath against his mouth. He remained where he was for a long time, caressing the side of her face with a gentle hand until he was certain that this time she was truly asleep. Then he managed to free his hand and return to the chair. He wondered if, when she woke, she would remember what had taken place. He needed to discover how her brother had died—only then would he know whether he would be able to keep his word to her. As for Edward Fustian, the world would be a better place without him. He closed his eyes, but it was some time before he fell asleep.

Rosamund woke just as it was getting light and turned over on to her side. Stretching out a hand, she felt for the man she expected to find at her side. Empty! She sat up and the pain in her head thumped in rhythm with the increased beat of her heart. She was terribly thirsty and could not remember getting into bed or aught of their conversation last evening. Where was Master Nilsson? Had he carried her to bed because she was drunk and, disgusted with her behaviour, left her to sleep alone? For this to happen now utterly depressed her spirits.

Her eyes pierced the dimness of the bedchamber and she was able to make out a figure in a chair. Now she became aware of his steady breathing and she slid soundlessly off the bed. She felt dizzy and her throat was tight with misery. This time there really was a need for a parting of the ways. For him to choose a chair rather than remain in the bed spoke much of how he must feel towards her.

She searched for her outer garments and boots and, by some miracle, found them without waking him. She did not pause to put them on, but cautiously went over to the door and unlocked it. She opened it a fraction, managed to ease herself through the gap and closed the door behind her. She would travel the rest of the way to London on foot; if God forgave her and answered her prayer, then she would find her godmother's house before dark. If she and Master Nilsson were ever to meet again, she prayed that he would not recognise his erstwhile travelling companion in Mistress Rosamund Appleby.

Alex woke suddenly and wondered what it was that had disturbed him. It was morning and his gaze darted to the bed. He saw that the bedclothes had been flung back and the bed was empty. He found the door unlocked and hurried downstairs, hoping to find Mistress Appleby taking the fresh air to clear her head. There was no sign of her and he hurried to the stables. His horse was still there, but she was nowhere to be found. Why had she deserted him now? Had she not been fully asleep when he had kissed her? He could think of no other reason why she had taken fright and cursed himself for giving in to temptation. He saddled up his horse and knew he had to find her before she ended up in trouble.

Rosamund thanked the carter who had been kind enough to give her a lift on the last stage of her journey and limped along Aldersgate Street. She glanced up at the threatening sky and knew she had to find her godmother's house before nightfall. But first she needed a gown to wear. Perhaps she could exchange her cloak for a used gown. Surely there would be a used-clothes dealer somewhere in London? But where exactly? She passed St Paul's Cathedral and Paternoster Row where shops sold rosaries in their hundreds. She paused to gaze inside a workshop and marvelled to see books being produced on a printing press.

She felt certain Master Nilsson would have been interested to see the printers at work because it had become obvious to her that he was an educated man. But she must not think of him, she had to hurry.

A short while later she had still not found a used-clothes dealer. She glanced up at the darkening sky and felt the cold sting of a snowflake touch her cheek; then a positive flurry of snowflakes threatened to blind her. She hurried, but soon realised that she was lost. Suddenly she heard a slithering sound and heavy breathing, then came a suppressed cough. 'Is there someone there?' she called. 'Can you help me?'

A figure loomed out of a doorway a few yards ahead. 'Depends on whether yer can make it worth me while,' said the man.

'What do you mean?' she asked with a tremor in her voice.

'What do yer think I mean?' he sneered.

A hand shot out and seized her arm. Her heart gave a frightening lurch and she managed to tear herself from his grasp. She made to run, but he caught hold of her cloak and dragged her back against him. Her hat went flying as he pinned her arms to her sides.

'What is it you want?' she cried.

'Coin to buy bread and a pallet for the night,' he replied.

'I have none. I'm just a poor lad who's come from the country to try to earn a crust.'

'Then I'll have to take yer cloak,' said that voice in her ear. His foul breath caused her to gag. 'And don't try any funny business or I'll choke the life out of yer.'

With shaking hands Rosamund attempted to unfasten the ties at her throat. But he grew impatient and dragged the garment from her, causing the ties to snap, before running off with it. Furious with herself for behaving like a frightened hen, she gave chase. After all, it was possible that he would lead her out of this maze of alleys. Instead, she ended up blundering into a wall. Her hands explored its surface and she discovered that it loomed high above her and carried on horizontally for what seemed an age.

Surely it must lead somewhere?

Rosamund jogged beside it, tripping over rubbish several times in the gathering gloom. At last she came to a gateway and was about to try to open the door when she heard footsteps on the other side. The door opened and a religious appeared. She gazed at Rosamund from beneath her wimple and suddenly her eyes widened.

'By the saints, Harry, where have you been these past six months?' she asked in a charmingly accented voice. 'Why did you have to go off the way you did? There was really no need. You won't know it, but Alex left London. Although perhaps you met with him on your travels?' she asked anxiously.

'I think you are mistaking me for someone else,' said Rosamund.

The nun looked uncertain and peered into Rosamund's damp face. 'Aye, I see now that you are not Black Harry, but you are very like him.' She placed a hand on Rosamund's chest and smiled straight into her eyes. 'Is it possible that you are kin to him?'

'I don't know a Black Harry. I had a brother once called Harry, but he drowned.'

The nun's expression altered. 'You must come with me. I know someone who would be interested to meet you.'

Rosamund felt a prickly feeling in the nape of her neck and suddenly knew this religious was perhaps not what she seemed. At that moment there was the sound of a man's voice in the yard behind her. Instantly, Rosamund recognised her stepbrother's voice. She shoved the nun against the door and then she ran like the wind along the passageway.

To her relief there came a turning and the next moment she arrived at a tributary of the Thames. She paused to catch her breath, but she knew she could not delay. She might be completely mistaken about the nun, but she definitely was not about that voice. Lowering her head against the swirling snowflakes, Rosamund began to walk uphill. So it was she did not notice the tall, dark figure coming towards her and blundered into him. Caught off balance, he swayed. She clutched his cloak, but he slipped in the snow and they both fell to the ground with her on top of him. He arched his body in an attempt to throw her off, but she was entangled in his cloak so that proved impossible. He reached up and pushed. Rosamund gasped, thinking that he must not have realised where he had put his hands and dragged on one of his arms. 'Master, will you desist and release me!' she cried in a panic.

On hearing that muffled voice coming from somewhere beneath his cloak, Alex could scarcely believe his luck. 'Master Appleby! Or should I say *Mistress Appleby*?' he said in a velvety tone.

Rosamund collapsed on top of him and lay unmoving, listening to the heavy thud-thud-thud of his heart and the gallop of her own. He knew her secret, but she deemed him the lesser of two evils. 'Master Nilsson,' she gasped. 'I lost myself in the back alleys and was robbed of my cloak and then I saw a religious, who thought I was someone called Black Harry. I find that very strange in the light of my having had a brother called Harry. Then whose voice did I hear beyond the wall but that of my stepbrother, Edward.'

'You mean Fustian was inside the Steel Yard?'

'Keep your voice down! So that's what that place is,' she murmured. 'I have heard of the head-quarters of the Hanseatic League, but never set foot inside. What was Edward doing there? I knew I had to escape. If he catches me now, then it will be your fault. You're lying on part of your cloak and I can't tug it free.'

'Will you be quiet! Now, if you will release your hold on my cloak we can free ourselves.'

Relieved, she tried to do as he asked, but one of her hands was caught beneath his body and it required effort to free it. He hissed at her to stop.

'But you're lying on my hand,' she explained in an undertone.

He muttered indistinctly, lifting himself up and glancing about him as he did so. He tried not to think about what was going on in his loins. Mistress Appleby might have stopped wriggling, but the damage was already done and he could only hope she was unaware of his arousal. What was it about this woman that she could stir up a whole host of conflicting emotions inside him at such a dangerous time? If Fustian came upon them now, then they would be at a huge disadvantage.

'That's better,' gasped Rosamund, stretched her cramped fingers. She felt a bump against her belly and shifted to avoid it.

Alex groaned and, making an enormous effort, raised himself higher, taking him with her. With a final thrust he managed to throw her aside.

Rosamund scrambled to her feet and took several deep breaths. Despite the cold and damp, she had felt a heat between them that had her wanting to fan herself. But now was not the time to think of such things. They had to get away. She had only taken a couple of steps when a noise to her rear warned her that they were not alone. She called a warning to Alex before she was seized from behind.

'Let me go,' she cried, fearing that she had been caught by Edward.

'Youse shut yer mouth and keep yer orders to yerself,' snapped an unfamiliar voice.

Rosamund could scarcely believe that she had been captured by another ruffian. 'Not now,' she muttered, struggling to free herself.

'We wants to know what yer've got in yer pockets,' snarled the man, twisting her right arm up her back. She cried out in pain.

'Hold fast there,' said Alex, drawing not only his own sword, but Rosamund's short-sword as well. 'Release her at once.'

'Another furriner giving his orders,' said a woman with a sniff.

'Just do as I say or I'll run you through,' said Alex.

The man who held Rosamund captive produced a dagger. 'Come one step nearer and I'll slit his throat.'

'You have too much to say for yourself,' growled Alex, and with one swift movement he knocked the dagger from the man's hand and then, with a twirl of the other sword, he caught him a blow beneath the chin with its hilt. The dagger flew off into the darkness and the man's hold on Rosamund's arm slackened as he slid to the ground.

'Hey, what have yer dun to him?' asked his accomplice.

Alex did not bother replying, but seized Rosamund's hand and dragged her away, hurrying her along the bank of the tributary until the woman's cries faded into the distance.

'Wh-where are we going?' asked Rosamund, needing to clench her teeth in an attempt to stop them from chattering. She could not see the way ahead.

Alex bit back an oath and removed his own cloak and wrapped it round her. His fingers brushed her throat as he tied the strings and she trembled.

'Keep still and be glad you're a woman,' he said brusquely. 'I wouldn't be so gallant if you were a man.'

'Why should y-you feel a n-need to be gallant when y-you must believe my behaviour w-w-wicked and unseemly?'

'I was taught by my grandmother to respect women. A habit I find difficult to break. Come, we must go carefully. I have friends who can provide us with a hot tub and dry clothing.'

'Where is your horse?' she asked.

'At their house. I stabled him whilst I visited a couple of places.'

'But I told you I had to see Lady Elizabeth

Stanley. Did you not think of going to her home in search of me?'

'Aye. But not immediately. Anyway, we are some way from her mansion.'

'I was looking for a used-clothes dealer in the hope of exchanging my cloak for a gown.'

'Then you are in luck,' said Alex, stepping carefully. 'Tell me, how did you reach London so swiftly on foot?'

'A man took pity on me and let me ride in his cart. I was limping because my feet were sore.' Suddenly she slipped in the snow and was saved only by the strength in his wrist.

'You should not have run away from me.' His tone was vexed.

'I had to because I believed you had a disgust of me for getting drunk.' She gripped his hand tightly, still concerned about slipping in the snow. 'Tell me, how did I betray myself?'

'Your eyes, your lips and the way you swing your hips when you walk—the timbre of your voice and not even a hint of a whisker on your chin. Of course, there was also the slip about your stepmother wanting you to marry Edward.'

'How foolish of me!' She sighed heavily. 'But why did you not mention it at the time? I see I made lots of mistakes, but I swear on my mother's grave that everything I told you about myself and my stepfamily is true.'

'If I did not believe that, then I would not be taking you to my friends. How old are you, Mistress Appleby?'

'I have seen twenty-two summers, not eighteen,' she said rapidly. 'Do you not think it strange that that religious mistook me for this Black Harry?'

'How did your brother die?'

'Lady Monica told me he drowned. His clothes were found close to a part of the river where he used to bathe.'

'Was his body ever found?'

'No, but she initiated a search.'

'It is still possible that he did not drown,' said Alex. 'I must tell you, Mistress Appleby, that you were crying in your sleep last night. You believed he was being carried away.'

Rosamund stopped in her tracks. 'You mean my dream of him being carried away was not a delusion, but real?' she asked in a strained voice.

'Aye. It can be the only answer to your not only being mistaken for this Black Harry, but also for your father seeing a likeness to someone in a past life in this same Black Harry.'

Rosamund's mouth fell open and then she clamped it shut and took a deep breath before saying in a rush, 'How do you know this about my father?'

'Because he spoke those words to me on the only occasion I met him.'

Rosamund experienced such a splurge of joy that it rocked her to her heels and she needed to clutch Alex all the tighter. 'I so want to believe it,' she said.

'Then you must because I deem it the truth.'

Tears welled in Rosamund's eyes. 'I remember my brother well. I loved him dearly,' she said softly. 'He was protective towards me and was brave and funny.'

'Do not expect him to be exactly the same as you remember,' warned Alex. 'That's if we ever find him. People change.'

'Not Harry,' she said firmly.

'How can you possibly know? I trusted him like you did. When I first knew him I believed he possessed all the qualities you mentioned. But he betrayed me for the love of Ingrid and a stolen cargo.'

'I don't believe my brother is a thief and you are saying that love changes people for the worst? I do not believe that either,' she said stoutly.

'I deem you have never been in love, Mistress Appleby,' he rasped. 'Passion, desire, lust can drive a man to do things that he would never normally do.'

'More fool the man,' she retorted. 'Oh, how I wish Father was here! This news would have made him so happy.'

Alex looked at her in astonishment. 'Your father treated you disgracefully. And he did not even say that that likeness was to his own son, but just someone in a past life.'

Some of her joy evaporated and Rosamund said, 'You would not know how badly my mother's death affected my father and then on top of those tidings came the news that Harry had drowned. I believe my stepmother—not that she was my step-mother then—told him that the grief had driven me mad. And it is true that I was bereft.'

'All the more reason for him to show you love instead of allowing that woman and her sons to try to sap your spirit utterly,' he said roundly. 'I am just amazed that they did not succeed.'

Rosamund was silent, touched by his champion-ing her in such a way.

Alex smiled. 'I can see I have taken your breath away. Time to move on, I deem.'

To her further amazement, he swung her up into his arms. 'What are you doing?' she asked. 'You must let me down.'

'Be quiet, woman! You have caused me enough trouble already. Now relax and let me make haste.'

Rosamund said no more. She might be shivery and exhausted, happy and sad and utterly astounded by the fact that Harry was alive, not to mention being vexed with Master Nilsson for doubting Harry's loyalty, but at least he seemed willing to still help her.

'These friends of yours…?' she asked.

'As I said earlier, Mistress Appleby, you are in luck. They make a living from buying and selling used garments. My friend, Walther, is Swedish and married to Maud, who is a Londoner, born and bred. They have been of great help to me and I know that I can always count on finding a bed at their house when I stay in the city.'

'Will they have a separate bedchamber for me?' asked Rosamund.

His arms tightened about her. 'You worry needlessly, mistress. I will explain just enough to satisfy them why you are dressed as you are. Now, do you feel strong enough to stand?' he asked.

Despite still feeling shaky, Rosamund said, 'Of

course. How can you ask after my surviving the journey we made together?'

He felt truly rebuked and set her down. After producing the key, he opened one of the doors and ushered her into a large yard. 'Beware of the washing lines.'

He stretched out a hand to her and she took it thankfully. He steered her between the lines towards a building at the far end of the yard, where light gleamed through the shutters. He knocked on a door and called out in the Swedish tongue. There came an excited voice and then bolts were drawn back. The door opened to reveal a man holding a lantern who addressed Alex in his own language. They spoke for several moments before Alex turned to Rosamund.

'This is my friend Walther. He welcomes you to his home.'

Rosamund thanked him in English and was relieved that he made no sign of disapproval of the way she was dressed. Even so she felt awkward and warm with embarrassment. Her awkwardness deepened when an older woman entered the room, but her primary attention was not for her, but Master Nilsson. Rosamund watched the woman smile at the sight of him.

'So, you have come back for your horse.'

'Aye, but I wish to ask more of you than stabling my horse.'

'Of course, anything you want.' She frowned suddenly. 'But you are soaking wet and…' She peered over his shoulder and whispered, 'Who is this you have brought us? One of your spies in need of a new disguise?'

Alex nodded. 'But do not speak of the work to her. Mistress Appleby is chilled to the bone and in need of a hot tub—as am I. You must also find for her several of your best gowns and the necessary accessories—we are to visit the Lady Elizabeth Stanley on the morrow. Can you provide us with bedchambers for this night? You will not lose by it.'

Maud nodded. 'Walther told me earlier that you have asked him to hire some men to keep a watch on Master William Fustian's house. We do not like the man. He would put us out of business if he could.'

Alex nodded. 'He has no liking for foreigners, which is strange when he has to do business with them. Anyway, he is unaware that Mistress Appleby is in my company so he will not come here.'

She nodded. 'I will go now and speak to the maids and have them fill tubs for you both.'

Alex rejoined Rosamund. 'I have explained your needs to Maud, Mistress Appleby, and she is having a hot tub made ready for you.'

'You did not tell her everything?' asked Rosamund, mortified at the thought of the older woman knowing she had spent nights, never mind days, alone with this man.

'Of course not. She believes you are a spy in disguise and in need of a few changes of costume.'

Rosamund gasped and put a hand to her mouth and said in a muffled voice, 'You jest!'

He grinned.

Rosamund felt a tap on her shoulder and turned to see Maud smiling at her. 'It is a pleasure to have you here with us, Mistress Appleby. I have ordered a maid to fill a tub for you, but first you will follow me to the parlour.'

Her friendly manner made Rosamund feel at ease. 'I appreciate your kindness in coming to my aid.'

'It is always a pleasure to help one's friends. You will take a cup of mead? No doubt you are hungry, too. I've smoked eel and bread.'

Rosamund's face lit up. 'You are generous. I have not eaten all day.'

'Then follow me. You can warm yourself by

the fire and I will have a maid bring food and mead whilst I see what I can find for you in the way of gowns for your latest assignment.'

Chapter Six

Rosamund nodded dumbly, glanced at Master Nilsson to see if he was coming as well, but he was in conversation with Walther. She followed Maud through an unlit chamber and into another room. There a fire glowed on the hearth and several candles provided extra light. She was shown to a cushioned settle and then left alone. She removed her wet gloves and placed them on the hearth to dry. Master Nilsson must be playing games with her. She was no spy!

A maid entered the room, carrying a tray upon which there was a platter of food and a drinking vessel. She slanted a curious glance at Rosamund as she set food and drink on the table and, then, with a whisk of skirts, she was gone.

* * *

By the time Rosamund had consumed the food and drunk the mead Maud had returned to the parlour. She bid Rosamund follow her and took her to a room containing a steaming wooden tub.

'This is where we wash the clothes that we buy. Some we just hang in the steam and clean any stains because washing would ruin the fabric,' she explained. 'You'll find all you need on the chair. I'll return in a short while.'

As soon as Rosamund was alone she stripped off her travel-stained garments. Then she tested the water with her elbow before lowering herself into its depths. For a moment she just sat there with her legs hunched up against her body, relishing the heat. Then she reached for the soap and gave herself a thorough cleansing, including her hair. As she did so, her thoughts were of Master Nilsson and how he had wrapped his cloak round her and lifted her off her feet. A picture suddenly flashed into her mind of a figure bending over her, crooning *'Little Rosie is crazy!'* A cold shiver ran down her spine and she was remembering someone holding her down whilst her stepmother forced her mouth open and spooned in the liquid. She could hear Edward asking his mother what effect the potion would have on Rosamund's mind. Loathing filled her and she so longed for them both to suffer for all they had put her family through that she vowed she would not rest until it came about. And she was convinced that Harry would feel the same.

She did not linger in the tub for long; by the time she had wrapped a drying cloth around her and was rubbing her hair dry, Maud returned with a woollen dressing robe. 'Goodness! How different you look already,' she said, holding out the robe to her guest.

Rosamund smiled shyly and slipped her hands through the sleeves and fastened the belt about her slender waist. Then she followed Maud from the room and up a flight of stairs.

'You will sleep here, Mistress Appleby,' said Maud, stopping outside a door.

Rosamund followed her inside, only to stop short when she saw Master Nilsson standing there. Alex's gaze washed over her and paused a fraction as his eyes rested on her cleavage. She had made a handsome young man, but she was even lovelier as a woman.

'I beg your pardon for invading your privacy. I saw a light in here and was curious. I stayed to approve Maud's choice of gowns,' he said.

With his eyes upon her in a way that made her

aware of her femininity, Rosamund drew the opening of her robe closer together. She looked down at the garments spread out on the bed and her dark brows knit. 'I do not have any money to pay for them,' she said.

'I will do so,' said Alex firmly.

Rosamund shook her head. 'I know you paid for my food and lodgings on the journey, but that was different. I cannot allow you to do this for me.'

'Why?' He seemed amused. 'Perhaps you have me written off as a pauper.'

She hesitated. 'You cannot be rich if you need to wander hither and thither far from your own country, taking *spying* work where you can find it and performing in front of whoever will pay you. I know you have spoken of your grandfather's business, but—'

'You still know little about my life,' said Alex in a mild tone. 'But if it bothers you, I will simply loan you the money. You need to make a good impression on her ladyship if you wish to obtain her support in delving into the circumstances surrounding your father's death. These gowns will not cost a fortune, but should be suitable for that purpose.'

Rosamund moved over to the bed and fingered

one of the gowns. Alex gazed over her shoulder and said, 'That is an excellent colour and will match your eyes.'

Rosamund felt her cheeks warm and was glad he could not see her face. 'Aye. It is the kind of dark blue I like,' she said casually.

She turned to speak to Maud about the blue gown, but realised she must have slipped out of the bedchamber whilst she and Master Nilsson were talking. 'Where has Maud gone? Now we are here in your friends' house, we must have a care for our reputations.'

He said seriously, 'You are right to be concerned about such matters, but Maud and Walther would not expect me to behave in any other way than honourably to a woman.'

'Tell me, when did you first realise I was a woman?' she asked curiously.

Alex leant against a bedpost where he could watch her expression. 'I suspected you were not all you seemed that first night back in the cave.'

She was taken aback. 'So soon!'

'Aye. But there is no need to feel that you must marry me. It is our secret that we spent several nights together.' The words were out before he could recall them and he wondered why he had mentioned marriage. It had not been in his thoughts at all.

Rosamund had not even considered the need for him to make a respectable woman of her, but she did now. The bedchamber appeared to tilt and then spin round so that she had need to clutch one of the other bedposts.

'I do not wish to be married right now. I have to find Harry and make my stepmother suffer by bringing Edward to his knees.'

Alex felt a vague disappointment that she had no desire to marry him. 'I am glad that you are a woman of good sense,' he said brusquely. 'Marriage would be a complication in my life that I can well do without.'

'Then that is settled and we will not refer to it again,' said Rosamund, pushing aside the garments on the bed and sitting down. 'It is not that I do not enjoy your company,' she added, toying with her fingernails. 'But naught happened between us that either of us needs to feel guilty about.' Her cheeks burned as she remembered how she had wanted him to kiss her and hold her. 'I am still chaste,' she added, a quiver in her voice, 'so let us move on to talk of other matters.'

Alex went to a dressing table upon which were

items for a woman's *toilette*. He picked up a comb and ran a fingernail along its teeth. 'As you are such a woman of good sense, I will broach a matter that is on my mind. Have you considered the likelihood of Lady Elizabeth refusing to help you and your stepbrother seeking you out and forcing you to go with him?'

Rosamund said, 'I do not believe that she will refuse me. I have not been completely honest with you concerning Lady Elizabeth. I kept from you that she is my godmother.'

Alex dropped the comb and whirled round to face her. 'Your godmother! Why did you keep this a secret from me?' he demanded.

'Because you would have questioned why the person I was pretending to be had a lady for a god-mother,' said Rosamund. 'I am certain there is that in your life that you have not told me—and why should you when we scarcely know each other? Besides, I have not seen my godmother since before my mother died. Yet I have this hope that she will welcome me like a daughter. Then when Harry comes home I could keep house for him.' She paused. 'Which reminds me of something that religious said when she thought I was Harry.'

Alex fixed her with a stare. 'What did she say?'

Rosamund concentrated. 'Something like *"Why did you have to go off the way you did? There was really no need. You won't know it, but Alex left London. Although perhaps you met with him on your travels?"'*

Alex swore beneath his breath in his own tongue.

'Obviously it means something to you,' said Rosamund.

He nodded. 'It was Ingrid you spoke to.'

'Ingrid! But isn't she the woman who—?'

'Aye. And it seems I have misjudged her.'

'And my brother? How upsetting! She must have taken the veil because you both broke her heart.' She could not prevent a touch of sarcasm invading her voice.

'I do not think so,' said Alex drily. 'A nun's habit was one of her favourite disguises.'

Rosamund could not believe what she was hearing. 'You're not saying that Ingrid is a spy, too?'

'I really should not be discussing such information with you,' said Alex, feeling he needed to be alone for a while. He made for the door. 'I must go and bathe,' he said abruptly.

'No! Don't go just yet,' said Rosamund, holding

out a hand to him. 'I would like to know how you met my brother.'

Alex flicked back a lock of damp, tawny hair and his expression was moody. 'All right. I will do so.'

Rosamund's heart was suddenly beating ten to the dozen.

'It was in the port of Visby in my own country twelve years ago. I found him hiding amongst some merchandise that had been carted to the port, ready to be shipped overseas for my grandfather,' said Alex. 'Harry looked half-starved and was covered in sores—his clothes were just rags. It was obvious that he needed help.'

'Poor Harry! Why was he in such a state?' she asked in distress.

'At that time we did not speak the other's language, but my grandfather knew enough English to discover that Harry had escaped from a pirate ship. I might have told you a little about pirate ships already. Anyway, one can encounter many a pirate ship in the northern seas—not that their captains would appreciate being called by that name. But you will find Scottish ships raiding English merchant vessels and English ones attacking their Scottish neighbours. It is not unknown for both to mistakenly attack vessels from my own country, as well as others from the Baltic.' He paused and held her gaze. 'It must be stopped, for it is disastrous for trade. That is why England and Scotland are signing a Pact of Perpetual Peace and Henry is marrying off his elder daughter to James of Scotland.' He frowned. 'But you will want to know what happened next to Harry.'

'Please.'

'We took Harry home with us and my grandmother fed him. That summer we spent getting to know each other. I taught Harry Swedish and he taught me English. We fished and sailed around the islands and were given work to do by my grandparents. Eventually Harry asked my grandfather if he could find him a position on one of his ships. This he did to their mutual satisfaction. Harry and I saw less of each other after that, but the friendship that was forged that summer remained and, when possible, we met up at various ports throughout Europe.' His voice trailed off and his expression was bleak. 'I've said enough. I will leave you. Sleep well.' He made for the door.

'No! Wait!' She hurried after him and seized his

arm. 'You cannot leave the story there. Tell me—where does Ingrid come in all this? Where did you both meet her?'

Alex allowed himself to be persuaded to sit down again. 'I met her in Stockholm at a masque. She was young, lovely, charming and I believed her to be a lady.' He fell silent.

'And was she a lady?' prodded Rosamund, wondering what he had been doing at this masque. Spying?

A painful smile played about his mouth. 'That's what she believes, but I doubt it is true. The next time we met I was with Harry and we were unloading a cargo in Visby. She looked just as lovely, but was not so well dressed. She gazed right through me as if she did not recognise me, but she spoke to Harry, asking him about the cargo.' He frowned. 'I could see that he was just as bewitched by her as I was that night in Stockholm. The next time we met was in Bruges and then London. It was then I began to have my suspicions about her.'

'What suspicions? She certainly travels a lot,' said Rosamund, almost enviously.

'That is because sometimes she has to leave a country swiftly. She is not a real lady, but lives by her wits and has a definite gift for disguise and getting men to talk.' He rose and said firmly, 'I believe I've given you enough to mull over.'

'Aye. But I would hear more,' said Rosamund, wondering how much secret information Ingrid had managed to get out of him. 'You will tell me more tomorrow?'

He did not answer, and this time, there was no keeping him.

Rosamund returned to the bed and perched on it. She had no doubt that Master Nilsson had saved her brother's life that day in Visby. For that she would be eternally grateful. She longed to see Harry and get some answers from him about this woman, Ingrid. It seemed to her that Ingrid had truly woven a spell over both men. But for what purpose? And did she know Edward? After all, hadn't she heard his voice at the Steel Yard? Surely he was the person who Ingrid implied would like to meet her? And where was Harry if Ingrid did not know of his whereabouts?

Rosamund prayed that he was still alive. It would have been far better for her never to have known that Harry had not drowned all those years ago than to discover now, after having such hopes of being reunited with him, that he was dead after all. She felt a lump in her throat and tears pricked the back of her eyes. She needed to talk to Master Nilsson about this matter, but no doubt he was thinking of Ingrid. Perhaps he was full of hope that they could be lovers again, now he believed her innocent of betraying him with Harry.

If only Rosamund had know it was she that was much on Alex's mind, then she might have felt much more cheerful. As he immersed himself in hot water and rested a leg on the rim of the wooden tub, he had been shocked to realise that he no longer wanted Ingrid. He had spent too many months thinking of her with Harry and feeling hurt. Of course, there were questions he needed to ask her, but somehow during the last week or more he had become accustomed to Mistress Appleby's company. He thought how enjoyable it would be sharing a large tub with her. But there was no way that he could have Harry's sister as his mistress. A pity, but there it was. He had promised to find Harry for her and he meant to keep his promise. There was still the matter of the message he had been sent and only Harry could explain that away.

Alex soaped an aching thigh muscle and imagined Mistress Appleby performing the task.

He realised that he was obsessing over her now it was in the open that he knew her for a woman. They were going to have to be careful what they said when they reached Lady Elizabeth's mansion. If she was to suspect that they had spent nights together, unchaperoned, she would think the worst. They had to dissuade her from such thoughts. He found himself considering telling her ladyship that he had enlisted Mistress Appleby as one of his spies. She would be useful at court with her gift of self-effacement, whilst keeping her eyes and ears open. He could guess what she would make of that notion. In his mind's eye he could see her pretty mouth falling open and those blue-violet eyes of hers widening in astonishment. 'You jest, Master Nilsson,' she would blurt out.

He grinned, imagining himself silencing her protestations by kissing those luscious lips. He recalled the feel of her satiny skin beneath his fingers and the swell of her breasts against his chest as they lay in the snow. A definite stirring in his loins caused him to cut short such imaginings and reach for the cold-water jug.

That night when Alex fell asleep he dreamed that he and Mistress Appleby were making love.

Afterwards he decked her out in silks and satins and velvet and the best amber jewellery from his country. He woke up with the words running in his head: *I give you a choice. You either marry me or be my lover spy.* It was then he realised just how desperate he was not to be parted from her and had to remind himself that he had once felt the same about Ingrid and that he no longer loved her.

Rosamund had also been dreaming, but hers were dark ones of her brother drowning and crying out to her to rescue him. She woke with tears on her cheeks and got out of bed and down on her knees and prayed that he was still alive and she would see him again.

She felt better after that and fell asleep once more. This time in her dream she was wearing a dark blue gown and on her raven hair she wore a silver circlet encrusted with gemstones of amber. Master Nilsson was facing her as he placed a ring on her finger. Strangely he was wearing a saffron-dyed tunic and a soft leather jerkin, but on his flaxen head he also wore a silver circlet. He was smiling tenderly down at her and then suddenly he vanished and in his place was her stepbrother's snarling face.

* * *

She woke in terror and this time she did not go back to sleep. She wondered what the dream could mean. No doubt her stepmother would have said it was a sign of her madness. On shaky legs, she went over to the window and drew back the curtain and peered outside. Daylight had come and the sun glistened on the snow in the yard. Her heart lifted and she told herself that she would believe that Harry was still alive. As she gazed down into the yard she saw Master Nilsson tending his horse.

The sight of him reassured her, but she could not help wondering if he had made time to go and take a look at her stepbrother's residence What had Edward and Ingrid been doing inside the Steel Yard? She must ask Master Nilsson what it was like on the other side of those high walls.

She moved away from the window and looked at the garments that she had placed on a chair before getting into bed, without having made the effort to try any of them on. She removed the robe that she had slept in and hastened to cover her nakedness with a cream, woollen under-gown. The feel of the soft, warm fabric gave her a *frisson* of pleasure. She pulled on the blue gown over it and the sensation when the skirts brushed her calves as she twirled round made her want to dance. The sleeves were puffed about her upper arms, but gathered tightly in a band just below the elbow, where they puffed out again to be gathered in embroidered bands at the wrists. She stretched forth her arms and did another twirl.

Then she frowned. What was she thinking of? She could only have this gown if Master Nilsson loaned her the money and loans had to be paid back. But she was going to have to wear a gown if she were to go with him to Lady Elizabeth's house, so she was going to have to accept being further in debt to him.

Having made that decision, she tried on several more gowns. She dithered over whether to take the dark blue one, but remembered what he had said about the colour matching her eyes. She selected another two gowns, one green and one saffron yellow, before also trying on stockings, garters, a couple of hats, shoes and boots.

She was combing her hair when there came a knock on the door.

'Mistress Appleby, are you awake? We must make haste.'

Her pulses raced. 'Aye. I am almost ready, Master Nilsson.'

'You have chosen some gowns to take with you?' he asked.

Rosamund hesitated and then opened the door. She caught a whiff of almond-and-honey soap and noticed he was clean shaven. His tawny hair curled about his ears and he had changed his garments and now wore a cream linen shirt beneath a russet doublet; his well-formed legs were clad in red hose. Her senses were roused; she realised that not only did she still want him to kiss her, but that she was desperate for his approval of her appearance.

Alex's breath caught in his throat at the anxiety in her eyes and he wanted to punch those who had given her such a low opinion of herself. 'Blue is a colour you should wear often,' he said, taking one of her hands and twirling her round. 'How lovely you look.' He felt some of the tension leave her and her obvious delight made him want to reassure her by taking her in his arms and kissing her. But he knew that he must keep a rein on his passions.

'You can have no notion of how different I feel wearing such a gown,' she said shyly.

'Your eyes are like sapphires. I scarcely recognise you as the same person who rode me down near Appleby Manor,' he teased.

'That seems so long ago now,' said Rosamund, blushing. 'But you must go downstairs, Master Nilsson. There is no need for you to wait for me. I will be down as soon as I have tidied my hair.'

'I am content to wait for you.' He released her hand and went over to the dressing table and picked up a net of silken blue threads. 'What a pretty trifle this is. You will wear it?' Rosamund eyed the hairnet and agreed that it was indeed pretty. He handed it to her. 'Have you chosen other gowns to take with you?'

'I have picked another two,' she answered, 'that is, if you are willing to fund me to that extent? I need boots and shoes and other fripperies, as well.'

'Of course I am willing.' He picked up the cloaks hanging over the back of the chair. 'You will have these?'

Rosamund gave them a fleeting glance. 'I need only one.'

Alex placed a fur-lined blue velvet cloak about her shoulders. 'Now how does that feel?'

Rosamund had noticed the cloak earlier, but had deemed it too costly to try on. Now she could not resist stroking the blue pile. 'I have never worn velvet before.'

'You will need a brooch to fasten it as it has no ties,' said Alex.

'I do not have a brooch.' She made to remove the cloak, but he stayed her with a hand.

'I have a brooch you can use. Please accept this cloak as a gift. I know you do not wish to be beholden to me, but I would like to see you wearing it.'

She would have refused him, only he lifted a fold of the material and brushed it against her cheek. 'Imagine wearing such a cloak in your stepmother's presence. Picture her gnashing her teeth in envy and fury.'

A faint smile replaced Rosamund's serious expression. 'You tempt me, Master Nilsson. But I cannot wear it now—it is an evening cloak.'

'Then wear this brown woollen one for travelling and we will take the blue one with us. Now tidy your hair and let us be on our way.'

Rosamund submitted to his will. When Harry returned, she felt certain he would willingly pay her debts. She pinned up her hair beneath the blue silk net, whilst Alex neatly folded the garments she had chosen.

She followed him downstairs and into the parlour where Maud and Walther were eating breakfast in front of the fire. Walther said something in Swedish to Alex, but it was Maud who translated his words. 'My husband says how lovely you are and I agree with him. You will have some bread and honey and ale?'

Rosamund thanked her, and was shown to the table. Maud left her for a moment, but she was soon joined by Alex and Walther. Whilst their host poured ale into drinking vessels, Alex produced a silver brooch from a pouch. He handed it to Rosamund and she gazed at it with interest because its design was unusual.

'What does it symbolise?' she asked. 'It looks like Christ's cross, only…'

'It was once an amulet of Thor's hammer,' said Alex. 'As you can see, it has been made into a cross in the form of a brooch.'

'You must value it highly,' she said.

He hesitated. 'It belonged to Harry. I bent to pick it up and it was then that I was attacked from behind.'

She paled. 'You've kept this because you believe it is evidence against my brother?'

Alex shrugged. 'I kept it because I did not wish to be rid of it. You can keep it.'

She was greatly moved by the thought of having in her possession that which had belonged to her brother. 'Thank you. I will take care of it until I see him again.'

At that moment Maud returned, along with a serving maid, so no more was said about the brooch.

When the meal was over and Rosamund came to look for the bundle of clothes, there was no sign of it. She spoke to Alex about it.

'Maud has tied it up with cord and it awaits us in the next chamber. We will collect it on our way out.' He stood and helped her to her feet.

Rosamund thanked Walther and Maud for their hospitality.

'We hope all goes well with your plans and look forward to seeing you both soon,' they said.

Chapter Seven

Alex and Rosamund spoke little as they rode through the streets to Lady Elizabeth's mansion, which was situated near the Strand. Two watchmen stood on guard at the gates. Alex dismounted and spoke to them. The gates were thrown wide and a stable boy summoned to tend to the horse. Alex led Rosamund to the entrance of the house and the door was opened to them by the butler. Alex handed him a missive that he had written last night in his bedchamber. He exchanged a few words with him and, after a curious glance in Rosamund's direction, the man showed them into a large hall and told them to wait while he informed Lady Elizabeth of their arrival.

Rosamund's heart was beating fast, but she did her best not to reveal her nervousness to Alex and gazed about the hall. She hoped that her god-mother would recognise her. But would Rosamund remember Lady Elizabeth? Suddenly her eyes alighted on a portrait on a far wall and she hurried over to take a closer look at it.

Alex followed her. 'Your godmother when she was young,' he said. 'I recall that I once visited here with my grandfather. It had slipped my mind until I saw the house.'

'Godmother was beautiful! I wonder if she has changed much.'

'She is an old woman,' said Alex in a low voice. 'This was here when I visited as a boy.'

'Her skin looks as soft as rose petals,' she murmured.

Alex rubbed his chin with his knuckles. 'Aye, it is a pretty picture.'

Rosamund darted him a sidelong glance. 'How did your grandfather come to be invited here?'

'If I remember rightly, it was due to her having visited Visby a few months previously. She had been widowed the year before and had decided she wished to travel. She commissioned some amber-and-silver jewellery to her own design. Grandfather took on the role of her agent and she asked him to deliver the commission in person. He decided it would be useful for me to visit London and so brought me along.'

'I had no notion you were so long acquainted,' said Rosamund.

'The lady scarcely noticed me.' Alex paused. 'We need to decide what to tell Lady Elizabeth. We cannot tell her the whole truth.'

Rosamund went over to the fire and removed her gloves. 'If we did so, she wouldn't want to have aught to do with me.' She held her hands out to the flames. 'Besides, we don't know what else she might have been told about me during her sojourn in Lathom House except that I was ill and slightly crazed in the head.'

'I do not believe you were ever crazy. Anyway, hopefully she will be sympathetic to one in your situation,' said Alex, joining Rosamund by the fire.

'I pray so. Do we admit to having met up north?'

'Have you any other suggestions? I believe it is always best to stick as close to the truth as one can,' said Alex.

'I had believed my godmother dead until the day I met you,' said Rosamund. 'I think Father had mentioned that she was very ill some years ago. I believe he expected her to die.' She sat down and smoothed out the kid gloves on her knee.

Alex's gaze rested on Rosamund's bent head. 'I presume your plan that day was to tell your godmother of how you were being treated at home and of your suspicion concerning the death of your father?'

'Aye.' Rosamund sighed. 'When you told me that she had already departed for London, it placed me in somewhat of a dilemma, as you well know.'

'But if you were pretending to be Master Wood, how did you plan to gain entry to Lathom House and speak to Lady Elizabeth?'

She shrugged. 'Does that matter now? I am more concerned about what I am to say to her when I see her.'

He nodded. 'We will tell her that we met outside Lathom where you discovered that she had already left for London. I told you that I was acquainted with her ladyship and intended visiting her. You decided to travel to London, so I offered you my escort as we were travelling in the same direction.'

Rosamund shook her head. 'It will not do. She will suspect that we travelled alone.'

'Not if we can tell her that we had company on the road,' said Alex firmly. 'She is not to know otherwise.'

Rosamund plucked at her skirts. 'It sounds feasible, but you have not said what your reason was for calling at Lathom House?'

Before Alex could answer, there was a sound behind them. They both turned to see a woman standing there. She was dressed in a plum-coloured gown and her red frizzy hair resembled a bird's nest.

'I cannot believe that at last we are to meet, Rosamund,' she gasped with a hand to her chest.

Rosamund realised that this lady must be her godmother and could only hope she had not over-heard their conversation. She rose to her feet and went to meet her. The lady seemed to glide across the floor towards her as if on wheels. Close up, Rosamund realised that the lady's face was painted white that gave her features a mask-like appearance. 'Lady Elizabeth?'

'Who else, my dear?' said the lady drily. 'I know I have altered somewhat, but it is still me beneath this paint.'

A flushed Rosamund apologised. 'I am de-lighted to see you again after all these years, Godmother.' She dipped a curtsy and then took the hand offered to help her rise.

'My appearance always gives people a shock,

whether it be for the first time or after an age,' said Lady Elizabeth.

'You are very understanding and I thank you for your welcome. I would have visited you at Lathom House if I'd been able to do so. But it was not easy escaping my stepmother's domination. By the time I did so, you had already left for London,' said Rosamund.

'That woman!' snorted Lady Elizabeth, rolling her eyes expressively. 'I am still angry that your father put her in my dear Jane's place.' She looked at Alex and her eyes softened. 'Thank you for your missive, my dear Baron. You are so like your grandfather. If you will be so kind as to be patient whilst I talk with my goddaughter, I will give you my full attention in a moment.'

My dear Baron, thought Rosamund, puzzled by the title. She watched him remove his hat and incline his tawny head. 'Of course, Lady Elizabeth. I understand what a pleasure it must be for you both to meet again after all these years.'

'Charming,' she said, touching his cheek with a finger before resuming her conversation with her goddaughter. 'So that woman asserted her will over you.'

Rosamund pulled herself together. 'You sound

as if you know the kind of woman my stepmother is,' she said.

Her godmother's eyes widened. 'My dear, your mother and I knew Monica McDonald when we were children. We all had kin living in the north.' Lady Elizabeth sat down and waved them to a settle. 'Jane refused to believe the rumours about Monica's wanton behaviour because she always believed the best of people. Anyway, Monica stayed on at Appleby Manor after Jane miscarried, supposedly to nurse her.' She sighed. 'Well, we know what happened after that! Monica's family was such a quarrelsome one and they were furious when she had an affair with her cousin's husband. No doubt it was that which made it impossible for her to return home.' She frowned. 'The whole lot of them were unstable and I knew Monica McDonald for what she was—a greedy, conniving madam.' She paused. 'I have heard that her lover is a widower now, so who is to say that she might not run off with him.' Lady Elizabeth grimaced and cracks appeared in the white paint and there was a peculiar smell.

Rosamund swallowed a cough and then hurried into speech. 'Thank you for telling me this story. My stepmother's background was always a mystery to me, for she seldom spoke of her family. Yet surely Father must have known something of my stepmother's past, so why did he marry her?'

'No doubt she tricked him into it. He was grief-stricken and lonely and most likely found it convenient to have a new *mother* for you close at hand.'

'She was no mother to me,' said Rosamund, her eyes smouldering. 'She told people I was mad and was going to have me locked up. She feared what I might tell them and that was why I had to escape.'

'I am sure she has plenty to hide and was, no doubt, jealous of you, my dear,' wheezed Lady Elizabeth. 'You have grown into a lovely woman, so like my dear Jane. I look a fright and know it. But when you reach my age, having survived the smallpox, then one must be forgiven for painting over wrinkles and pockmarks.'

Rosamund felt both pity and admiration for her. 'Father told me years ago that you were ill and expected to die. It was not until I heard my stepmother mention you that I realised you were still alive. I knew then that I had to see you.'

'Well, I am glad you made the effort, my dear. My intention in trying to get in touch with you was so we could become better acquainted before it is too late.' She patted Rosamund's hand and then turned to Alex. 'My dear Baron, I was so sorry to hear of the deaths of your grandparents. Your grandfather in particular was helpful to me on several occasions. I am delighted that we are to work together and you are to be part of my troupe. I do hope you will like the costumes for the dance. They are black and silver and there will be such carolling that it will surely gladden the hearts of the royal family and their Scottish guests.'

Rosamund wondered what they were talking about, but there was no mistake about him being a baron because her godmother had addressed him by that title again. Of course, it might be all of an act if he really was a spy. Whichever was the truth, it was obvious to her that here was an example of Master Nilsson's duplicity. He had not been honest with her.

'I presume there will be time for rehearsals?' he was asking.

'The members of my troupe will be here this afternoon,' informed Lady Elizabeth. 'If you are to take part, then I will partner you. But time enough to sort that out later and for you to learn…' she paused to catch her breath and patted her bosom '…your steps…and see what gossip you can rake through for information. We will leave for Richmond in the morning—' She broke off again, her chest heaving.

Rosamund gazed at her anxiously. 'Are you all right?'

'I am as well as can be expected in the circumstances' she gasped. 'I have decided that the troupe will wear masks to create an air of mystery. What is your opinion, my dears?'

'It sounds exciting,' said Rosamund.

Alex said politely, 'I am certain it will delight their Majesties and the Scottish lords and archbishops.'

'I am glad you deem it so.' Lady Elizabeth winced and rubbed her forehead with a trembling hand. 'I have such a megrim coming on. I will have to take my potion soon.'

Rosamund stared at her anxiously.

Lady Elizabeth forced a smile. 'You must not worry about me, my dear. You know, when I heard your father had died, I could not help thinking it was a pity he did not go sooner in place of my dear Jane and your poor brother.' Her eyes were suddenly damp and she took a kerchief from the velvet pouch that hung at her waist and dabbed her eyes before flicking white flakes of paint from her gown.

'I must tell you some good news, Godmother,'

said Rosamund, glancing across at the Baron. 'My brother, Harry, is not dead as we believed.'

Lady Elizabeth raised her head and fixed her with a hard stare. 'I don't understand. What sorcery is this? Your father told me fifteen years ago that he had drowned.'

Alex said, 'He was deceived. I met Harry twelve years ago in Visby. I will not go into all the details now, but he had escaped captivity aboard a pirate ship and was in need of a friend. After I missed seeing you at Lathom House, I met Mistress Appleby who was on her way to visit you. It came as quite a shock when we introduced ourselves because, just the same as yourself, she had believed Harry had died fifteen years ago. Now there was I informing her that I knew him and believed that Sir James had recognised him last time he was in London. Whether they met I do not know, because Harry disappeared and Sir James died unexpectedly.'

'I believe Father was murdered,' said Rosamund. 'And I believe my stepmother had Harry abducted.'

Lady Elizabeth drummed her fingers on the arm of her chair. 'This is all too much for me to make sense of right now. I do know that woman was ambitious for those sons of hers and gave the elder an exalted idea of himself. I remember thinking that they should be stopped. You know what this means?' she said breathlessly. 'Harry is the rightful heir and can evict that woman from Appleby Manor and get rid of the sons, as well. We have to find him.'

Alex smiled. 'Of course.' He glanced at Rosamund. 'My hope is that he is plying his trade in the ship my grandfather bequeathed him when he died.'

'You did not tell me that your grandfather willed my brother a ship,' said Rosamund, startled.

Lady Elizabeth let out a cackle. 'Good for Harry. The Baron must have thought well of him. Let us hope he will soon return. In the meantime I will mention this whole affair to my kinsman when we are at Richmond,' she wheezed, nodding her head vigorously and then groaning and holding it with both hands. 'You and I have matters to discuss, Baron. Rosamund, you must be weary after so much travelling. I will have a maid show you to a bedchamber. You must rest and will be summoned when the midday meal is ready.'

Rosamund felt she had been summarily dismissed, having noted that her godmother had called Master Nilsson Baron again. She supposed it was possible that at her age and in her state of health that she was confusing him with his grand-father, the baron. She wondered what the business was that they needed to discuss. The purchase of more amber jewellery, perhaps? She left them alone and went upstairs with the maid.

Lady Elizabeth leaned back in her chair and closed her eyes. 'So, Baron, your natural father wants my help,' she murmured.

'Aye.' Alex stared at her with a mixture of sympathy and exasperation, wondering what his father was thinking of when he suggested this interesting, but sick, old lady as a fellow conspi-rator. 'Have you ever met him? He said you are kin by marriage to the wife of one of his allies.'

'Cicely. She married Lord Mackillin. Like me, they are getting old,' she said mournfully.

'You are not too old to help ensure future peace between Scotland and England,' said Alex politely.

She opened her eyes and leaning forward, patted his knee. 'It was your grandfather who told me that Earl Douglas was your natural father. He was proud of you and often spoke of your sense of diplomacy and your courage.' Her voice was barely above a whisper. 'He is a loss to me, but I presume you will settle down soon and take the reins of the business into your own hands?'

'Eventually,' he said after a moment's hesitation. 'Right now it is my plan to prevent members of certain clans from destroying the proposed alliance between England and Scotland. I was interested to hear you say that your goddaughter's stepmother was a McDonald. We must keep our eyes and ears open and ensure that any plot they might conjure up will be thwarted. It is possible they will enlist those Englishmen who wish King Henry's rule to fail.'

'Sons whose fathers supported the Yorkist cause and whose lands were taken from them when Richard was defeated at Bosworth,' whispered Elizabeth. 'Young lords of noble birth who will have pledged their allegiance to Henry, not only to regain some part of their father's lands, but to be in a position where they know what is happening at court. I have one such lord amongst my troupe of dancers. I am not saying he will turn traitor, but it may serve you to have him watched.'

'His name?' asked Alex, his eyes narrowing.

'Lord Bude. He is fair-haired and handsome like you, but younger.'

'You will introduce us?'

'Of a certainty.' She smiled. 'I will introduce you to the troupe this afternoon. My health is not good, as you can see, but I will manage the steps as long as you follow my lead and do not rush me.'

Alex would have needed to be blind and deaf not to have noticed she had difficulty breathing and could not conceal his concern. 'You do not have to do this, Lady Elizabeth. I deem that your god-daughter could be of use to us.'

Her smile faded. 'I will not have her putting her life at risk. Do not stop me playing my part just because I am old and ill. I would gladly die in the service of my country. Now, I would appreciate your help in getting up from this chair and out of this hall.'

He did as she requested and she clung to his arm as they crossed the hall to the door. 'I suspect I do not have much longer to live,' she gasped, 'that is why I wanted to see Rosamund while I was staying at Lathom House.' Her expression was wistful. 'Unfortunately I caught a chill and could not leave the house. I would that I—I had made the effort sooner, but her father never approved of me.' She paused. 'I need to retire to my bedchamber for a while and take the potion that my physician prescribes. I must rest if I am to initiate you into the dance this afternoon.' They paused in the entrance. 'You will stay here, of course, Baron, until we leave for Richmond.'

'I will happily do so,' said Alex gravely. 'It has occurred to me that Mistress Appleby's stepmother might visit Lathom House and ask whether her stepdaughter left for London in your company. She will receive a negative reply, but she still might decide that her stepdaughter has followed you to London. It is possible that she will travel south herself to inform her elder son that Rosamund has escaped. It is likely that he might reason that she will have come here.'

Lady Elizabeth gave him an exhausted look. 'You are suggesting that either or both of them might present themselves at my door. The nerve of that woman! What is her son's name? I have forgotten.'

'Edward Fustian. He is a member of the Royal Company of Mercers.'

'I will warn the servants not to allow either of them entry.'

'I would go further and have them deny that either of us have been here,' said Alex, grim-faced. 'I do not want him to know just yet that I am acquainted with either you or Mistress Appleby.'

'You will be our secret weapon,' she chuckled conspiratorially.

'Aye.'

Alex noticed a couple of servants approaching and was relieved to hand over their mistress to her maid. As he went upstairs with the male servant, he thought how he and Rosamund had managed to escape being questioned by her ladyship about how they had travelled to London and in whose company, although the sick woman might yet still do so. He and Rosamund should have discussed their answers further, but it was too late to do so now.

Rosamund wasted no time joining her godmother at the table in her parlour when the summons to the midday meal came. She felt rested and was eager to get to know Lady Elizabeth whilst the opportunity was available. No mention had been made about Rosamund travelling to Richmond with the other two, so she could only presume that she would stay here at her godmother's mansion in London.

'I hope you do not mind eating in here, my dear,' said Lady Elizabeth, 'but it is much warmer than the hall and easier for the servants.'

'I do not mind at all,' said Rosamund, smiling

across the table. 'I hope you are feeling better.' It was hard to tell by looking at her painted face.

Lady Elizabeth's eyes smiled at her goddaughter. 'I feel better for seeing you, my dear. Tell me, what do you think of the Baron? An interesting, attractive man, is he not? He will make some fortunate woman an excellent husband.'

Rosamund's smile faded. *So Master Nilsson was definitely a baron like his grandfather before him.* 'I suppose he would. But why do you mention this to me?' she asked casually.

Lady Elizabeth did not immediately reply, but leaned forward and seized her goddaughter's arm with a claw-like hand. 'How old are you, Rosamund? I'm afraid I have forgotten what year you were born.'

'Two-and-twenty,' she answered.

Her godmother sighed. 'I thought as much. Of course, you are old enough to find a husband for yourself, but in the circumstances you could do with a little help.'

'Why do we talk of husbands?' asked Rosamund, her mind in a whirl. 'Has he spoken to you about my needing to get married?'

'Certainly not!' Her godmother looked at her keenly. 'Why didn't your father choose a husband for you years ago, when you were in the first bloom of womanhood?'

'I deem he believed my stepmother when she told him I was mad,' said Rosamund sadly. 'She wanted me to marry Edward, but thankfully, Father would not allow it. As for William, he said that no man would want to marry me. Not only was I ugly, but I was too much of a bad bargain for any man to take on.'

'What wicked things to say to you, my dear, and not true,' said Lady Elizabeth indignantly. 'Well, you've escaped them now and you will marry.'

'No. You must not concern yourself,' said Rosamund hastily. 'Besides, I have no dowry.'

'No dowry! Does the Baron know this?'

Rosamund stiffened. 'I do not remembering raising the matter with him. Why should I?'

'Because he is your best prospect. He does not need the money, but with a dowry you will not feel like a beggar maid when you accept him. I will send for my lawyer instantly and he will deal with this matter of a dowry before we leave for Richmond.'

Rosamund was stunned. 'No! You must not do this. I do not wish to marry and, even if I did, I have decided that I will wait until Harry's return before doing so,' she added rashly.

Lady Elizabeth gave her a shrewd look. 'Has the Baron compromised you, my dear?'

Rosamund gasped. 'Certainly not! How can you suggest such a thing? The Baron is an honourable man.'

Her godmother's eyes wore a satisfied expression. 'So he has proposed marriage to you?'

'I did not say that!'

'No, you did not, but I can imagine that he is determined that you will not suffer by your both succumbing to temptation. I do not blame you for being charmed by him. He is just like his grandfather, irresistible.'

'No! It was not like that at all,' cried Rosamund, jumping to her feet. 'I am chaste.'

A spasm twisted Lady Elizabeth's face and she removed her hairpiece and scratched her almost-bald pate. Rosamund could only stare at her. 'Close your mouth, dear. You look like a fish,' said her godmother, replacing her wig. 'So he asked you to marry him and you tell me you are chaste.' Her tone was thoughtful.

Rosamund was angry and embarrassed and attempted to change the direction of the conversation. 'It was extremely rude of me to stare at you in such an ill-bred manner.' Her voice was terse.

'No more than I was in removing my wig in your company, but it itches so at times and that makes my head ache even worse.' Lady Elizabeth paused. 'Don't be angry with me, my dear. I am only interested in your well-being. I did, after all, notice that neither of you arrived with servants, nor did you mention having company on the road. In the circumstances, you would be a fool to refuse him.'

Rosamund clenched her fists. 'He has not asked me to marry him and there is no need for him to marry me. I am chaste and I do not wish to marry him.'

'Why not? He is rich, handsome and charming.'

'Because…' Rosamund's voice trailed off. She could not tell her godmother that the Baron was in love with another woman. Most likely she would not believe her.

'I understand,' said Lady Elizabeth, shaking her head. 'Young women are always full of romantic notions. You wish to be wooed.'

Rosamund had not thought of that as a reason for refusing the Baron's proposal, but now she decided that it was as good a one as any other, so she acknowledged there was some truth in Lady Elizabeth's words.

Her godmother nodded. 'You must come with us to Richmond Palace for the celebrations. There should be time enough there for the Baron to woo you in the proper style.'

Chapter Eight

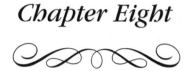

A thrill raced through Rosamund at the thought of being wooed by the Baron. 'You mean I can accompany you to the royal palace without prior permission?'

Lady Elizabeth gave a laugh that sounded like rustling dry leaves. 'I am related to the royal family and they are accustomed to my starts and fancies. In truth, they consider me a little mad at times and I would not deny that on occasions a certain mood takes me and—' Her expression changed. 'Here comes the Baron! He really is a fine figure of a man. I have not told you, but my troupe of players are all noble men and women. It is as the queen requested.' She hailed Alex. 'Come, sit with my goddaughter. I have decided that Rosamund will accompany us to Richmond.'

Rosamund watched his face to see if he was pleased or not, but he wore that bland expression that made his thoughts unreadable. What would he think if he knew about their earlier conversation?

'I already had it in mind that Mistress Appleby should accompany us,' said Alex, seating himself at the head of the table between the two women. 'She will be much safer at Richmond.'

'Good. I am glad we agree,' said Lady Elizabeth placidly. 'Here comes our meal.'

Rosamund knew that she should be relieved that her godmother and the Baron were in agreement. Yet now she felt oddly put out by the fact she appeared to have no say in what should happen to her with these two people for whom she had strong feelings. She watched as the servants began to serve boiled hare in a sauce that proved to be made from ale, pepper, bread and onions.

Lady Elizabeth began to separate the meat from the bones. 'My dears, I am thinking that God granted me ten extra years of life so that I could be of help to you both.' She broke off for several moments and Rosamund held her breath, thinking that her godmother might be about to reveal all to the Baron. Instead she continued with a change of subject. 'I hope you are both hungry. I asked for *toste rialle* to be made for pudding. No doubt you have tasted it, Baron. I first did so in Calais.' She signalled to the servant to pour the wine and drank off a draught all in one go.

'What is *toste rialle*?' asked Rosamund, thinking she could not help but be fascinated by all that her godmother did. How could she down her wine so swiftly when there were times when she seemed hardly able to breathe?

'It is a paste of sugar, spices and sweet wine,' said Alex, smiling at Rosamund as the lady paused to wipe her chin with her napkin.

'There is more to it than that,' said Lady Elizabeth, 'there is quince, raisins, nuts and flour spread hot over white bread and sprinkled with sugar.' She smacked her lips.

'It sounds delicious,' said Rosamund, quite affected by the Baron's smile.

Lady Elizabeth nodded. 'I want you to have some pleasure in life, Rosamund dear, because I fear you have been dreadfully unhappy. That is why you must marry a rich man.'

Alex almost choked on a morsel of meat and had to wait for the coughing to subside before saying, 'You have been discussing marriage with Mistress Appleby?'

'Aye. I have decided what she needs is a child-less widower,' said the lady.

Rosamund stared at her in astonishment.

'I do not agree,' said Alex, putting down his knife. 'I wonder at your making such a pro-nouncement, Lady Elizabeth.'

'I shall tell you why,' wheezed the lady. 'I was younger than Rosamund when my parents chose a much older man for me. My head was full of nonsense. I was convinced I would be happier with a young, brave knight in shining armour. I wept on my wedding night. But when George died I inher-ited all his money and was still young enough to enjoy being rich.' She beamed at them both.

'It is vital that a man should be able to support his future wife, but there should be affection and respect and trust in a marriage,' said Alex, glancing at Rosamund before giving Lady Elizabeth his attention once more. 'You were ob-viously not happy living with your husband if you set about enjoying yourself once he was dead.'

'I agree with the Baron,' said Rosamund bravely.

'You feel like that because you are young, my dears,' mumbled Lady Elizabeth through a mouthful of food. 'Your blood gets heated and it is lust that drives you, not wisdom.'

Rosamund felt her cheeks burning and quickly lowered her gaze to her platter. What would her godmother say next? She hoped the Baron did not think that she had poured out all that had happened between them to Lady Elizabeth.

'You embarrass Mistress Appleby,' hissed Alex.

'If my goddaughter is to marry, Baron, then she needs to know what to expect when bedded by a young man driven by his animal passions. That is, if she does not know already.'

There was a whimpering sound from Rosamund.

'You will stop this,' said Alex in a furious whisper. 'Are you mad?'

'I do not mean to offend, Baron, but I suggest you remember your manners, too,' said the old lady, giving her attention to her dinner. 'You are a guest in my house and should not speak to me in such a way. I understand you are under a great strain and I will forgive you and say no more. Now, let us eat up this good food.'

Alex wondered what she meant by his being under a great strain, but at least she was as good as her word and did not speak again. But she had created an atmosphere that made him reluctant to break the silence. What had Rosamund been saying to her? Had she lied about what had taken place on their journey to London? He felt so angry that he was tempted to storm out of the parlour and go to stay with Walther and Maud. He glared at Rosamund, who flushed to the roots of her hair, but there was an expression in her lovely eyes that kept him glued to his seat.

Rosamund was all of a-quiver, remembering how she had felt when she and the Baron were caught in that forced embrace in the snow. Were her feelings then love or lust? What was he thinking? It was obvious he was angry and she did not blame him. No doubt he would never ask her to marry him and she realised that she might just enjoy finding out about love in his arms. This despite his having deceived her about his station in life.

By the time the meat course was cleared away and the dessert placed in front of them, Alex and Rosamund had calmed down a little and were able to enjoy the delicious confection set before them. More wine was poured and comments made about the food and weather. Rosamund asked when the troupe would be arriving.

'They will soon be here, as will the musicians,' said Lady Elizabeth. 'You must come and watch the Baron being taught his steps. I swear he will be in trouble if he treads on my toes.'

The words had scarcely left Lady Elizabeth's lips when a servant came hurrying into the hall and whispered in her ear. No sooner had the meal been cleared away than a young woman entered the hall, carrying a black-and-silver gown over her arm. Her eyes alighted on Lady Elizabeth and she hurried over to her. She was followed by several other young men and women. The women reminded Rosamund of butterflies because their skirts fluttered and they were dressed in a variety of colours.

'Lady Elizabeth, I bring bad tidings,' trilled the first woman. 'Lady Joan cannot join us. She has caught a fever and is abed. She begs your pardon for disappointing you.'

Elizabeth uttered a *tsk* of annoyance before saying, 'Poor Lady Joan, I hope she will soon be well. It does make matters awkward. The figures will not be right for the dance and we have so little time to find someone else to take her place. The Baron here will partner me.'

The group stared at Alex and one of the ladies smiled. 'Introduce us, Lady Elizabeth.'

'This is Baron Dalsland from Sweden. His

grandfather was a great friend of mine and brought me many precious jewels from his country,' said Lady Elizabeth.

'Has he danced before?' said another lady with bold eyes.

'But of course,' said Alex, smiling down at her. 'I would be of little use as a replacement if I could not.'

'I will take you in hand,' said the bold-eyed lady.

Rosamund, sitting on a chair in front of the fire, watched this light flirtation with startled eyes and more than a little annoyance.

'That will be unnecessary,' said Lady Elizabeth firmly. 'I will allow no dalliance during the dance. I have said that I will partner the Baron.'

'What about this young lady?' asked one of the men, noticing Rosamund.

'Oh, I cannot dance,' she said hastily.

He laughed. 'I do not believe that is true. Everyone can dance.'

'Not me,' said Rosamund firmly.

All attention was now on Rosamund. 'I could teach you,' said the fair-haired man who had spoken. 'The steps are not so difficult and you could fill Lady Joan's place. We do not have to perform for another three days, so you could perfect the steps in no time. May I introduce myself? I am Lord Bude.'

Rosamund could not resist looking at Alex to see what he thought of the young man's suggestion. He was frowning. Obviously, he believed she was not good enough to dance with an English lord before royalty.

'I deem it a wonderful notion,' said Lady Elizabeth, much to Rosamund's surprise. 'May I introduce my goddaughter, Mistress Rosamund Appleby, lords and ladies. Her parents are dead and she has recently come to live with me.'

The party eyed Rosamund with as much interest as they had the Baron. The lady who had broken the news about Lady Joan, said, 'It is fate! You are of the same height and have the same colouring as Lady Joan, Mistress Appleby, and, as Lord Bude has said, the steps are not difficult.'

Alex wanted to disagree. Bude was the name Lady Elizabeth had mentioned earlier as a man who might possibly turn traitor. He was obviously of a flirtatious manner; if he was as poor as her ladyship had said, then he would be on the lookout for a wealthy heiress. Perhaps he thought Rosamund might inherit her godmother's fortune. How was Alex to know that her head would not be turned by this handsome young lord? He could not allow that to happen.

But before Alex could make a move on the young lord, one of the ladies approached him.

'I know something of your homeland, Baron,' she said. 'I admired Lady Elizabeth's amber jewellery and she told me it was made in Sweden. I asked my father if he would buy me such a set, but he refused. He said I needed a rich husband if I wanted such trinkets.'

'Hardly a trinket, Margaret, if your father cannot afford such jewellery,' said one of the other ladies. 'It must be worth a fortune.'

'Enough!' said Lady Elizabeth, clapping her hands. 'We are here to dance. My goddaughter will attempt to fill Lady Joan's position.'

Rosamund opened her mouth to say that she had not agreed, but it was too late. Already Lord Bude was reaching for her hand and her godmother was nodding in her direction. 'You had best try on Lady Joan's costume this evening in case it needs altering, Rosamund, my dear. We will walk through the dance several times to give you and the Baron a chance to familiarise yourselves with the steps without the music.'

Rosamund took a deep breath as Lord Bude's

soft, white hand clasped hers. 'Now pay attention, Mistress Rosamund,' he said in her ear. 'No one expects you to be as good as the rest of us, but no doubt your pretty face will make up for any faults.'

Immediately Rosamund wanted to tug her hand out of his grasp and resume her seat by the fire, but the other dancers were already calling out instructions. She did her best to comply with what they said, but there were too many voices telling her what to do and she stepped on Bude's toes more than once.

She glanced up at him, apologizing, and instantly was aware that his eyes were gazing down her cleavage. She lost all desire to do well and made a complete mess of the steps when the music began and she was supposed to dance in earnest. It was a relief when the wheezing Lady Elizabeth eventually signalled a halt.

Concerned about her, Alex led her over to the settle and made her sit down. She whispered to him to tell the others that there would be another rehearsal tomorrow evening at Richmond. He did so.

The musicians and dancers departed, chorusing their farewells. Only Lord Bude lingered. 'Perhaps I could give you a private lesson this evening,' he suggested, taking one of Rosamund's hands and kissing it.

'I think not, Lord Bude,' said Alex, removing Rosamund's hand from the other man's grasp. 'Mistress Appleby has had a long journey and needs her rest.'

Bude scowled. 'Surely Mistress Appleby can make her own decisions? I really don't see what it has to do with you, Baron?'

'But that is because you are unaware that the lady and I are betrothed,' said Alex politely.

Only by a blinking of the eyes did Rosamund betray that she was more surprised than Bude to hear those words. His lordship muttered an apology and with a terse good night left the hall.

'Why did you tell him that we were betrothed?' demanded Rosamund, as soon as Bude was out of earshot.

Alex was asking himself the same question. It would have been wiser if he had allowed Rosamund to encourage Bude to discover if he had any dealings with those with treacherous intent. 'He is a fortune-hunter,' snapped Alex. 'Do not take what I said to heart. I still have no intention of getting married until I am thirty.'

A sharp laugh escaped Rosamund. 'Then you

should have remained silent. You are forgetting that not only do you wish to be avenged on my brother, but also that I have no fortune.'

'He knows that Lady Elizabeth is extremely wealthy and that you, her goddaughter, have recently come to live with her. It is obvious Bude smells money when he looks at you.'

Two spots of colour appeared high on Rosamund's cheeks and she tugged her hand free. 'You are insulting. Did you not consider he might find me comely?'

'Bude cannot afford to be swayed solely by a lovely face,' he said harshly.

'Why should I believe you? He is a lord of the realm, whilst you are a foreigner, unable to trust me with your real identity.'

Alex realised that he had hurt her and his voice was gentler when he said, 'I did not trust those lords and ladies with it either.'

She frowned. 'You mean you are not a Baron?'

'Ach! I have that title in my own country. I inherited it from my grandfather, as well as his estate and his business.' He hesitated. 'But I have another name that my father gave me and it is not Nilsson.'

'Are you going to tell me it?'

Alex hesitated. 'Why do you think I am here, Rosamund?'

Her eyes darkened. 'I am in no mood for guessing games,' she said shortly. 'If you are already rich, then I presume it simply amuses you to entertain and to spy on people.' She turned away from him and went over to the chair where Lady Joan's costume had been placed and picked it up.

'Come here, if you please,' said Alex quietly.

She glanced at him and he smiled at her in such a way that her heart seemed to move inside her. 'Give me a reason why I should, Baron?'

He walked slowly towards her and stopped a few inches away. 'If you want to perform before the King and Queen, then perhaps you should practise the steps one more time.'

His closeness was having a strange effect on her. 'You mean with you?' Her voice sounded husky.

'Why not?' He took the costume from her and placed it on the chair. Then he reached for her hand and clasped it firmly. 'One always starts with the left foot,' he said. 'There are four double forwards and then we face each other and drop hands. Double steps back, and then forwards. Let us do that and then we'll try the next part.'

At first she could not concentrate and she muffed her steps and her fingers trembled in his grasp. 'Relax, Rosamund,' he murmured against her hair. 'This is not a matter of life and death. You are meant to find pleasure in the dance.' She nodded and tried to concentrate on her steps and not on the effect he was having on her. 'That's better,' he said. 'Now we do a quarter-turn left and then double forwards, turn right around and double forward back to where we began.'

Rosamund followed his lead and eventually managed the steps without watching her feet. They came to a halt and she laughed. 'I can do this.'

'Of course you can,' said Alex, grinning.

'What next?'

'We now face our partner as we are doing and I turn on the spot. Then you do the same.' She did so and then he took both her hands and they slip-stepped up the hall.

'I think I remember what comes next,' said Rosamund, and proved she did.

Laughing, they came to a halt. 'Ach! That was good,' said Alex. 'You make an excellent dancer when you stop worrying.'

'Thank you.' Rosamund's eyes were luminous as she looked up into his face.

Suddenly, as if drawn together by an invisible cord, they moved closer until their bodies touched. Gently at first they kissed. Rosamund had never enjoyed anything so much and did not want him to let her go. Then a snore that turned into a wheezing cough caused them to spring apart.

'I must go,' murmured Alex, so aroused that he knew that if he did not cool down then he would not be able to answer for the consequences. He made for the door, only to be stopped by Lady Elizabeth's breathless voice.

'I have been thinking, Rosamund, that I would like to see you married before I die.'

Alex turned and looked at Rosamund and then at the white-painted face staring at them both over the back of the settle. Lady Elizabeth smiled grotesquely. 'What say you to an official betrothal before we leave for Richmond, Baron?' she gasped. 'My lawyer will be here soon. He is to make provision for a dowry for my goddaughter and could draw up a betrothal agreement at the same time.'

Alex walked slowly over to the settle. 'You overheard what I said to Bude? You were only pretending to have dozed off?'

'I cannot sleep without my potion, for I can

scarcely breathe,' panted Lady Elizabeth. 'I would like to see Rosamund's child born before I—'

'What child?' asked Alex, frowning.

'There is no child,' cried Rosamund, going over to her godmother.

'There could be,' said Lady Elizabeth in a faint voice.

Alex's eyes narrowed. 'Enough of such talk. You should be in bed.' He went over to the settle and scooped the old woman up into his arms. 'Rosamund, open the door,' he commanded.

She hastened to do his bidding, wondering what the Baron was making of all this talk of a child. Before she could ask if he knew where her godmother's bedchamber was, her maid suddenly appeared.

'What has happened?' she asked anxiously.

'Lady Elizabeth has over-exerted herself,' said Alex. 'Lead the way to her bedchamber and we will follow.'

The maid nodded and almost ran in her haste to reach her ladyship's bedchamber that was fortunately on the ground floor. Once there, she drew back the bedcovers and Alex laid her ladyship down.

'Bring me my potion, Hannah,' gasped Lady

Elizabeth, her eyes rolling in her head. 'And, Rosamund, you stay with me.'

The maid hurried out.

Rosamund glanced at Alex, who was standing the other side of the bed. She knew this was not the right time to try to explain to him her godmother's conviction that he had seduced her on the journey to London.

'Sitting up will improve Godmother's breathing. You hold her whilst I pile up the pillows behind her.'

There was much Alex wanted to ask Rosamund, but knew it would have to wait. He moved swiftly to comply with her request and watched Rosamund deftly heap several pillows behind her godmother. Then he eased her gently against them and Rosamund tucked in the bedclothes so that she was snug and warm. Then she drew up a chair and sat beside the bed and took one of her godmother's hands in hers.

'Should we send for your physician?' she asked.

Lady Elizabeth moved her head slightly from side to side and closed her eyes. 'Send for the priest,' she whispered.

Rosamund's heart sank. She did not want to believe that she was about to lose her godmother when she had scarcely had a chance to get to know her. She glanced at the Baron's stern face, but before she could even ask, he was on his way.

To her relief he was not gone long.

'It is done,' he said, wondering if it was his imagination that her ladyship's breathing seemed a little easier now. He hated to see anyone suffer in such a way and walked over to the window and gazed out. He remained there, thinking about what Lady Elizabeth had said about Rosamund's child. He did not want to believe that she was not the innocent he considered her to be. She had insisted there was no child. But if that was true, then why did her godmother believe there could be? Was he missing a trick here?

He glanced towards the bed and caught Rosamund staring at him. *What was she asking of him?* He turned away and gazed out of the window, wondering with part of his mind if the lawyer would arrive at the same time as the priest. If Lady Elizabeth's condition worsened, then what was Alex to do? She had obviously decided that he was the husband she wanted for her goddaughter. If she was dying, would she expect a wedding instead of a betrothal? This had never been part of his plan when he had agreed to do what his natural father had asked.

Hannah reappeared, carrying a golden goblet on a salver. Alex turned and watched the maid and Rosamund help Lady Elizabeth to drink the potion. Would it ease her suffering and enable her to live a while longer? He could only pray it would be so. They eased Lady Elizabeth back against the pillows and watched her close her eyes.

Rosamund sat back in the chair and took her godmother's hand in hers once more. She was aware that her godmother's breathing was still audible, making almost a whistling sound. But hopefully the potion and rest would improve her condition. She glanced over at Alex; as if sensing her eyes were on him, he turned. But he did not have a smile for her. Could the kisses they had shared mean so little to him? Did he believe in this mythical child and that she had been impregnated by someone else? She watched him go over to the maid and speak to her, then the maid left the room.

Alex resumed his watch at the window, but his body was turned slightly towards Rosamund. He was remembering how much he desired her and how he had compromised her. She was Harry's sister! Were these three things reason enough for him to suggest making an old lady die happy and for him to possibly father another man's child? Maybe her stepbrother's?

But before he could make a decision, a slurred voice from the bed said, 'I was thinking, if you are both willing you could marry, instead of getting betrothed. The priest would say the words over you for the bequest of a tidy sum for his church.'

Her words caused Rosamund's heart to begin to thud in her breast. She did not want the Baron to be forced into marrying her. 'You are not going to die, Godmother,' she said, a quiver in her voice.

'You cannot guarantee that, my dear,' gasped Lady Elizabeth. 'You are not the Almighty. Is it that you would refuse a dying woman and a fortune?'

'I do not want your money,' said Rosamund quietly. 'But I would make you happy.'

Lady Elizabeth said, 'Good. What do you say, Baron? Or is it that you were only toying with my goddaughter's affections?'

'No!' cried Rosamund.

Alex darted a glance at her and for a moment their eyes met and he knew what his answer was going to be. 'I will ignore that slur on my honour, Lady Elizabeth, and I will take your goddaughter as my wife.' He might not love or trust her completely, but he did believe that if there was a child then Fustian had raped her. He felt sick at the thought.

'No slur was intended, Baron,' gasped Lady Elizabeth. 'As soon as Master Jamieson and Father Thomas arrive, they are to be brought here.'

'It will be done, Lady Elizabeth.' Alex's voice was calm despite his racing heart. It was possible that tonight he and Rosamund would be husband and wife. He gave his attention to the view from the window once more.

Chapter Nine

Alex did not have long to wait before noticing a soberly dressed man of middle years and a younger man Alex presumed was his clerk approaching. He informed her ladyship and she asked him to go and greet them and explain the situation.

No sooner had he gone than Rosamund became aware that her godmother seemed to have gone off into a doze. She felt nervous, hoping this was not the prelude to a deeper sleep. The room was quiet, except for the sound of the sick woman's laboured breathing. Rosamund wished that she and her godmother could have met years ago when she was younger and in good health. It seemed an age before Hannah entered the bedchamber with a flagon of wine and a branch of lighted candles. She placed the candelabra on a table close to the bedside before pouring some wine for Rosamund.

Alex entered the bedchamber a few moments later with the lawyer and his clerk. They were followed almost immediately by the priest. From the lawyer's demeanour, it was obvious to Rosamund that Alex had explained all that was needful. As for the priest, he approached the side of the bed opposite to the lawyer. Instantly, Rosamund rose and gave up her seat to him. She moved over to the window with her goblet of wine, aware that Alex stayed by the bed. Obviously, he intended not missing a word said between her godmother, the lawyer and the priest.

Indeed, that was Alex's intention and he could not help thinking that he and his father had not reckoned on this happening when they had made their plans that had involved Lady Elizabeth. Still, he was determined to ensure that her wishes were carried out where Rosamund was concerned.

He looked around for her and saw that she had gone over to the window and was gazing outside. Her face looked drawn and sad and he wanted to crush Fustian beneath his heel. He prayed that her godmother would live long enough to enable them to plight their troth.

Two hours later, Alex knew that he need not have doubted her ladyship's staying power. As soon as he and Rosamund had spoken the words that would bind them together until death, her ladyship had beckoned Hannah over and mouthed that she must serve wine to all those present. Then she reached out a hand to the newly married couple and congratulated them. 'I hope you will have many happy years ahead of you,' she whispered.

Tears trickled down Rosamund's cheeks as she thanked her godmother. It was difficult to believe that she and the Baron were wed. She found herself twisting her godmother's silver-and-amber ring around her finger in an agitated manner. Tonight would be her wedding night. But even as the thought made her feel apprehensive and excited at the same time, she realised that it was unlikely that she and her new husband would have the opportunity to share a bed that night. How could they both leave her godmother when she lay dying?

The lawyer drank his wine and said he would send his clerk with the papers in the morning for her ladyship. The priest said he would come back later as he had a mass to conduct. Alex saw them out and then returned to the bedchamber where Rosamund had resumed her place at her godmother's side. She rose when he entered the room.

'What do you wish me to do, husband?' she asked, looking docile.

He was suspicious of such meekness. 'What I wish and what I must do are in conflict with each other,' he said, frowning. 'We must take turns to sit with her during the night.'

'Shall I take the first watch?' asked Rosamund.

'Aye. I will partake of supper and then I will come and relieve you, so you can dine.'

'I am not hungry,' said Rosamund.

His frown deepened. 'You must eat to keep up your strength. It will not do for you to be ill,' he rasped.

'Then I will eat,' she said, wondering about the depth of his concern.

'Good,' he said, and left the bedchamber.

Rosamund returned to her post, but this time she knelt at the bedside and prayed not only for her godmother, but her new husband and herself, as well as Harry. Then she sat back on the chair and, as Lady Elizabeth appeared to be sleeping, Rosamund allowed her mind to wander. She did not need a title, especially a foreign one. How did a Swedish baroness behave? How should she address her new husband, by his title or—by the name he had spoken in the brief service?

Alexander. Was that his real name? She wondered if they were legally married if he had not used his proper one. Had the Baron considered such a possibility so he could have the marriage annulled?

Suddenly she was remembering her dream last night. How long ago it seemed now and yet she could recall it vividly. At least it had not been a premonition. The Baron had not turned into her stepbrother during the wedding ceremony. She experienced a cold feeling in her belly simply by thinking of Edward.

She stood up and went over to the window and saw that it was almost pitch-black outside. On such a night might murder be done. She shivered. What was she doing thinking such thoughts? She drew the curtains and returned to her godmother's bedside.

Shortly after the Baron entered the bedchamber and asked if there was any change in Lady Elizabeth's condition. Rosamund shook her head. 'My fear is that this sleep might be one from which she will not wake,' she whispered. 'But she is in God's hands and we must trust that He will do what is best for her.'

'If she recovers this time, it would make sense if she stopped painting her face,' said Alex.

'Perhaps you should suggest it to her, husband,' said Rosamund, lifting limpid eyes to him.

He stared at her fixedly. 'You are her goddaughter. It is probably more fitting if the suggestion came from you.'

'I doubt she will listen to me as she is accustomed to having her own way. She was so looking forward to attending the celebrations at Richmond and so was I,' said Rosamund softly. 'I suppose it will be out of the question going there now.' She stood up. 'You will wake me if I fall asleep so I can keep my watch, won't you?'

He inclined his head. 'Of course! But go now and eat and rest.'

Rosamund nodded. She kissed her godmother's cheek and reluctantly went to eat her lonely supper.

Alex took her place at the side of the bed. He had no intention of waking his wife if she were to fall asleep. *His wife!* It felt odd saying those two little words, but they did mean that he now had the right to protect her. But what about the child her godmother insisted that she was carrying? The one Rosamund denied having conceived? He was in a quandary because he could be completely wrong about Fustian having raped her. But if he had done so, then most likely she would find the sexual act repulsive. It made sense not to consummate the match just yet until her condition was known. What if she was not to be trusted and encouraged her stepbrother and all that she had told him was false? He was weary and his head was in a muddle. He settled himself in the chair for what would surely be a long night.

Rosamund was tempted to disobey her husband and return to her godmother's bedchamber after finishing her supper. She did not wish to go to a lonely, cold bed where no doubt her thoughts would guarantee she would be unable to sleep. He had not wanted to marry her and perhaps he thought that she had deliberately led her godmother astray in order to trap him. The notion made her feel angry, but thankfully, after a second goblet of wine, she could scarcely keep her eyes open. She made her way to her bedchamber and got into bed and instantly fell asleep.

Alex started awake. The hard lines of his body were tense—he had been dreaming of Rosamund. Despite the mask she wore, he was convinced it was his wife. Yet every time he drew closer to her, she retreated in a way that reminded him of the movements of the dance. Did this mean he was going to lose her? He rubbed his eyes and looked towards the bed. The candles in the candelabra had guttered out and dawn was not far off. He could see the outline of the lady in the bed and, *thank God*, she was still breathing. He stood up and stretched, wondering what had woken him. Perhaps a noise outside. Had the priest returned and not managed to rouse the house in order to gain entry?

He went over to the window and drew back the curtains and rubbed at the frost on the glass with his sleeve and peered out. He saw a slight, dark-haired figure hurrying in the direction of the stables. Immediately he thought the worst—Rosamund regretted the vows she had made last night and was running away. He had to rouse Hannah so she could sit with Lady Elizabeth whilst he went after his wife.

As he strode along the passage he could smell baking bread. When he reached the hall there was a serving wench sweeping the floor. He called to her and she came scurrying over to him and asked how was her ladyship.

'She is asleep, but I've had to leave her for the moment. Will you fetch Hannah to sit with her?' he asked.

'Aye, Baron!'

Alex left her and hurried to the stables where, to his relief, he discovered that his horse was still in its stall. He was returning to the house when he heard someone hail him. He turned and saw Rosamund.

'You did not send Hannah to wake me as you promised and I know the reason why.' She smiled faintly. 'You dozed off, so I let you sleep. Godmother's breathing sounded so much better that when I heard shouting outside I decided to investigate.'

'I saw you from the window and thought you were regretting last night and had decided to run away.'

She stiffened. 'Where would I run to? I see you still do not trust me. I am not so ungrateful towards Godmother or frightened of you that I would run away,' she said coldly and turned away.

'Forgive me! I woke suddenly and obviously I was not thinking rationally.' He reached out and touched her face. 'You are cold. You must get inside without delay.'

'And what of you?' asked Rosamund, warmed by that gesture. 'You must rest whilst I sit with Godmother.'

'Hannah is with her. You mentioned hearing shouting. Did you find out from whence it came?'

'No. I decided if anything untoward had happened, then the guards would have investigated.'

'You went as far as the gates?'

She shook her head. 'I did not want to be out too long.'

'Then I will go and speak to them after I have seen you to the house.'

'I can see myself indoors,' she replied. 'If you are concerned, go immediately.'

She turned away and hurried to her godmother's bedchamber, hoping that she would be no worse than when she had left her. To her delight she found that Lady Elizabeth was awake and speaking to Hannah. Instantly, she broke off from what she was saying and greeted her goddaughter.

'So there you are, my dear,' she gasped. 'I wondered where you and the Baron had gone.'

'I heard shouting, so I went outside to investigate,' said Rosamund. 'I did not see anyone, but the Baron is making a further search.' She smiled. 'How are you feeling now, Godmother? You sound so much better than you did last even.'

'I realise now that it was foolish of me to dance,' said Lady Elizabeth ruefully. 'If we are to go to Richmond, then I know I will have to be sensible.'

Rosamund was surprised. 'You are still considering attending the celebrations?'

'Of a surety. It could be the last time I have the opportunity to share in such an occasion.' Her voice was mournful.

'But won't you find the ride exhausting?' asked Rosamund with concern.

Her godmother shook her head and then had to straighten her wig. 'No. For I will travel by barge. You and the Baron may wish to ride,' she wheezed, resting against the pillows, 'and you may do so, for I am certain you have much to talk about and would prefer to be alone.'

Rosamund did not deny it. 'But who will take care of you?' she asked anxiously.

'My dear! I never travel anywhere without a whole host of servants. Hannah here will not leave my side.' Lady Elizabeth leaned over and patted the woman's arm.

'If you are certain that is your wish. When must we depart?'

'I must wait until my lawyer arrives. I gave him firm instructions that he must have his clerk and copyist prepare the documents for me to sign this morning,' said Lady Elizabeth.

Rosamund took her hand. 'I have not expressed

my gratitude for your generous gift of a dowry. I do appreciate your kindness very much indeed.'

Lady Elizabeth smiled. 'I am glad you were sensible enough to fall in with my wishes by marrying the Baron. Now leave me alone for a while and send him to me as soon as he returns.'

Rosamund marvelled at her godmother's stamina, courage and determination. She kissed her cheek and left the bedchamber. There was no sign of the Baron in the parlour or the hall and so Rosamund went outside, thinking to give him the news of her godmother's decision, but he was nowhere in sight. She decided to put on her boots and a cloak and go as far as the gates.

On arriving at the gates Alex had found only one guard on duty. He was stamping his feet and blowing on his fingers and was a different man to either of those guarding the entrance yesterday.

The guard suddenly noticed him and said, 'Who goes there?'

'I am Baron Dalsland and I am a guest of Lady Elizabeth's,' said Alex.

'Ahh! You'll be the foreigner who came yesterday with her ladyship's goddaughter.' The guard's eyes were alight with curiosity. 'Rumour has it in the guardroom that you and the young lady were wed last night.'

Alex did not deny it.

'And is Lady Elizabeth in better health this morning?'

'I believe so.'

The guard grinned. 'It's not the first time she's had her lawyer and the priest out and us thinkin' she were on her death bed. Always manages to rally round so far.'

'I am pleased to hear it.' Alex asked the man whether anyone had come through the gates that morning or if he had seen anything suspicious during the night.

The man pursed his lips and scratched his head. 'Now there's a question. Josh, who's new and from the north, was checking the perimeter wall earlier. He said there were bits of mortar and brick dust on the ground, as well as a broken branch from a tree. It's as if someone had tried to breach the wall.'

'I'd like to speak to this Josh,' said Alex.

'He'll be here later,' said the man.

Alex thanked him and decided to take a walk and see for himself if aught of interest was happening at the Steel Yard or Fustian's house. Hopefully, by the time he returned, the other guard would be back on gate duty and he could have a word with him.

Rosamund arrived at the gates without seeing anyone. She hailed the guard on duty and asked if he had seen the Baron that morning.

'Aye, Baroness.' He looked at her with interest. 'The Baron, your husband, went out.'

Being addressed as Baroness gave Rosamund an odd feeling and caused her to feel tied to the Baron in a way she had not done so far. Her dark brows knit and she gnawed on her lip, wondering where he could have gone. She thought of Ingrid and was suddenly uneasy.

'Ahhh! I remember where he was going now. I shall go and find him,' she said brightly, and slipped out of the gateway.

She noticed that there were several pairs of footprints in the snow and had no trouble distinguishing those of her husband's boots from the others. First, they were larger, second there was a jagged cut on the leather of the left one. She had noticed such marks when he had left footprints in the mud near a stream several times. It was also a fact that the footprints looked to be the freshest. She began to follow them and managed to do so all the way to a gateway in the Steel Yard, close to the quayside.

She drew her hood further over her head and gazed at the open gates. There were no guards and few people going in and out. Why had the Baron come here? Was it because he expected to find Ingrid here? She felt desolate and stood a moment, trying to decide what to do. The sun was rising in the sky and there was little heat in it, but maybe it was strong enough to soon melt the snow and destroy her husband's footprints. She made up her mind and headed for the gates.

Once inside, she saw that the Steel Yard was like a proper little village with workshops open for business, shops, houses and a church. Despite the earliness of the hour and the weather, there was much hustle and bustle going on inside, but when people called to each other it was as if she had stepped inside Babbel and she could not under-stand a word. Dismayed, she realised also that people's feet had already turned the snow into slush here and she no longer knew which direction her husband had taken.

Frustrated, she decided to make for the church to find some peace and pray. Once inside, she stood in the gloomy interior lit by a few candles and sent up a prayer. Then she made for the door, only to pause at the sound of voices. She could not make out what was being said, but one of them was definitely female. She melted into the shadows as two people appeared at the far end of the church. Her eyes caught the gleam of a man's fair head in the candlelight before he put on his hat. He had his back to her so that she could not see his face, but with a jerk of her heart, she realised there was something familiar about him. She heard the woman say something and, although, Rosamund had heard Ingrid speak only the once, she recognised that voice. Even as she stood there, she saw the woman draw the man's head down towards hers and they kissed.

Rosamund could not bear to watch them any longer and blundered out of the church, heedless of the noise she made. She ran towards the gates, sliding in the slushy snow and almost losing her balance a couple of times. She was aware that she drew attention to herself, but did not stop until she was through the gates and heading towards the Thames. There she stopped to catch her breath and gaze out over the river at a yellowy wintry sun reflecting on the surface.

How could Alex kiss Ingrid when only a few

hours ago he had sworn fidelity to herself? He might have acted as if he hated the woman he believed to have betrayed him, but obviously the tidings that Rosamund had brought him yesterday had melted his fury, and he had not been able to resist her when he saw her again.

Tears filled Rosamund's eyes and trickled down her cheeks. She wiped them away fiercely with the back of her glove and began to trudge towards the Strand. She felt cheated and utterly miserable and kept her head down so no one could see her tears. She was within yards of the gates of her godmother's mansion when a hand seized her shoulder from behind. She tried to turn round, but that hand was relentless and its fingers bit into her flesh through her cloak and gown. A terrible fear seized her and she was unable to cry out for help as her hood was drawn back.

'So it is true,' hissed a hated voice against her ear. 'What a foolish woman you are! Will you never learn that you cannot escape your destiny? You were mad to believe you could. Accept, Rosie, that one day I will have you. You will be my slave and beg me to be merciful to you.'

'Let me go!' she gasped. 'You are too late!'

'You are talking of your betrothal to that

Swedish fool. Don't get too fond of him, Rosie. He doesn't have much longer to live.'

Rosamund felt faint and struggled to stay conscious then suddenly she was free. She staggered and fell over in the snow. Edward's voice came to her on the breeze. 'I'll see you again soon, Rosie, and when I do there'll be no escaping me then.'

She tried to get up, but was trembling so much that her feet kept slipping. Then she heard a voice saying, 'Mistress Rosamund, are thee all right? That man! He reminded me of Master Fustian. What was going on there?' The next moment she was being lifted up by two strong arms and gazed in disbelief at the stocky young man staring anxiously into her face.

'Joshua, it can't be you! Oh, this is all too much.' She burst into tears.

Laughter rumbled deep in his throat. ''Tis me, and I'm right glad to see thee, Mistress Rosamund.'

She clutched his arm and smiled through her tears. 'I never thought I'd see you again. I feared that she might have done away with you.'

'Naw, Lady Monica just gave me my marching orders. If it weren't for thee, I'd have left when thy father died.'

'It's like a miracle,' she whispered. 'What are you doing here?'

'I'm one of Lady Elizabeth's guards.'

She gazed into Joshua's broad face with its broken nose and could not be more pleased. 'How did this happen?'

'When Lady Monica turned me off, I goes to the Earl of Derby and asks can he give me some paid labour. He had nuthin'!' Joshua pulled a face. 'But as luck would have it Lady Elizabeth was staying there with her entourage, so I got gabbing with me mate here.' He jerked his head in the direction of the other guard. 'He told me that one of the other men had taken ill and died. So I just stepped into his shoes.'

'I am so pleased,' said Rosamund, remembering how Joshua had grieved for Harry as much as she had done. She was about to tell him the news about her brother, when the other guard spoke up.

'I hate to remind yer, Josh,' he said, 'but this here lady's husband is the Baron. Best not be too familiar.'

'Lor! Thou's right, Will. I'd best be keeping me distance.' Josh moved away from Rosamund to take up a position the other side of the gate.

She was now feeling extremely peculiar. She had run the gauntlet of so many differing emotions in the last hour that, having lost the support of

Joshua's arm, she needed to rest a moment, so leaned against the gatepost.

'Surely we don't have to stand on ceremony, Josh? I'm still the same person you knew back at Appleby,' she said in a low voice.

'I doubt it, Mistress Rosamund. I mean, Baroness,' he said, standing at attention. 'For thee to be here means thee has changed.'

'I *don't* feel different towards you, but I suppose it is true that I have changed. At least the Baron believes so. I must tell you, though, that—' Her voice broke off at the sound of approaching footsteps. She began to tremble afresh. Was it her husband or her stepbrother returning?

The priest stopped and smiled at her. 'I saw your husband a short while ago, Baroness. He told me that Lady Elizabeth has survived the night.'

'Indeed,' said Rosamund, attempting to put some steel into her spine and a welcome in her voice. 'She opened her eyes and spoke to me and I am sure that she will be pleased to see you.'

'What a strong will she has, but she might yet have a relapse, so I must make haste and pray with her. You will accompany me?'

Rosamund glanced at Joshua, but he was staring straight ahead. She decided to tell him about Harry later. Her legs were feeling shaky, but she managed to walk beside the priest to the house. She lingered in her godmother's bedchamber only until the lawyer arrived. Then she asked to be excused and went upstairs to her bedchamber, where she collapsed on the bed.

She attempted to blank out all thought of the last hour, but it was impossible for her to do so. Her fear and pain was too great. Her husband loved another woman and her stepbrother had found her and was determined to punish her for running away. She thumped a fist into the pillow, thinking she would rather die than be taken by him again. But how had Edward discovered that she was here with the Baron? Had Ingrid told him? Had she had time? Thinking of her husband with her brought tears to Rosamund's eyes again.

Perhaps she should kill herself. Belladonna would do the trick. She gasped. What was she thinking of! What purpose would killing herself serve? She would fight them both, Edward and that woman who would steal her husband.

Chapter Ten

Rosamund sprang off the bed. She also had to consider Harry. She longed to see her brother again—what if he returned to England, only to be told that he'd had a sister, but she was dead. There was also Richmond to see! She was supposedly riding there with her new husband today. Was there any way she could escape being alone with him, knowing that he had betrayed her within less than a day of them plighting their troth? She felt that ache in the region of her heart again and determinedly tried to ignore it. Had she not survived years of lack of love and bullying? Why was she getting so fussed? Their wedding had taken place to please her godmother, so maybe she was expecting too much of him in wanting him to remain faithful. But the thought of him kissing another woman still hurt.

A sigh escaped her. She would go down and discuss the journey with her godmother. Pray God that she had not had a relapse and was well enough to go to Richmond. She hoped the gowns in her possession would be sufficient for her stay at the royal palace. She was apprehensive about what lay ahead. Presumably the troupe would still be part of the entertainment, but with her godmother no longer able to dance, would the Baron still take part? She remembered how much she had enjoyed dancing with him yesterday and the kisses they had shared. Obviously, they had not meant anything to him. It was then she recalled her godmother suggesting that she try on Lady Joan's costume. Would it be worth doing so? She would see if the gown was still on the chair in the hall because, if they were to go to Richmond, she would need to pack it.

Rosamund searched for the black-and-silver costume, but it was not there, so she hurried to her godmother's bedchamber and was pleased to find her sitting in a chair with a metal box on her knee. She marvelled at her powers of recovery.

'There you are, my dear,' wheezed Lady Elizabeth, closing the lid of the box and turning the key in the lock. 'Am I to presume that the Baron has not yet returned?'

'Aye. Surely he cannot be much longer?' said Rosamund brightly. 'He was not clad for outdoors. I hope he does not catch a chill.'

Her godmother smiled. 'You already sound like a wife. As soon as he returns you must have breakfast and set out for Richmond. I still have a few matters to deal with before I can leave. They will have made ready a suite of rooms for me and my entourage. In case I am delayed, I will write a message with instructions that you and the Baron are to have one of the finest bedchambers. After all, you were cheated of your wedding night,' she added with a twinkle in her eyes. 'Tonight I want all to go well for you both.'

'What if the Baron does not return?'

Lady Elizabeth's eyes clouded. 'Don't be gloomy, my dear. I haven't gone to all this trouble to see you married to have my plans thwarted. If he has not returned within the hour, I will send some of the men to make a search for him. In the meantime, I will give orders to have my barge made ready. As long as there is no trouble with the tides or the river freezing over, then all will be well.'

'Perhaps I should travel by barge with you?'

Her godmother gave her a sharp look. 'There is no need for you to fear being alone with the Baron now you are married. He will take care of you as I intended.'

Rosamund was starting to wonder if her god-mother's difficulty with breathing last evening had been feigned, but decided it was best not to speak her thoughts. She did not wish to disillusion the old lady about the man she put so much faith in. Instead, she said lightly, 'I had forgotten that the Thames was tidal.'

'It is, indeed, but we are miles from the sea. The horse ferry at Westminster will take you across to the south bank. Unless the weather worsens, the journey should only be of a few hours' duration. You will arrive there well before nightfall,' said Lady Elizabeth.

No sooner had she finished speaking, than there came a knock. 'Enter!' she called.

The door opened and the Baron entered. He looked at his wife and said without preamble, 'I hear you left the grounds in search of me. You should not have done so. One of the men said you were attacked opposite the gates.'

Lady Elizabeth looked at Rosamund in astonishment. 'You made no mention of this to me.'

She flushed. 'No. I did not want to distress you, as it was, one of your guards came to my rescue.'

'I am truly shocked that you should be set upon so close to my gates.'

'I am sure it will not happen again,' said Rosamund, not wanting to upset her further by telling her the identity of her attacker. 'I had naught to steal.'

Alex frowned. 'Even so, it was foolish of you to go out alone. If the guards had not seen you, then you might have been seriously hurt.'

'I would prefer you not to make a fuss,' she said stiffly, annoyed that he should scold her. Where had *he* been when she needed him, but out meeting his former lover? 'I shall not do it again,' she added, an angry gleam in her eyes.

Alex wondered why she was so vexed with him. Was it not natural for a husband to be concerned about his wife's safety? 'I should hope not. Anyway, I bring tidings.'

'What tidings?' asked Lady Elizabeth eagerly.

'Lady Monica and her party have arrived in London.'

It was just as they had expected, but the news caused Rosamund to feel quite sick. 'How do you know this?' she asked.

'I have been having Fustian's house watched and I was fortunate enough to see his wife,

Marion, with an older woman whom she addressed as Lady Monica.'

'She must have ridden like the wind to get here,' said Rosamund, thinking it was not surprising the Baron had been out so long if he'd visited both the Steel Yard and her stepbrother's house.

'Or flew on her broomstick,' muttered Lady Elizabeth.

Alex smiled and pressed his wife's shoulder gently. 'You must not fear them. I have the right to protect you now.'

'Spoken like a true knight,' said Rosamund lightly.

Lady Elizabeth sighed. 'Just the kind of husband I wanted.'

Alex stared at her. 'You certainly seem to have made a miraculous recovery, Lady Elizabeth.'

'The power of prayer,' she said piously, touching the amber-and-silver crucifix hanging from her girdle. 'I deem that God has healed me in order that I can make the journey to Richmond. Hopefully I will be able to leave within a few hours. As I have already said, I will travel by barge, so as not to exert myself too much. I have suggested to Rosamund that the pair of you ride to Richmond as soon as possible. We need to make certain that one of us arrives at the palace to execute your father's plans.'

Rosamund thought she must have misheard her godmother's words. Had the Baron not told her that his father had played no part in his life? So what were these plans they were talking about?

'I see the sense in what you say, Lady Elizabeth, but if you fail to reach Richmond, then I will have to reconsider our plans,' said Alex. 'I say that Rosamund could still be of help to us.'

'I do not know of what you speak,' said Rosamund. 'What I wish to know is whether I will still be taking part in the dance? If so, I must inform you, Godmother, that Lady Joan's gown has gone missing from the hall.'

'Do not concern yourself about it,' said the older woman. 'Most likely one of the servants has picked it up. I will see to it that it is packed with my baggage, along with the masks I have ordered, which are yet to be delivered.' She clapped her hands together. 'Now, enough said, my dears. You must eat before setting out on your journey. Breakfast will be served in my parlour,' she wheezed. 'Baron, your wife can explain to you my plans for your arrival at Richmond. Go now! I must write a message for you to take with you.'

Rosamund and Alex accepted their dismissal

without comment and left the bedchamber for the parlour. She sat down at table, but he went over to the fire and held his hands out to the blaze. 'It is still very cold out. You must wrap up well.'

Rosamund wondered how he could speak of such mundane matters when he was such a deceiver. 'Godmother said that we are to take the horse ferry at Westminster and cross to the south bank. We should reach Richmond before night-fall,' she said in a colourless voice.

He slanted her a frowning glance. 'You are still upset by what happened outside the gate, I deem. You must not go out alone again.'

'We have already had this conversation,' she muttered.

'Aye. But where did you go when you went out in search for me? I saw no sign of you.'

She thought he sounded suspicious and her hurt deepened. 'Perhaps you weren't looking for me, but someone else?'

Before he could reply, a servant entered and placed food and ale on the table. It was not until the man had left that Alex said, 'You make that sound as if there was something wrong in doing so. I told you where I have been.'

She reached for bread and salted pork and said

firmly, 'Are you certain you have told me all that you did?'

'Is this what marriage is about?' Alex picked up the jug and poured the ale. 'I suspect that you are going to tell me you saw me somewhere else.'

'From what you have just said, you did go somewhere other than to spy on my evil stepbrother,' she said, a flush on her cheeks. 'You certainly missed seeing him when you were seeing someone else.'

Alex was astounded. 'Of what are you accusing me?'

'I saw you with that religious in the church in the Steel Yard. You were in an embrace and she was kissing you!'

'You're mistaken. If I had an assignation with Ingrid, I would certainly not arrange to meet her in her nun's habit in a church,' he said firmly.

He sounded so positive that Rosamund was immediately filled with doubt. 'But he seemed familiar and definitely reminded me of you.'

'It was not me.' His voice was carefully controlled. 'Now I'd like to know what you meant by my missing seeing your stepbrother?'

Rosamund felt ashamed of her suspicions. But if it was not the Baron who had been with Ingrid, who had it been?

'Well?' demanded Alex, slapping the table with the flat of his hand.

She started and looked at him and the expression in his eyes caused her to take a deep breath. 'It was Edward who attacked me. He-he threatened me and you.'

Alex's expression altered. 'Did he hurt you?' he rasped.

'No doubt I shall be bruised where he seized me, but he was more intent on—on telling me that I would never escape him and you were going to die.'

Alex swore. 'How did he know I was here? I was so careful.'

'He seemed to know there was something between us.'

'You mean he knows that we're wed?'

'No, I feel sure he did not know that and I did not enlighten him. He did think us betrothed, though.'

Alex was silent and then said, 'Eat your breakfast. We need to leave soon.'

'Might it not be best if we travelled by barge with Lady Elizabeth?' asked Rosamund.

'No. It is possible that she might have a relapse and be unable to make the journey. It is vital that we reach Richmond as soon as possible.'

'Because of these plans to do with your father?'

He did not answer, but carried on eating his breakfast.

She took a mouthful of ale and forced some food down. At least she could be glad that he had not been unfaithful to her so soon. The ache in her heart had abated and she felt much better. 'You said that you spoke to the guards.'

'One of them.'

'You did not speak to Joshua?'

'No. He must have been the other one.' He cocked an eyebrow. 'Why?'

'What is your opinion of him?'

'He seemed a sturdy fellow. Why do you ask? Do you think he could be the spy in the camp?'

'No! Joshua is no thief.'

Alex frowned. 'You know this man?'

She smiled. 'I have known Joshua all my life. He is the man I pretended to be—Master Joshua Wood, woodcutter. He taught Harry about wood-craft and they used to practise swordplay together with wooden swords. That was until Father bought Harry a short-sword. He grieved with me when we believed Harry to be dead.'

'Why did you not tell me this earlier?' he said mildly, not wanting her to suspect that he was a little envious of the obvious affection that she bore this man.

'I only discovered he was here a short while ago. You may ask the other guard about our meeting.' She reached for the honey.

'Did you speak of Harry to him?' Alex bit into bread and smoked pork.

'I would have done so if the priest had not arrived just then,' replied Rosamund.

He nodded. 'Best that you do not tell him. If he was such a friend to Harry, we do not wanting him taking off in search of him.'

Rosamund's expression lightened. 'I had not thought of his doing so. But why should he not help us?'

'Because Lady Elizabeth needs him here.'

Rosamund fell to thinking, remembering him saying, *Is this what marriage is about?* when she had doubted him. 'Do you regret marrying me?' she asked bluntly.

'What a question to ask me,' said Alex. 'Why? Are you regretting the match we have made? It is not too late for an annulment, if that is what you want. I will be honest and say that I believe your godmother tricked us into marriage because she believes you are carrying my child. I only pray that she will live long enough to realise her mistake.'

Rosamund heaved a sigh. 'She might believe that is so, but we both know that I am not carrying your child. Maybe she has regrets about her own childless state and wants me to have a child so she can be a proxy grandmother.'

'That's understandable. She has made you the recipient of most of her fortune. If all she asks in return is for you to provide her with a proxy grandchild, then the least we can do is to grant her wish,' he said, sounding exasperated.

'So *you* don't want an annulment?' murmured Rosamund, aware of a sudden welling of happiness.

'Not at the moment,' he said, shaking his head. 'Perhaps it makes sense for me to take a wife now instead of waiting until my thirtieth birthday. I could be dead then.'

Rosamund's happiness faded. 'What a thing to say! You have destroyed my appetite. I will go and fetch my baggage and hopefully I will not have been widowed by the time I return. You will not forget my godmother's message before we leave?' She did not wait for his permission, but hurried from the room.

'Damn!' Alex threw down his own napkin and

went after her, but she was already out of sight. She must have run like the wind, he thought. He had no idea of the whereabouts of her bedchamber, but was determined to reassure her of his affection and his determination to stay alive before they left for Richmond. He could so easily imagine the atmosphere between them on the journey if he did not put matters right.

He tried several vacant bedchambers on the first floor before he reached one that was locked. From inside came the sound of pacing feet and a voice muttering, 'If I am widowed, what good is it if Godmother leaves her money to me? Edward will find some way to get at me and the money. I might as well be dead now.'

'Rosamund, open this door,' commanded Alex, worried by what he had overheard. 'We must talk.'

There was a long silence before she answered him. 'We have talked enough. It is obvious to me that you do not know how to handle a wife.'

'That is most likely true because I have never had a wife before,' said Alex patiently. 'But there could be that in our future that would make us both happy. Tell me, Rosamund, have you ever slept with a man?'

'Who have you in mind besides yourself?' She

laughed a mite hysterically. 'If you suspect that Joshua and I might have had a youthful liaison, then you are mistaken. Joshua never laid a finger on me, unlike that cur, Edward.'

Alex felt a familiar anger at her mention of Edward. 'Unlock the door, Rosamund,' he said in a gentle tone. 'We cannot waste time arguing like this if we are to go to Richmond.'

He heard a bolt being drawn, and the door swung open. He noticed the tearstains on her face before she turned away and picked up her baggage. He experienced a rush of compassion and wanted to protect her not only from other men's angry attentions, but his own.

'Give that here,' he said.

She handed the bag to him. 'Are you going to beat me when we get to Richmond?'

Alex dropped the baggage and kicked the door shut behind him. He seized her by the arms and drew her against him. 'How can you believe that I would beat you?'

'A husband owns his wife. He is free to do with her what he wills,' she said on a sob. 'Edward beats Marion and he would have done the same to me if Father had not forbidden it.'

Alex had difficulty controlling his rage, thinking

she was in a real muddle, but knew it would be a terrible mistake for her to see his anger explode. 'Rosamund, Rosamund,' he whispered against her ear. 'I would not treat you so cruelly. When I hold you in my arms like this, I want to make love to you, not beat you.' He nudged up her jaw with his chin and covered her lips with his own and kissed her gently. He wanted her, but was certain that whilst she was in such an emotional state that matters between them could go badly wrong. 'But now is not the time,' he said softly, releasing her and reaching for her baggage. 'I will meet you downstairs.'

Rosamund was mollified, but she would have preferred him to go on holding her and speaking in that gentle, caring voice. 'You will not forget to ask Lady Elizabeth for the missive you are to hand to the controller of the royal household?' she reminded him.

'I had forgotten,' he said wryly. 'I can see it is going to be useful having a wife. Thank you.'

He left her alone to collect herself and returned to the bedchamber that had been allotted to him last night. He put on his hat and cloak and picked up his gauntlets and saddlebags and went downstairs.

After saddling up his horse and fastening on the

pillion seat, he led his steed to the front of the house and went inside in search of Rosamund and Lady Elizabeth.

Her ladyship was not in her bedchamber, but he found her in the parlour eating bread and honey. He half-expected to be asked why he had taken so long preparing for the journey. Instead, she simply handed him a sealed parchment and wished him a safe journey. He thanked her, but paused to ask whether she knew that one of her guards had worked as a woodcutter on Appleby Manor.

'No, I did not know that,' she said, showing interest. 'I presume you are talking about the man that my captain of the guard hired while I was staying at Lathom House.'

'Aye. Joshua Wood. It has occurred to me that you have a man here who would recognise Rosamund's stepfamily on sight.'

'What are you suggesting?'

'If he is the man Rosamund believes him to be, then he will have their measure and warn us if he should discover anything that could be a threat to us.'

She nodded. 'I will send for him as soon as you and Rosamund have left for Richmond and speak to him. I pray God that we all have a safe journey.' She offered him her hand.

He raised it to his lips and kissed it.

As he turned away, Rosamund entered the parlour. He thought she appeared much calmer. 'So you both are here,' she said. 'I have come to say farewell for the moment, Godmother. I look forward to seeing you at Richmond.'

'Come closer, my dear,' wheezed Lady Elizabeth. 'I would kiss you farewell.'

Rosamund did as asked and was aware of her godmother's close scrutiny as she kissed her cheek. 'Have faith, my dear,' said Lady Elizabeth. 'Now go and enjoy each other's company.'

Rosamund thanked her and followed in Alex's wake. When they arrived at the gates, Rosamund was disappointed not to see Joshua on guard, but she made no mention of him. However, they had not travelled far when Alex said, 'I spoke to Lady Elizabeth about Joshua Wood.'

'What did you say to her?' She could not conceal her apprehension.

'I told her that you trusted him and that he could be useful. If Fustian were to return here or his mother or brother, he would recognise them and know what to do.'

Relief flooded her being. 'Thank you. I beg pardon for misjudging you.'

'I have misjudged you on several occasions, so I ask your forgiveness.'

'It is important that we trust each other,' she said awkwardly.

Alex nodded, considering being more open with her. Sooner rather than later he would need to tell her that he was the bastard son of a Scottish earl— he was not looking forward to doing so.

Chapter Eleven

Despite having visited London once before, Rosamund had never travelled as far as Westminster and she was determined to enjoy the experience despite her worry over Edward's threat. Her husband, on the other hand, seemed unconcerned about what her stepbrother might do and also appeared to know exactly where he was going and who lived where. He pointed out the riverside residences of the bishops of Exeter, Bath and Wells, as well as the palaces of the prelates of Carlisle, Durham and Norwich.

'One expects a king to live in a palace. But there is something amiss with the church, whose task it is to preach a gospel of self-sacrifice and love for the poor and needy, when its leaders are living in such luxury,' said Rosamund. 'I don't suppose you will agree with me.'

'Why should I not?' asked Alex. 'It is true that as we near Westminster you will see the hospital of St Mary Rouncelwell, but then comes the Archbishop of York's manor. There should certainly be more provision for the homeless, sick, elderly and poor and I believe change is coming.'

Rosamund was glad that they saw eye to eye on what she considered an important matter, but was curious to know more. 'What do you mean by change? Is it that you believe the rich and proud will repent of their ways? I find that difficult to believe.'

'Some will, but it is those who are educated and can read and want change that will foment it. Holy writ is being printed in such great numbers that there will be those who will speak out against the church and demand reform.'

'It has already begun,' said Rosamund with a stir of excitement. 'I remember Joshua's father talking about the hedge priests that his grandfather had told of to his father. They wandered the country preaching equality for all men and an end to war. They had read the gospels for themselves and paid a terrible price for saying the church was corrupt. Many were burnt alive.' She shuddered.

Alex was surprised that his wife knew of such horrors and should be willing to talk about them.

'From what I have learnt from history, it is that change nearly always involves bloodshed,' he said. 'I doubt if even a king could reform the church without rebellion and suffering. Shall we speak of other matters? I would that you were not made unhappy with such thoughts.'

'You would have me blind to the truth?' she asked.

'No. But we have talked enough of such a disturbing subject,' he said firmly.

Rosamund was silent for a while, but felt rejuvenated by their conversation so far. 'Tell me, have you ever been to Richmond before?' she asked.

'I have not been inside the palace, but I have seen it from a distance. It is similar in design to Lathom House.'

'Is there a reason for the palace's similarity?'

'I have forgotten who told me that the King so admired Lathom House that, after the Palace of Sheen was severely damaged by fire six years ago, he decided to have a new one built to a similar design. He renamed it Richmond because he and his father were once Earls of Richmond.'

'I presume they were named after the Richmond in Yorkshire,' said Rosamund. 'I am glad I will be able to compare the two buildings for myself.'

He nodded. 'Look, there is the ferryman. Fortunately the boat is on this side of the river, so there will be no delay in his taking us across to the other side.'

It was as he said and soon they were set ashore on the south bank of the Thames. Here was St Thomas's Hospital, as well as Bermondsey Palace whose lands stretched as far as Lambeth. They took the road to Putney and rode in silence for a while, busy with their own thoughts.

Rosamund determined not to think too far into the future because that meant worrying about what steps Edward would try to take to punish her and destroy her husband. Of course, she should not be underestimating the Baron and remembered thinking that here was a man strong enough to deal with her stepfamily. She really should have more faith in him.

She allowed her mind to drift into imagining what it would be like travelling to Sweden to begin a completely different life in a foreign country. She would need to learn Swedish if she was not to be solely dependent on this rich, well-travelled husband with an estate and a business to oversee. This Baron whom she had known less than two weeks. It was a daunting prospect. And what about

Harry? What if he did not return to England by the time the Baron decided they should visit his homeland? Perhaps she should discuss that with him when the time came.

She glanced at Alex. 'You said earlier that you have seen Richmond Palace from a distance. For what reason did you travel upstream away from the sea, and the business affairs that might interest you there?'

Alex wished that Rosamund had not asked that question. He sensed that she would know if he prevaricated and he had a growing conviction that his wife could match his grandmother for intelligence and courage. She was no mad girl, but a woman who thought deeply about important matters.

'I have some knowledge of the area due to having travelled by boat as far as Thistleworth,' he said.

'What is at Thistleworth?' she asked.

'Syon House. It is an abbey of the Bridgettine Order and but a league or so from Richmond.'

'I have not heard of that Order before,' said Rosamund, her interest roused. 'I would hear more.'

'It was founded by St Birgetta of Sweden and is open to both men and women.' He did not add that it was there that he and Harry had taken Ingrid last year. She had told them that she was one of the saint's true descendants, despite Birgetta's line having died out with the death of her granddaughter, Lady Ingeborg Knutsdotter, the Abbess of Vadstena. He remembered Ingrid staying at the convent, saying it was a place she liked to retreat to when possible.

'Is Birgetta the Swedish name for Bridget?' asked Rosamund, rousing him from his thoughts.

'Aye.'

Rosamund was reminded of the girl destined to marry William. 'I wonder if my stepbrother's intended bride travelled to London in Lady Monica's train,' she said. 'Her name is Bridget McDonald.'

'It could be useful meeting her,' said Alex. 'But first we need to have our thoughts fixed on events at Richmond.'

Rosamund felt her stomach tighten with nerves at the thought of performing in front of the royal family and their guests.

'What if I am still expected to dance with Lord Bude?' she asked.

'Then you will do so and see what you can glean from him,' said Alex. 'It is surprising how much information a person can drop when they are not thinking about what they are saying.'

Rosamund said, 'You want me to act as one of your spies?'

'I would rather you had naught to do with him, but it would be useful to know what is in his mind,' he replied.

Rosamund nodded. Then she forgot all about Lord Bude—suddenly she caught her first sighting of Richmond Palace. She gasped in admiration.

'What a fairy-tale place. It looks far grander than Lathom House. See how its white stone walls gleam in the sun and how its towers are capped with pepper-pot domes and cupolas. I can easily imagine a damsel in distress imprisoned by her cruel father calling down to a brave knight to rescue her. Is there a moat?'

Alex laughed. 'I didn't realise you could be such a romantic. I have heard there is the remains of one, although a bridge now links that part of the palace to the fountain courtyard. You'll gather from its name that it has a water fountain, which it was once described to me as a pleasure to listen to on a hot day. Apparently the courtyard is flanked by a great hall and a chapel.'

Rosamund said, 'One presumes that the proxy marriage ceremony between the Princess Margaret and the King of Scotland will take place in the chapel?'

'One would think so, but according to Lady Elizabeth the event will be in the royal apartments that are separated from those housing the officials and guests.'

'It is a huge place. I should imagine several large kitchens will be needed, as well as huge butteries, wine cellars and everything else that is necessary to tend the needs of such a huge household,' said Rosamund, her eyes wide with the wonder of it all. 'And what of the gardens? I used to escape to the herb garden whenever possible at Appleby.'

'I believe there are very special gardens here. A large one encircled by two-story galleries, open at ground level and enclosed above. There the court can walk and play indoors when the weather is foul. During fine weather there are flower beds to admire and there is also a tennis court.'

A memory surfaced of Harry and Josh hitting a ball back and forth over a rope stretched between two trees. 'I remember my father telling Harry and me that King Henry discovered a liking for the game in his youth whilst exiled in France.'

'I have played it on occasions, but more for the honour of winning than purely to wager money on a game of chance.' Alex remembered a perspiring Harry determined to trounce him and win the favour of Ingrid, who was watching on the sidelines.

'You have painted a fascinating picture of the palace for me. You must have listened well to all that was told you,' said Rosamund lightly.

'I have a great interest in architecture.' Alex had no intention of being drawn into telling her that it was Ingrid who had somehow managed to get herself invited to Richmond—he did not want his wife dwelling on events in his past that were over and done with. It was true that he had listened avidly to Ingrid's description of the palace. In the past there had been times when his life had depended on his prior knowledge of a building and he had learnt much that could prove useful.

'Perhaps you would enjoy a walk along the river before we go inside,' he suggested. 'You will get a different view of the palace from there.'

Rosamund agreed and they dismounted. The sun was shining and the snow was beginning to thaw. She was of a mind that the river was a pretty place to take a stroll. His shoulder brushed her arm and she felt a tingle of pleasure at that brief bodily contact. They walked for a while. Then she noticed a barge being rowed upstream.

'Do you think that craft has come from London?' she asked.

'It is possible.' Alex's eyes narrowed against the sun as he gazed at the boat. Suddenly he placed an arm around her shoulders and drew her away from the river's edge. 'If I am not mistaken, that is your stepbrother leaning over the side!'

Rosamund experienced a cold feeling in the pit of her stomach and was glad of the comfort provided by her husband's strong arm. 'What is he doing here? I had thought we could escape him! Surely he could not have been invited?'

'We shall soon find out if the barge ties up at the royal quayside.' Alex ushered her over to where their horses cropped the grass beneath the bare branches of a willow tree.

'What does he have that the King might want?'

'It is well known that King Henry loves gold and silver. Fustian might have provided the King with a costly gift out of his own purse to present to one of his Scottish guests,' said Alex. 'By doing so he wins the King's favour and is invited to the celebrations, although by taking this step he will have given the King the impression he is a very wealthy man.'

'Wealth that my father amassed and which really belongs to Harry,' said Rosamund in a tight voice.

'At least Edward has to pay heavy taxes on the merchandise he brings into the country.'

'Only on that which he imports legally,' said Alex.

Rosamund stared at him. 'You suspect him of smuggling?'

Alex's expression was grim. 'Aye. I also believe that he is probably involved in piracy himself. He could use his ships to attack other ships that sailed out of London. It would not be difficult for him to discover what cargoes they would be carrying and when the ships would leave port. He could have the merchandise smuggled in farther north along the coast. I was lacking a reason as to why he should take such risks, but when you spoke of him wanting to be Lord Mayor of London, that provided me with the information I wanted. All I need is proof.'

'Just like I need proof that he killed Father. You know what makes what he is doing so much worse?' She did not wait for Alex's answer. 'Not only has he stolen what is my brother's, but the motto of the Royal Company of Mercers, of which he is a member, is *Honor Deo*! Honour God! Edward is not a man of honour and deserves to be shunned by that noble company.'

'Ssshhh! Calm yourself.' He brushed his lips

against hers. 'It looks like the barge will soon be tying up and its passengers disembarking. I do not want him to see us.'

'Why? He knows that we already know each other and that I must be aware that Harry is alive, so what is the use of us hiding? He would not dare to try to destroy us in full view of people.'

'I need to know if he has another purpose in coming here. Maybe to meet one of his mother's kinsmen. If I am right in my suspicions, then Fustian will not wish the peace pact to go ahead,' said Alex. 'It is best if we avoid coming face to face with him for the moment.'

She understood; besides, the less she saw of her stepbrother, the better she would like it. They walked on in silence, leading the horses. A thought suddenly occurred to Rosamund. 'When do we dance before the royal family?'

'Not for a couple of days and we will be masked,' said Alex. 'There is no need for you to fear Edward. If he were to catch you unawares, remember, I will not be far away.'

'Of course.' She was determined not to be frightened of Edward any longer. At that moment she could have said honestly that, with the Baron by her side, she no longer feared her stepbrother. No doubt it would be a different matter if she was to encounter him in a dark passage.

They retraced their steps and, much to their surprise, were fortunate to arrive at the palace at the same time as Lady Elizabeth and her entourage came into sight. She was being carried in a litter by four strong-looking men and only her eyes betrayed her weariness.

'So there you both are. I am so glad to see you arrived safely,' she said. 'I left within the hour after your departure.' She stretched out a hand to her goddaughter. 'So, Rosamund, my dear, what do you think of the King's palace?'

'It is indeed impressive,' answered Rosamund. 'I cannot wait to see what it is like inside.'

'There is much to see that is fine.' She added in a low voice, 'There are those who say that the King is miserly but, believe me, he was not frugal when it came to decorating Richmond. It is now the finest palace in the kingdom. I was here with my kinsman and his mother, the Countess of Beaufort, for poor Prince Arthur's wedding. Now that was a sumptuous affair. Whilst I doubt that Henry will part with as much gold and silver as he did then, nevertheless, I am certain he will not stint on spending what is necessary to impress our Scottish neighbours.' She indicated that they ride beside her litter and so they led her entourage along the red-brick outer wall to the main gateway that looked out over the Green.

Men-at-arms stood on guard, but as soon as Lady Elizabeth was announced, she and her party were allowed inside the walls. It seemed no time at all before an official was welcoming them and minions were summoned to attend to their needs. Lady Elizabeth asked whether certain people had arrived and the replies she received seemed to please her. Then she asked if a chamber could be made available for her troupe to rehearse in that evening.

Rosamund lost sight of the Baron in the throng and decided he would be able to find his way to the suite of rooms set aside for Lady Elizabeth and her entourage. A servant showed her to the bedchamber that was to be the Baron and Baroness Dalsland's for the duration of their stay. Rosamund experienced that odd sensation at being addressed as Baroness again and thought, for the first time, that along with her title came responsibility. She now had the power to help those so much poorer than herself. Lady Elizabeth had put one of her maids at Rosamund's disposal and she felt slightly ashamed of the few clothes she had for her to stow away in the oak armoire and chest. She thanked the girl and dismissed her.

Then she spent a few moments admiring the craftsmanship of the beautifully carved furniture and richly embroidered hangings and coverlet on the bed. A fine bed. She eased off her boots and hung up her cloak and hat before lying down. She decided the mattress must be stuffed with feathers and fell to dreaming of her husband making love to her as she listened to the crackling of the log fire. If only he really could love her, then she would be happy. But of course, their marriage was no love match, but one conveniently arranged by her godmother.

'Are you comfortable?'

Rosamund started at the sound of her husband's attractive tones and sat up.

'No, don't disturb yourself.' Alex tossed his hat on a chest and removed his outer clothes and boots before lying down on the bed beside her. Rosamund was intensely aware of him and felt her insides quiver as he reached out and took her hand. 'Your godmother plans to take a nap before the evening meal. She has decided we will take our meal here in her own apartment and it will be prepared by her own cook. She has already discovered that the King and Queen are to sup with their Scottish guests in their private apartments, no doubt in preparation for the ceremony tomorrow. After supper there is to be rehearsal for the performance the day after tomorrow.'

She glanced at him. 'Did you tell her that my stepbrother is here?'

'Didn't you?' He rolled onto his side so that he faced her.

'No. There was no opportunity to have a private word. She was speaking to her servants and having them take messages to the troupe and the musicians.'

'Then we will tell her later. In the meantime, perhaps we should also rest after our disturbed night—'

Alex drew his wife towards him. He was expecting a little resistance on her part, but she snuggled up to him like a kitten. 'Rest, you say,' she murmured, tentatively placing an arm across his chest. So trusting, he thought, stroking her hair and fondling her ear. After the shock of seeing Fustian, he had immediately wanted to challenge him and fight with him to the death. Instead, he had known he must wait until he got him alone.

He planted feather-light kisses down the side of her face and then kissed her mouth in a leisurely fashion. She returned his kiss and then rubbed her cheek against his unshaven one. He sensed she winced and reminded himself that he must shave later. He lightly touched the outline of her breast in the blue gown. He felt the peak tighten and he plucked it gently. A sleepy sigh escaped her and he unfastened the buttons on her gown and slid his hand inside and caressed that perfectly shaped orb. Several moments passed before he realised with a rueful smile that she had drifted into sleep. He made himself comfortable and within a short time he also was asleep.

Rosamund woke slowly and realised with part of her mind that someone was moving about in the bedroom. She sat up suddenly and cried, 'Who's there?'

'No need to fear,' said Alex, coming and sitting on the bed. 'It's time to get up and join Lady Elizabeth for supper.'

Rosamund yawned and stretched. 'How long have I been asleep?'

'Do you feel rested?' he asked.

'Aye.' She stared up at him with a puzzled expression.

'Then you have slept long enough.' He smiled

and helped her off the bed. 'Do you wish to change your gown?'

'Perhaps.' She glanced at the bed and wondered. 'Did you sleep?'

'Aye.'

Supper was almost over by the time Alex and Rosamund had finished telling Lady Elizabeth about Edward Fustian's arrival at Richmond Palace.

'He will not be the only one hoping to gain the prize of Lord Mayor of London,' she wheezed. 'Several will have paid a pretty penny for the honour of attending the celebrations in the hope of winning that role. You can be sure that the King will be watching them all and have courtiers strategically placed to listen to conversations, so as to deduce which of them is willing to pay the highest price for such a position.'

'The Baron thinks that he and I should keep out of Edward's sight until we have proof of his infamy,' said Rosamund.

Lady Elizabeth's eyes nearly popped out of her head. 'Don't tell me you suspect Fustian of having something to do with the other business, Baron?'

Alex and Rosamund exchanged looks.

Immediately, Lady Elizabeth said, 'Forget what

I said. Time is moving on and we have the rehearsal to attend.'

Easy enough to say *forget,* but Rosamund could not do so. Her husband had asked for her help and she intended giving it to him. She resisted looking his way as they rose and left the apartment to go to the place where several musicians were already in position and tuning up their instruments. The room was adjacent to a much larger chamber from whence came the sound of laughter and loud voices.

'I wonder what is taking place in there?' asked Rosamund of no one in particular.

'Go and see, my dear, and come back and tell me,' said Lady Elizabeth. 'Then we shall close the door so we will not be disturbed.'

Rosamund did so and decided that it was another party rehearsing for their part in the pageant. She noticed the livery on a banner and closed the door and turned to see her godmother in a low-voiced conversation with the Baron.

Rosamund sat down a little away from them, close to a curtained alcove. She tapped her foot in rhythm to the music and tried not to feel excluded. After all, her father had not shared every part of his life with his wives and had often spent time away from home. Besides, it was possible that

Alex was telling Lady Elizabeth what they had discussed earlier or perhaps not. She felt insecure again, but waited until she was certain they had finished their conversation before making her way towards them.

'The company next door have a banner displaying the livery of the Royal Guild of Mercers,' said Rosamund.

Alex glanced at her. 'Did you catch sight of Fustian?'

'No, although, perhaps he will attend later.'

Alex nodded. 'We will just have to stay alert in case he should pass through here.'

'I have heard that the Mercers' Guild is financing a grand finale to the pageant,' said Lady Elizabeth.

'I wonder what it will entail,' said Rosamund.

'There is bound to be a tournament with young knights joining the lists to prove how brave they are,' replied her godmother. 'I have never particularly cared for jousting since my brother was killed.'

At that moment members of the troupe began to arrive.

'Where is Lord Bude?' asked Lady Elizabeth.

'None of us has seen him,' said one of the ladies. 'What shall we do?'

'We shall go on with the rehearsal without him,'

said Lady Elizabeth. 'I will sit out and the Baron will partner my goddaughter.'

The lords and ladies lined up for the dance.

Alex took Rosamund's hand. 'You remember the movements of the dance?'

'I am certain you will put me right if I have forgotten them,' she replied.

He gazed at her intently. 'I deem you are vexed about something?'

She almost said, *how perceptive of you.* Instead, she shook her head and then gazed down at her feet.

Alex drew in his breath with a hiss, but there was no chance to sort the matter out. The musicians struck up. This time when they danced together she went through the motions without enthusiasm. She expected her husband to mock her performance, but he did not say a word.

'Excellent,' said her godmother, stifling a yawn. 'Perhaps a little more picking up of the feet, Rosamund. But no doubt you are tired. There will be too much making ready for the proxy ceremony in the morning for another rehearsal. And by evening, I doubt any of you will be fit to dance after the celebrations. So we will have a dress rehearsal the following morning.'

They all agreed and the musicians and the troupe drifted away.

Lady Elizabeth turned to Rosamund and Alex. 'I was too kind to you, my dears. Both your performances were leaden. Why do you not go through the steps again? There is plenty of space for you to practise now the others have left.'

Alex raised his tawny eyebrows. 'Well?' he said.

'It is what Godmother wishes,' replied Rosamund, her cheeks flushed.

So once again they performed the movements of the dance and this time Rosamund concentrated on picking up her feet and humming the music. Her husband surprised her by beginning to sing in his own language and slowly she relaxed and began to enjoy herself. They repeated the dance until she was quite out of breath and then he called a halt.

It was in the following silence that they heard voices on the other side of the door. Alex caught his wife's eye and suddenly he seized her hand and drew her into the alcove close by and pulled across the curtain. She stood trembling in the curve of his arm with her cheek pressed against his chest. She could hear the steady thud of his heart as the door opened.

'So you agree the plan should work if the other fails?' asked Edward.

'I don't see why it shouldn't, laddie. I shall have a wee word with yer kinsman. He feels much the same as we do about this damned alliance—and there are others who share his sentiments and will do what they can to prevent it from succeeding. But if we can put some money into our own pockets, who is to gainsay—?' The voice stopped abruptly. When it spoke again, it was in a whisper. 'Who's this?'

'I can't say, but she looks a perfect fright,' sneered Edward. 'Although…wait a moment. This must be Lady Elizabeth Stanley. I have heard that she paints her face.'

'Do yer think she might have heard us talking?' hissed the Scotsman.

'At her age—she's probably as deaf as a post. I did hear that she would be here,' muttered Edward.

'Why's that?'

'She's kin to the King's stepfather, as well as being godmother to my stepsister. Mother was supposed to deal with Rosie, but I will have to do the deed myself.'

Rosamund drew in her breath and instantly Alex pressed her head against his chest.

'What was that?' asked the Scotsman.

Rosamund could scarcely breathe and was aware that Alex was reaching for the dagger at his belt.

Chapter Twelve

Before Alex could release Rosamund and face the two men, there came a sudden break in the snoring and a sleepy voice said, 'Where am I? You—you two men! Who are you?' wheezed Lady Elizabeth.

'You are in the Palace of Richmond,' said Edward loudly. 'Am I correct in believing that you are Lady Elizabeth Stanley?'

'You are. But you have not answered my question. Who are you?'

'Ma name is Sir Andrew Kennedy,' said the Scot.

'You are a Kennedy. Now why does that surprise me?' said her ladyship in a vague tone. 'And you, sir, are obviously English. Have we met before?'

'No, Lady Elizabeth,' said Edward.

'Well, it is of no matter. You can help me up, seeing as how they all appear to have gone.'

'Who have gone?' asked the Scot.

'My troupe of dancers. You will see them perform the day after tomorrow.' There was the sound of rustling silk and Lady Elizabeth's rasping breath. 'Now you, Sir Andrew, can give me your arm. When you get to my age, a woman needs a man to keep her on her toes.'

There was the sound of retreating footsteps and Lady Elizabeth's breathless voice and then silence. Rosamund tugged on Alex's arm and looked up into his shadowy face. 'We must follow them. What if they were to hurt her? You heard what Edward said.'

Reluctantly, Alex set his wife aside and opened the curtain. 'We will not approach them unless it is absolutely necessary,' he said firmly. 'We are Fustian's intended victims, so I doubt they will hurt her.'

'They might do so if they decide she heard them plotting,' said Rosamund, glancing at her husband's face in the light of the wall lantern. 'I wonder to what plan they were referring. If Godmother had not chosen that moment to wake up, we might have found out.'

'She deliberately made a show of being wakened to distract from the noise you made,' said Alex, leading the way along the passage. 'I wonder if your stepmother's treacherous kinsman is another McDonald, working for the previous chieftain of the clan, John of Islay, one time Lord of the Isles and Earl of Ross? I doubt the present lord would be involved in such a plot.'

'How do you know of these people?' whispered Rosamund.

'I keep my eyes and ears open,' he said smoothly. 'You know how to do that, do you not, Rosamund?'

'By not asking so many questions, but just staying quiet and listening,' she murmured. 'There are more people who wish England and Scotland to stay divided than I thought. What do you deem is their plan?'

'That is something we have to find out,' said Alex, caressing her cheek with the back of his hand.

'We?' she asked. 'You still want me to help you?'

He nodded. 'Although there is a certain amount of risk involved.'

'It cannot be any more dangerous than Edward plotting to get rid of me.'

Alex nodded. 'We will discuss this later.'

Rosamund felt a lift of the heart. It seemed that he was going to take her into his confidence after all. Right now she was curious to know why her godmother had considered it strange to see a Kennedy at Richmond.

They arrived at the apartment to find Lady Elizabeth sitting in a chair, drinking from a steaming goblet with Hannah in attendance. She looked up and smiled. 'So there you are, my dears.' She turned to her maid. 'I'll call you when I need you.'

'I am so glad you are safe,' said Rosamund, kissing her godmother.

'You are a good child.' Lady Elizabeth stroked her cheek. 'So smooth.' She sighed. 'I presume you two were hiding behind that curtain and heard what took place?'

'Aye,' said Alex, closing the door and putting his back to it. 'How much of their conversation did you hear?'

'We decided that you were only pretending to be asleep when those men entered the chamber,' added Rosamund.

Her godmother did not answer, but took a sip of her potion before saying, 'What an ill-mannered fool your stepbrother is to insult me and to talk so openly about his plans for you. I will speak to Derby about him and he will quash his ambitions.'

'Not yet,' said Alex firmly. 'We need to discover what his and the other's plans are.'

Lady Elizabeth deliberated. 'The King could have them tortured,' she said with relish.

'But surely that would damage the peace agreement and play into their hands?' said Rosamund. 'Too long our countries have waged war across our borders. We are neighbours and should be allies.'

Lady Elizabeth sighed. 'You are right.'

'Tell us what you know about this Kennedy,' said Rosamund.

'I think you should go to bed,' said Lady Elizabeth, 'and leave this to the Baron and I.'

Rosamund glanced at her husband.

'I say she stays,' said Alex.

His wife gave him a dazzling smile and he felt a catch at his heart, wanting to take her into his arms again.

Lady Elizabeth frowned. 'But what about her safety? What about the child?'

Rosamund was about to say there was no child when her husband indicated with a slight shake of the head that she be silent. 'A man should not have secrets from his wife,' he said smoothly. 'I see no harm in Rosamund knowing what you have to say.'

Lady Elizabeth appeared slightly flustered by that remark. 'If that is what you think, but I am depending on you to keep them both safe.'

'Trust me.' He waved Rosamund to a settle and sat beside her. 'Begin,' he said.

Lady Elizabeth sucked in her cheeks, cracking her paint. 'The King of Scotland has a mistress, Janet Kennedy. No doubt her family would rather a proxy marriage did not take place between James and Princess Margaret. Perhaps in their wildest dreams the Kennedy clan imagine that the son Janet Kennedy bore King James could follow in his father's footsteps. After all, the King has given the boy the title of Earl of Moray.'

Rosamund glanced at Alex to see what he thought of this information.

'I doubt King James would legalise his affair with Janet Kennedy. To favour them would cause war amongst the clans,' he said.

Lady Elizabeth nodded. 'You are probably right. I have heard that she has had other lovers amongst the Scottish hierarchy. One of the powerful Earls of Douglas has been rumoured to have shared her bed.' She fixed Alex with a stare. 'One wonders if he could have fathered more than one bastard.'

Alex scowled at her. 'I think it would be best if we did not discuss the Earls of Douglas.'

'Why? It was your grandmother who insisted that she was the best person to—'

'Enough, Lady Elizabeth,' said Alex, ruthlessly cutting through what she had to say. 'This has naught to do with the matter under discussion.'

'Is it possibly that the Kennedys, Douglases and McDonalds might work together to destroy the peace?' asked Rosamund.

Alex sighed heavily. 'Definitely not. It was a McDonald chieftain, the previous Earl of Ross, who behaved treacherously towards the border Douglases in the present King of Scotland's father's reign. The McDonalds committed murder after signing a treaty with the Yorkist King Edward. They would help him regain his throne and in return he promised to help them defeat the Scottish king, as well as give them land and gold. Edward never kept his side of the bargain and the Earl of Ross suffered defeat at the hands of the present King of Scotland, lost his lands and title and vanished into obscurity. It is possible that he is behind this plot to destroy this chance of peace between England and Scotland.'

'Such intrigue between our countries,' said Rosamund, shocked, but fascinated none the less.

'Do either of you believe that my stepbrother and Kennedy's plan is to prevent the proxy wedding taking place?'

Alex shook his head. 'It presents too much of a risk with so many people around. Kennedy spoke of them lining their pockets. It sounds to me that our plotters' aim is not only to destroy the peace pact, but...' He paused for several moments before continuing, 'Let us consider the costly gifts that King Henry will give to his guests. The plot could include them relieving the homebound Scots nobles of those treasures.'

'But that might not destroy the peace,' said Rosamund.

'That's true,' muttered Alex, 'and from what the Kennedy said about lining their pocket, that was just an afterthought.'

The three of them fell silent, pondering on what their enemies' plan might be. Then Rosamund said, 'The marriage!'

Alex stared at her. 'What do you mean the marriage?'

'If the marriage was not to take place, the alliance would fall apart,' she said. 'I mean the proper marriage between the new Queen of Scotland and King James. Where will it take place?'

'Edinburgh,' informed Lady Elizabeth, her eyes gleaming. 'Are you saying their plan could be to prevent Margaret from ever being joined to James?'

'She could mean murder,' said Alex, gazing at his wife as if bewitched. 'They could be planning an attack on the young Queen's train as soon as they cross the Scottish border. Her murder would destroy any chance of peace between the two countries. Either side of the border would do to destroy the peace pact. I am stunned, wife, by the sheer breadth of your imaginative powers.'

Rosamund beamed at him. 'Then I haven't wasted the time spent locked up by my step-mother, when all I could do to occupy myself was to think and think and dream of what I would like to do to her if I was free.'

'We should inform the King,' gasped Lady Elizabeth, who was looking exhausted.

Alex shook his head. 'We have no proof. It is naught but guesswork on our part. We must wait and find out when the journey to Scotland is to take place and set a trap.'

'If you insist, Baron. I am for my bed,' said Lady Elizabeth, 'but I tell you now that I might have other ideas on the morrow.'

Rosamund rose to her feet. 'I am sorry that we have kept you awake. You've had an exhausting day.'

'It cannot be helped, my dear.' Lady Elizabeth patted her hand. 'God put me in the right place so that we could hear those villains plotting. If you could assist me out of this chair, Baron. And, Rosamund, please, call Hannah.'

Alex helped Lady Elizabeth to her feet and Rosamund summoned her maid to come and attend to her. Immediately Hannah came running. Alex and Rosamund went to their bedchamber. There a fire still glowed on the hearth and several candles provided more light.

Alex locked the door, thinking that this would be the first night they would spend together as husband and wife. He watched Rosamund wander over to the bed and push aside a hanging. Then he heard her draw in her breath noisily.

'What is it?' he asked, alerted by that sound to reach for his dagger.

'Someone has been in here.'

He hurried over to her.

Rosamund laughed. 'I don't think you will need the dagger. Most likely it was the maid who put the costumes on the bed.' She held up a black gown and flourished a black mask. 'Yours is here, too. Shall we try them on?' she asked.

'No. It is late and we will be able to see more clearly how we look in daylight.' Alex tossed his costume on a chest at the foot of the bed.

Rosamund placed hers beside his and then shot him a tentative glance. He interpreted that look as one of nervousness and thought how she would have delayed getting into bed with him by trying on the costumes. It was going to be a long day tomorrow and they would need to have their wits about them.

'What would you have me do on the morrow?' she asked. 'Would you like me to pay heed to Kennedy's whereabouts and with whom he talks and eavesdrop on their conversation?'

Immediately alarm bells rang in Alex's head. 'No, I would not. You will stay with Lady Elizabeth and keep out of trouble. You heard what she said about not risking your life and that of the baby.'

Rosamund's face fell. 'But there is no baby, so you do not need to worry too much about me. What about these Earls of Douglas? If you point them out to me, then perhaps—'

'No. They are not here.'

'Is that because King James is not pleased about

having a rival for Janet Kennedy's favours and does not trust them?'

'I am not in the Scottish king's confidence,' rasped Alex, turning his back on her.

Rosamund stared at his back and wondered what she had said wrong. Slowly, she began to undress. 'Is it that you do not approve of the Douglases? This talk—'

'Enough, Rosamund!'

'I don't understand. I thought you trusted me now you're allowing me to be involved in gathering information?'

He did not respond, but blew out the candles and marched over to the bed. Disappointed, it was several minutes before she joined him there. He had allowed her the same side as that which she had occupied during their journey to London and he was not facing her. She swallowed a sigh and climbed into bed. She remembered now that he had cut off her godmother when she had been about to say something about the Earls and their bastards, which meant that it was not only herself with whom her husband was annoyed. Hopefully he would be in a better frame of mind on the morrow and she might discover what it was about the Douglases that put him in such a mood.

Alex was furious with himself. Why couldn't he just accept that his father had not wanted the inconvenience of a baby bastard son after his mother had died? It was not as if he had suffered because his grandparents had provided for all his needs. He should not have behaved so ill mannered either to his wife or Lady Elizabeth. Her words about keeping his wife and baby safe played over and over in his head. He felt a sudden longing for it to be true that Rosamund was carrying his child. He thought about his doubts about her chasteness when Lady Elizabeth had spoken of Rosamund carrying a child. How many times had Rosamund denied the truth of her godmother's words? Surely there would be no need for her to do so once she had his ring on her finger if all she had wanted was a father for Fustian's child?

He turned over, but Rosamund had wrapped herself so tightly in the bedcovers that it was obvious that she did not wish to have aught to do with him that night. He sighed and knew that he would have to wait until tomorrow to sort the whole matter out.

Rosamund was the first to wake. Perhaps it was a cock crowing that disturbed her. Instantly, she was aware that her husband was snuggled up against her back with his arm about her. So he had recovered from his bad mood and she rejoiced in it. She remembered longing for him to hold her like this on the journey to London and relaxed against him. She realised he was wearing his shirt, but it had ridden up so that she could feel his naked thigh pressed against the back of her thigh. It gave her a delicious thrill. She had no idea when the proxy wedding would begin, but was certain her godmother would tell the maid to wake them in plenty of time.

She closed her eyes, but could not get to sleep again, so she deliberated over which gown to wear for the ceremony. Eventually she decided on the dark blue one with the fur-lined blue velvet cloak, fastened with her brother's silver brooch. She wondered how Harry would feel about her being alive and married to the man who had saved his life. She did not doubt he would be pleased. If only she could see him again, he would be able to answer all the questions that no one else could. She prayed for his safety and then hummed a snatch of the dance music. She had a feeling of warm contentment. Was this akin to happiness and would it last?

'What are you thinking?'

Her husband's question startled her into saying, 'What should I be thinking? How did you know I was awake?'

Alex caressed her calf with his big toe. 'You were humming. I always think, when someone answers a question with a question that they are avoiding telling the truth.' His voice was light.

Her brow puckered. 'You think I'm not being honest with you?'

'How can I tell if you do not answer my question?'

She thought about that and said cautiously, 'I was thinking about what to wear for the ceremony and decided on the dark blue gown and the blue velvet cloak.'

'Could you not have told me that straight away?'

'I thought you might have considered me frivolous.'

'Deciding on what you are to wear for an important occasion is not frivolous. It shows sense.' He lifted her dark hair and kissed the nape of her neck. 'Besides, why should I disapprove of you being frivolous on occasions? From what you have told me of your previous life, you were seldom light-hearted and you showed good sense in what you had to say in our discussion last night.'

Rosamund turned in his arm and smiled at him.

'Thank you. I am glad that you have forgiven me for overstepping the mark. I should not expect to know all your secrets.'

A smile cleaved his cheek. 'But you would like to do so?'

She thought about that and replied, 'I think it depends on the secret, but I will not press you. I— I must learn to do well all that a wife must do. Lady Elizabeth spoke of your grandmother and I wish I could have met her. I would like to be like her.'

He frowned. 'I would rather you be yourself than someone else. My grandmother was not perfect.'

'You expect me to be perfect?'

'No!' he exclaimed vehemently. 'For I am not perfect.'

Rosamund wanted to ask why he thought that, but did not have the courage. As it was there was a knock on the door that brought their conversation to an end.

'Time to get up,' said Alex.

He would have liked to have stayed longer in bed with his wife and risk bringing up the subject of babies. Instead, they turned away from each other and climbed out of bed.

The fire had gone out and it was cold in the room. Rosamund picked up the jug and hurried over to the door and opened it a few inches. She was about to ask the maid to bring some hot water, but saw a jug of steaming water had been placed on the floor. She carried it inside. 'No doubt all the servants are rushed off their feet this morning.' Her eyes alighted on their dance costumes. 'Do you think we have time to see if they fit?'

Alex rasped a finger along his unshaven jaw. 'You can try yours on whilst I shave.'

'Don't you normally have a man to do that for you?' she asked, watching him take a leather package from a saddlebag.

'At home in Sweden,' he answered.

'What is your home like? Is it large and well furnished, fitting for a Baron?' She felt in such a good mood that day that she was not going to torture herself with thoughts of Ingrid. She picked up the black silk gown sewn with silver stars and saw that there was a sleeveless surcote to wear over it. She had not noticed it before.

'My grandfather once had a house in Visby, but now trade has dropped off so I sold it after Grandmother died. I have yet to buy another town house.' He glanced round at her. 'There is no rush for me to do so as I have a manor house in the country.'

'When will we go there? Is it possible that Harry might sail to Sweden rather than return to London?' Rosamund eased the gown over her head and pulled it down over a fresh white linen undergown. She tied up the silver ribbons that tightened the bodice and smoothed the sleeves down to her wrists.

'It is possible,' said Alex cautiously. 'It depends on the cargo he is carrying. If he does not return to London by the time spring is here, then we will cross the northern sea in May in the hope of finding he has made landfall there.'

'You said that his ship was given to him by your grandfather,' she said, fastening the surcote. 'That was very generous of him.'

'Aye, it was, but Harry had worked hard for the business.' Alex wiped his chin with a cloth and turned to look at her. A slow smile lightened his rugged features. 'You look enchanting. I'm reminded of a night sky.'

She gave him a delighted look. 'Do you think that was what Godmother was thinking when she designed the costumes?'

'Perhaps. Let me see you wearing the mask?'

Rosamund complied with his request, but had difficulty fastening the strings at the back. Alex performed the task for her and then twirled her round so that she faced him. 'Would you recognise me?' she asked.

His eyes narrowed. 'If I were not expecting to see you and it was by candlelight and there were other ladies dressed the same and moving in the dance? I think not.'

'I'm not sure the same could be said of you,' she added, removing the surcote. 'You're taller than the other men and your hair is longer and fairer.'

'I am not cutting my hair,' he said firmly.

'You could wear a wig,' she suggested as she tugged at the strings of the mask.

'Here.' He untied it for her and murmured against her ear, 'You are not suggesting I borrow one from Lady Elizabeth?'

Rosamund chuckled. 'I would like to see her face if you were to do so. Have you worn a wig in the past?'

'On occasions when I have needed a special disguise.' He picked up his mask and held it against his face. 'What is your opinion?'

She met the glitter of his eyes through the eyeholes. 'How different a mask makes one appear.' A shiver ran through her.

'There is naught to be frightened of,' he said

sharply. 'Now we must stop wasting time and get ready for the ceremony.'

'I beg your pardon. I did not mean to waste time, but—'

'Quick, Rosamund! Out of that gown and on with the one you are wearing for the ceremony,' he said, slapping her lightly on the bottom.

She feared that she had displeased him, for he was still frowning when he picked up the velvet cloak and swung it about her shoulders and fastened it at the throat with Harry's brooch. Once that was done, he escorted her from the bedchamber.

'Do we stay together? Edward is sure to be there and might see us,' she said, a tremor in her voice.

'Perhaps it is wiser to put a little distance between us during the ceremony,' said Alex, taking her hand. 'But do not look so anxious. All will be well.'

She determined to smile more often and told herself that she was looking forward to the day's events. After all, how many of the King's subjects were able to attend such an occasion?

Lady Elizabeth was waiting for them and Rosamund thought she looked regal, dressed as she was in a pale green satin gown sewn with pearls. She suggested that they partake of bread and honey and wash it down with ale before making their way to the Queen's great chamber. 'One just does not know how long these occasions will last,' she said hoarsely. 'What a pretty gown, my dear,' she added.

Rosamund thanked her. 'You look magnificent.'

Her godmother shrugged. 'I would swap all my gowns to be your age again.'

She sat at table with them and gossiped about those who would be at the ceremony, mentioning names she considered obedient to the King. There were others that she would not trust an inch. Alex listened, but spoke little. As for Rosamund, she tried to commit to memory as much as she could of her godmother's revelations.

'Has Bude arrived?' asked Rosamund.

Alex darted her a glance.

'Indeed, he has,' said Lady Elizabeth. 'He sent a message asking me to forgive him for not attending the rehearsal last night. He added that I could depend on him on the day.' Rosamund and Alex exchanged glances. 'No need to look like that, my dears,' continued Lady Elizabeth. 'I have told him that you are partnering each other, so he will be dancing with me.'

Rosamund looked concerned. 'I thought you

had decided not to dance again. Remember what happened the other evening.'

Her godmother pouted. 'Stop fretting. Nothing is going to happen to me.'

Chapter Thirteen

Rosamund was determined not to be nervous as they made their way to the Queen's great chamber. There, a dazzling array of men and women was gathered. She had never been in such illustrious company. She had no idea where her stepbrother was and could only pray that he could not see her, squashed as she was between her godmother and an unknown lady. She wished it was her husband the other side of her, but respected his decision to keep his distance for the moment.

Rosamund watched with lively interest as the twelve-year-old Princess Margaret entered with her five-year-old sister, the Princess Mary, as well as the Queen, who was large with child. There was a fanfare of trumpets as the King and Henry, Prince of Wales, followed them into the chamber.

Accompanying them were the Archbishops of Canterbury and York and the Scottish lords and clergy who had their parts to play. Her godmother whispered in Rosamund's ear that it was Patrick Hepburn, the Earl of Bothwell, who would act proxy for the King of Scotland. He was accompanied by the Archbishop of Glasgow and the Bishop Elect of Murray.

The purpose of the ceremony was announced with great pomp and the proceedings began. As it was asked whether there was any impediment why the alliance should not take place, Rosamund found herself holding her breath, remembering what her godmother had told her about the King of Scotland's mistress. Perhaps Kennedy would speak out at this point, but the moment passed without incident.

Soon after Princess Margaret spoke her vows loudly and clearly to the Earl of Bothwell, finishing with the words, 'Therefore I plight and give to him in your person, as procurator aforesaid, my faith and troth.'

There was a burst of music from the royal trumpeters and in the adjoining chamber minstrels began to play. Rosamund pitied the new Queen of Scotland. She was so young to have to leave her family and country without having met her husband. Terrible to be a pawn in men's games and for her life to be at risk. But before Rosamund could be completely overcome by a fit of the dismals, her godmother told her that they would have to be making a move now that the royal family had led their Scottish guests to another chamber where a sumptuous banquet was spread for all.

Rosamund had barely sat down next to her godmother when she caught sight of her stepbrother. She was filled with a familiar dread. Fortunately, he was not looking her way, but talking to a nun in a white habit. Immediately, she thought of Ingrid and wondered was it her. If so, what would the Baron make of the two of them sitting next to each other? Suddenly, as if he had sensed her eyes upon him, Edward turned his head and stared directly at Rosamund.

She forced herself not to look away and reminded herself that her husband was somewhere in this hall, keeping his eye on her. Edward smiled his wolfish smile and she continued to stare at him dispassionately, despite her throat feeling so tight she felt as if about to suffocate.

The nun placed a hand on Edward's arm and put her mouth against his ear. There was something so intimate about that gesture that Rosamund's suspicions were roused. She watched his lips move and then the nun looked in Rosamund's direction with a startled expression on her lovely face that turned to fear.

Rosamund was so surprised that she could not look away. Then she felt a hand on her shoulder and looked up into her husband's face. 'Do you see her? That is Ingrid sitting at Fustian's side,' he said.

'Aye. I see her,' said Rosamund, her trauma intensified by the anger in his face. 'They must have been together in the Steel Yard that evening I was lost.'

'Aye. Your swine of a stepbrother and the woman I was fool enough to allow to worm secrets out of me,' he said. 'I am glad I know her now for what she is—untrustworthy and an adulteress.'

Rosamund was relieved to hear that was how he felt about his erstwhile lover. 'Does she ever wear anything other than a nun's habit?'

'Aye. She is a woman of many guises, is Ingrid.'

'What is she doing here with Edward dressed as a nun?'

'If there is gain to be made, then I deem she has a part to play in the conspiracy,' said Alex in a low voice, sitting next to Rosamund. He placed his arm about her shoulders, despite continuing to stare at Edward and Ingrid, and brought his head close to Rosamund's. 'I am convinced now that she did play me false.'

'You mean with Edward instead of Harry?'

'Aye.' Alex's eyes glinted. 'I am glad I changed my mind about keeping my distance. I decided I was not having him smirking at you and believing you defenceless. I want him to know that I am your husband.'

His solicitude was comforting. 'Why is she dressed like a nun here?' she whispered. 'How did she get an invitation?'

'It is for us to find out,' said Alex. 'I remember her telling me that she was placed with the nuns after her Danish mother died, but as soon as she was old enough she escaped the convent walls because she found she had no gift for the religious life. It was too dull. Besides, she could not bear women *en masse* day after day.'

'Did you not mention there were the nuns at Syon House, not far from here?'

He nodded. 'Obviously Fustian must have summoned her here for a purpose dressed in such garb. We need to discover what it is.'

Rosamund gazed at his taut profile and her heart ached for love of him. 'Perhaps I should go and make conversation with her and Edward. I could act like a lack-wit and that way they might reveal more than they would to you?'

'No. Your stepbrother knows you are not crazed, however much he might have said so in the past. He also must know you detest him and I am certain by now he suspects that I am aware of his illegal activities. Let us just keep our eyes on them and wait for them to make the first move.' He kissed the side of her face. 'In the meantime, let them see that we are enjoying ourselves in each other's company.'

'If that is the game you want to play,' she said, wondering if the kiss was part of it.

'This is no game, sweeting. This is deadly serious. So, what shall we talk about? You choose.'

How could she start a conversation when her head was in a whirl? But, hesitantly at first, she began to talk about the proxy ceremony and of the clothes worn by the royal family. Whilst they ate, they discussed the food and he told her of the great fish that he and Harry had pulled out of the waters of his own country. In between courses, they discussed jewellery and furniture, dancing, music and architecture.

Every now and again, she noticed he would look

surreptitiously at Edward and Ingrid to see what they were doing. And all the time Rosamund wondered why it should still hurt that her husband had once loved Ingrid. She felt so tense that her head ached as she strained to make her voice heard and catch his words against the background noise of music and other chattering voices. She wished the banquet would end.

Fortunately there came the moment when the King gave permission for people to move about whilst the royal family retired for a short while. It was then that Alex noticed Edward leaving the hall and told Rosamund that he was going to follow him.

'That might be what he wants,' she said. 'He might lie in wait for you and—'

'He generally gets someone else to perform his foul deeds,' said Alex, his eyes hard and bright as gemstones. 'You stay here and keep your eye on Ingrid. I also need to send a message.'

Rosamund watched him stride from the hall. Her godmother and the lady on her right had risen as soon as the royal family had left the chamber and now she was alone at the table.

A group of tumblers entered the hall and began to practise their moves. She watched one of them perform a double-back somersault and then several cartwheels. She marvelled at his agility.

'Mistress Appleby?' said a rich, deep voice with a light foreign accent.

Startled, Rosamund looked up and saw Ingrid standing a couple of feet away. The light was better here than it had been in the church and outside the Steel Yard and the face was older than she had thought. There were creases at the corners of the pale blue eyes and lines between nose and mouth. Even so, Ingrid was still a lovely woman.

'Sister—?' enquired Rosamund politely.

'Sister Birgetta.' She inclined her head. 'I would like a word with you, if I may?'

'If you are acting as my stepbrother's emissary, then you can tell him that I do not wish to hear what he has to say,' stated Rosamund, proud that her voice was steady.

Ingrid sighed. 'Master Fustian told me it was hopeless, but I refused to believe him. He said that you were obedient to the church's teaching, so I thought I could act as peacemaker between the two of you.'

'What would you have me do?' asked Rosamund lightly. 'Agree to meet you in a quiet place where he would creep up on me and carry me off to his mother, who would lock me up, then poison me?'

Anger flickered in Ingrid's eyes, to be replaced almost immediately by sadness. 'He told me you needed taking care of because you were a crazed woman. I see it is true, for we saw you in company with a dangerous man. Unlike Master Fustian, who is a good man and wants to look after you.'

So Edward has already told Ingrid that I am crazed. 'You obviously do not know my step-brother as well as you believe you do,' said Rosamund. 'I have known him a lot longer than you, Sister. He is a cruel thieving cur and he has stolen what belongs to my brother.'

Ingrid appeared to not have heard what Rosamund said because her eyes were fixed on the silver brooch at her throat. 'Where did you get that brooch?'

'The Baron gave it to me. It belongs to my brother, Harry.'

'But what is this you say?' Ingrid gave a tinkling laugh. 'Your brother is dead.'

'Have you proof of that?' said Rosamund with disdain. 'His body was never found, you know. I am certain he still lives.'

Ingrid laughed. 'Because the Baron has told you

so? I would not believe him if I were you. He is a spy and is for ever deceiving people.'

If Rosamund had not already known her husband was a spy, then this revelation might be expected to shock her. 'And what is your reason for deceiving people? Linger here a while and tell my husband to his face that he is a deceiver.'

Ingrid's face blanched. 'Your husband! I deemed you were only betrothed.'

'Then you have been wrongly informed. Baron Dalsland and I are married.'

'I don't believe it. There has been no time.'

Rosamund's eyes gleamed with a sapphire light. 'I married him two days ago in front of a priest in my godmother's bedchamber.'

Ingrid's lips tightened into a thin line. 'Your godmother! She is the one with the white painted face? Why did you marry the Baron in her bed-chamber? Perhaps she has not long to live and thought to provide you with a protector,' Ingrid said in pitying tones. 'You cannot really believe a real baron would marry you without some incite-ment. Besides, he should be arrested and thrown into a deep, dark dungeon. He is a pirate and has attacked English ships. I will see to it that he is arrested,' she said passionately.

Rosamund could feel a megrim coming on, but her curiosity was roused. 'How can a nun have my husband arrested?'

Ingrid smiled. 'Now you ask a sensible question and I will give you an answer. I will speak to the new Queen of Scotland and ask her to deal with the matter.'

'You are acquainted with her Majesty?' asked Rosamund with genuine surprise.

Ingrid drew herself up and there was an odd expression in her pale blue eyes. 'I am a representative of the Bridgettine Order at Syon House, where prayers have been said for the Princess Margaret daily. They will continue, even though she is now Queen.' She smirked. 'I was appointed to bring her a wedding gift because I have royal blood in my veins. It is a specially printed copy of the gospel of St Luke. She was delighted.' Ingrid tucked her hands in her wide sleeves. 'Now I will go and have a word with the Queen and you may come with me.'

'I would rather not,' said Rosamund, wondering what the Baron would make of this news. 'I can see my husband coming. You had better go.'

Ingrid's self-satisfied expression altered and she hurried away, only to collide into one of the tumblers and send him flying. She steadied herself and suggested loudly that he pick himself up, then she left the hall.

'Frightened her away, did I?' said Alex, looking grim.

'She as good as said that she has the ear of Princess Margaret—I mean, the new Queen of Scotland.'

Alex's expression was suddenly alert. 'Did she say how she managed that?'

'Apparently the nuns pray daily for the Princess Margaret and Ingrid was chosen to bring a present for her from the convent.'

'She has retreated to the convent in the past, so perhaps some of what she told you was true.' Alex sat down next to his wife and grinned at her. 'I don't know how you extracted that information from her, but it is possible that she could worm herself into the royal confidence and end up in a position where she is able to discover the date of departure and the route Queen Margaret and her entourage will take to the border.'

Rosamund was warmed by his praise. 'I am glad I please you. I can add to the information I have already given you and tell you that she was going to ask the new Queen to have you arrested for piracy.'

'Did she now?' Alex whistled. 'She would need to provide proof and no doubt she believes

Edward could do that due to his own involvement.'

'He did tell her I was crazed and she wanted to take me to him.'

Alex's gold-brown eyes flamed with anger and he took Rosamund's hand and held it firmly. 'You have given me at least two reasons why I should kill him. The pair of them remind me of the mythical serpents who inhabited the underworld Isle of Naastrand, dripping venom on suffering sinners.'

Rosamund gazed down at their linked hands. 'Mockery and criticism and cruelty over a long period does poison one's confidence and could drive them crazy.'

He raised her hand to her lips and kissed it. 'But those hurts are now in the past. Right now our concern must be that the new Queen of Scotland does not come to any harm.'

'We will tell Godmother and she will warn her,' said Rosamund.

'No,' said Alex firmly. 'We need to catch our conspirators in the act and must have definite proof. Those involved are people of position and power.'

'So is my godmother.'

'I would not deny it, but despite her position and

her connection to the royal family, some regard Lady Elizabeth as being a little mad. She has admitted as much herself. We must be patient.'

She nodded and winced with the pain in her head. 'Tell me—were you able to follow Edward?'

'Aye. I saw him in conversation with Lord Bude.'

'Lord Bude! Could you hear what they were saying?'

'Unfortunately, no. Why do you ask?'

Rosamund felt the colour flood to her face. 'I have just realised that it is possible that I mistook him for you in the Hanseatic church in the Steel Yard.'

'You mean he and Ingrid were locked in an embrace?' He laughed. 'Now, is he being ensnared by Ingrid to work for the conspirators or is he already one of them and she has a fancy for him? Even I would admit he is a handsome man. He also has a title, which always impresses Ingrid. I wonder what Fustian would make of it if he knew of that embrace?'

Rosamund thought he did not sound the least bit jealous of Bude. 'Do you still want me to indulge in conversation with Lord Bude at the dress rehearsal?'

'If you can, but don't worry if you can't.'

She nodded and then frowned, giving a little shiver before massaging her forehead.

Alex looked at her with concern. 'Are you cold? Do you have a megrim?'

'Aye. The noise and the smoke and…there is a draught.'

'Then let us slip away before the royal family returns. I, too, have had enough of people and noise.'

A relieved Rosamund said, 'What about Godmother?'

'If we see her on the way out, we can explain that you are not feeling well.'

'Do we tell her about Edward and Ingrid?'

'Of course. But that can wait until later. Right now you need a quiet, dark room to lie down in.'

As they made their way to their bedchamber, Rosamund was aware that her husband's hand was on his sword hilt. It was as if he was prepared for any sudden attack on them. Fortunately, they arrived at their destination without any unwelcome surprises. It was pure joy to kick off her shoes and stretch out on the bed and close her eyes.

The fire was still burning. Obviously, a servant had put more logs on it and there was a bucket of them at the side of the hearth. Not wanting

Rosamund to get chilled, Alex put a couple more on the fire. Anxiety gnawed at his innards. He had never felt this worried about anyone before. Neither his grandparents nor Harry or Ingrid. What if this megrim was a sign of a serious illness and she died? He remembered her being out in the snow without a cloak and how her teeth had chattered.

'Are you cold still?' he asked.

'I do feel a little shivery.'

He hurried over to her and sat on the side of the bed and placed a hand on her forehead. He was relieved to find that it was not burning hot.

'Perhaps you would be better sitting by the fire.'

She sat up as if he had given her an order. 'If that is what you want me to do?'

He smoothed back her hair from her forehead. 'I want you to do whatever makes you feel better.'

'As long as I do not have to open my eyes.'

Alex slid an arm beneath her and lifted her up and carried her over to the chair by the fire. He sat down with her on his knee. 'How is this?'

'Fine.' Rosamund rested her head against his shoulder. 'Are you comfortable?' she murmured.

'Aye.' He was aware of the soft curve of her breast beneath the velvet cloak against his arm and the silky hair brushing his chin. 'We have been married only two days, but it seems longer,' he murmured.

'Is that good or bad?'

He smiled. 'I do not believe it is a bad sign.'

'Is it not strange that some days go by like a flash and others, like today, have so much fitted into them? Ingrid was angry when I told her you were my husband. She said a Baron would need much inducement to marry me. I should have mentioned Godmother's dowry.'

'I have no need of your dowry, but it would have impressed Ingrid. I would have liked to have been there when she told Edward that we were married.'

Rosamund opened her eyes to look into her husband's face. He was grinning. She touched his cheek. 'You have a good face.'

He took her hand and brushed her knuckles with his lips. 'You have a lovely face.'

She smiled and lowered her eyelids again. 'Edward will not like it that I am a Baroness.'

'The new Baron and Baroness Dalsland. I can hear us being introduced at a masque in Stockholm.'

'Were the old ones happy?' asked Rosamund.

'They respected each other and seemed content,' he replied. 'Although it was a grief to them that only my mother survived infancy. Sadly she must have been a disappointment to them.'

'Why do you believe that?' She yawned and closed her eyes. 'Did they say so?'

'No. But she presented them with only one grandchild and he was the illegitimate son of a foreigner.' Alex's voice sounded sad.

Rosamund's eyelids fluttered open and she stared at him. 'What are you saying?'

'I should have told you before we were wed, but there were others present and I did not want them to know that I was a bastard,' he said in bitter tones. 'Neither could I risk them knowing the name of my father.'

'Is this the secret you would not tell me?'

'Aye. My father is a Scottish earl, but I did not know of his existence until six months ago.' Alex found it easier to say than he had ever imagined. 'My mother was his mistress for several years and I was the result of their union. She died soon after my birth and I was sent with a wet nurse to my grandparents' home in Sweden. I grew up believing my father was a Swedish hero who had been killed in battle. It was his name I used most of my life. My grandmother did not tell me the truth until she was on her deathbed.'

Rosamund was moved almost to tears. 'How terrible for you to believe yourself one person and then discover you are someone else altogether.'

Her sympathy warmed his heart and he hugged her close and covered her mouth with his and gave her an enthusiastic kiss.

Rosamund felt her megrim ebbing away as she returned his kiss. She was aware of a tide of pleasure creeping over her. Of their own volition her arms wound themselves around his neck.

He lifted her off her feet and carried her over to the bed, where he placed her down without breaking off the kiss. He lay beside her and when he did bring the kiss to an end, it was so he could press kisses down the line of her throat. His fingers undid the fastenings on the front of her gown. She stilled, but when he proceeded to kiss her lips once more and he made no move to remove her gown then she relaxed. He nibbled her ear. A tiny giggle escaped her and he flicked his tongue around its shell-like rim whilst undoing the ribbons at the neck of her undergown. He eased the garment from her shoulders. Aware of his arousal, Alex prayed she was not. He must keep himself under control and concentrate firmly on giving his wife pleasure. He had to make certain that she was unable to think of anything else but the sensations she was experiencing.

He kissed her again and darted his tongue along the inside of her lower lip. Immediately he sensed their mouths had all her attention and took the opportunity of lightly caressing her upper left breast before circling its centre with a single finger. He felt her breath catch and chose that moment to lower his head and nuzzle her nipple. She gasped, but did not pull away. He was glad, for he was receiving as much pleasure as she appeared to be. For a while his mouth lingered in this area that caused so much gratification for them both whilst he removed her clothing.

Rosamund was in a daze of delight by the time she realised she was stark naked and her husband's tawny head was pressed against her belly. The words *what are you doing?* died on her lips as he kissed her hip bone and she felt his fingers penetrate that part of her that she had been determined once not to surrender to any man. She protested, but he reached up and silenced her with a kiss as his caresses began to work a subtle magic within. Her breath came fast as she felt a gradual build up of pleasure. Her body was still thrumming when he moved away.

She reached out to him in silent protest and watched him remove his clothes. She had never seen a man naked before and she told herself it was to be expected that her gaze would fix on that part of him that proclaimed his manhood. But he did not allow her time to wonder at its size because he returned to her, but this time he slowly and carefully eased that part of him inside her. She gasped, but the pain of his entry was not as great as she had expected. This time there was little gradual build up as he gained possession of her and she heard him groan as he seemed to explode inside her, creating a pleasure so exquisite that she thought her body would not be able to contain it.

Chapter Fourteen

Afterwards Alex and Rosamund lay in a tangle of arms and legs, reluctant to move. He knew now for certain that she had told the truth about the woodcutter not having touched her; also, his fear that Fustian might have raped her was completely allayed. Whilst riding astride on horseback might have stretched her a little, her maidenhood had been intact.

Rosamund stirred beneath him and he lifted his head from her shoulder and gazed down at her as she opened her eyes. He waited for her to speak, but she seemed only able to stare at him and he did not doubt that he had pleasured her. He smiled wryly, guessing she would not know how to thank him for it. No doubt she might be feeling a little discomforted by finding such delight in carnal behaviour. He was tempted to thank her because it had been as good as he had hoped and would be even better next time. His eyes searched for the washstand and drying cloth and he removed himself.

Rosamund watched surreptitiously as her husband washed that part of him that now lay limp. She marvelled at the wonders of the human body. How was it that a child could grow from the act that they had just performed? A child! Lady Elizabeth might get her way after all. Now she was tied to the Baron for fairer or fouler until death parted them. She could not wait to repeat what they had just done. She had not expected to be swept away on such a tide of—of carnal pleasure, and she was certain he must have enjoyed it, too.

There was something about this Swedish baron husband of hers that called to something inside her and it had overcome any resistance that might have lingered from knowing that they had both been tricked into marriage. She felt that she had reached a oneness with him that almost convinced her that she would never feel lonely again. It was only as she was drifting off to sleep that it occurred to her that he had not told her the name of his Scottish father.

* * *

The following morning, they were roused by Lady Elizabeth. 'Come on, lie-abeds,' she wheezed. 'I wish I could sleep the way you two do. You'll need to put on your costumes for the dress rehearsal. Not that I'm expecting everyone to turn up.'

'Why not, Godmother?' asked Rosamund, wishing she could share with her the pleasure she had felt in having the Baron make love to her for the first time.

'I shall tell you over breakfast. It will be on the table in my parlour within half an hour. I also wish to know what happened yesterday that caused you to disappear without a word to me. And, Baron, a message has been delivered for you.'

Alex drew Rosamund close and kissed her before reluctantly releasing her and getting out of bed. He wished there was time to make love to his wife again, but other matters demanded his attention. He wrapped the bedcover around him and delayed long enough to go over to the window, draw back the curtains and gaze out.

'What can you see?' asked Rosamund, reaching for her undergown and slipping it on.

'I can see little at the moment due to the mist.

Hopefully it will lift.' He turned and faced her. 'You have not forgotten I wish you to try to draw Lord Bude out to talk about your stepbrother?' His expression was sombre.

'I have not forgotten.' Rosamund had not expected to suffer that sinking feeling whenever Edward was mentioned again. Somehow she had believed that what had happened last night between her and her husband had completely destroyed her fear. 'I meant to ask you…' She paused, watching him sluice his face in cold water.

'What is it, Rosamund?' He looked at her.

'You did not tell me the name of your father.'

Alex stilled. 'Can you not guess?'

The question prevented her from asking him again and instead set her thinking about who could his father possibly be.

Alex turned away and began to put on the black-and-silver costume. 'I never wanted to meet him. I only did so because my grandmother insisted on my doing so before she died. It is he who asked me to find out what I could about those whom he suspected of plotting to destroy the peace pact. In return, I am to have the house and land on the Scottish coast that he gave to my mother.'

'That is indeed generous of him,' she said drily.

'I presume if I am in a position to be able to guess his name that it has been mentioned?'

He smiled. 'Clever Rosamund.'

Rosamund was pleased by the compliment and reached for the black-and-silver gown and pulled it on over her cream linen undergown. 'I presume your natural father was already married when he had an affair with your mother.'

'Aye. To my shame.'

'Why your shame? It was not your sin,' said Rosamund firmly. 'I suppose one could say that at least he was being considerate of his wife if you weren't there as a constant reminder to her of his adultery.'

'I have never viewed my rejection in that light before,' said Alex, staring at her with dawning comprehension. 'Do you really believe that was his reason for sending me away?'

'It does not matter what I believe. What is important is what can make you feel better about yourself and your father,' said Rosamund, searching for a comb to tidy her hair. 'If you are to spend time in the house he has handed over to you, then surely it would be more pleasant if you could accept your father for what he is. After all, he must have been very fond of your mother to have given her a house and land and she must have been fond of him to have not requested of the Queen to return to her own home.'

'I never thought I would hear anyone say such words to me,' said Alex. 'My grandmother only thought of what he might give me.'

'Did he give you the name Alexander?'

'I believe it is one of his baptismal names.'

'There you are, then,' said Rosamund cheerfully. 'He must have accepted that you had a right to it.'

'I believe he is a doughty fighter, as was his father before him. I suppose it's possible he was named after the great Alexander of Macedon who conquered a large part of the known world in his day.' He glanced at Rosamund as he picked up his mask. 'He travelled as far as India in Asia. Harry thought that a great adventure.'

Rosamund looked at her husband in dismay. 'You do not think that he has gone to India?'

Alex looked taken aback. 'The thought had not occurred to me.'

'Then I pray that it did not occur to him either.'

'Aye. Now we *must* go. I am not accustomed to such long discussions before breakfast.' He softened the words with a smile.

'Neither am I,' she said.

They entered her godmother's parlour where Lady Elizabeth confessed to feeling a little groggy that morning. She handed Alex a missive.

'Are you certain you are well enough to dance, Godmother?' asked Rosamund, watching her husband move over to the window to read his message out of the corner of her eye. 'After all, you already know the steps and I suspect it is only for my sake that this rehearsal is necessary.'

'You could well be right, my dear,' said Elizabeth, adjusting her wig. 'Do you know there is to be the first of many tournaments this morning? No doubt our young lords and ladies will wish to watch the jousts.'

'I find no amusement in watching men seeking to maim or to kill each other for a purse or to prove their manhood,' said Rosamund, spreading honey on bread.

'I am glad we agree on that,' said Lady Elizabeth. She turned to Alex. 'So, what news do you have for me?'

He placed the missive in a pocket and told Lady Elizabeth about Ingrid and Edward and Lord Bude. The old woman listened carefully, wheezing an exclamation every now and again.

When he had finished she was silent for what seemed a long time. Eventually, she said, 'I will speak to my kinsman later today about what you have told me. I will leave it to him to decide whether the King should be informed. A watch will be kept on those we suspect. I doubt this Ingrid will have been able to win Margaret's confidence so swiftly that she would attempt to persuade the King to have you cast into a dungeon.'

Soon after that decision was made they left the apartment, wearing their masks. Her ladyship had said that it would spoil the air of mystery and the dance if anyone were to recognise them beforehand. Despite her conviction, several people wished Lady Elizabeth a good morn. She ignored them. Obviously it took much to disguise such a well-known personage. But Rosamund was of the opinion that the mask made her almost invisible.

They reached the rehearsal chamber and, although the musicians had arrived and a few people had drifted in dressed in costume, it was as Lady Elizabeth had foretold and several members of the troupe were absent. Lord Bude was one of them.

Lady Elizabeth said, 'I wonder what has delayed

him this time! Rosamund, you will dance with the Baron and I will save my strength.'

Rosamund was glad that Lord Bude had failed to make an appearance because she had not amassed that much confidence that she felt at ease attempting to glean information out of a young English lord. Still, she experienced pleasure dancing with Alex.

It was as the group was dispersing, having arranged where to meet for their part in the pageant later, that Lord Bude arrived with Edward. Rosamund was taken unawares. She was a girl again, wanting somewhere to hide from her stepbrother.

Alex reached out a hand and caught hold of Rosamund and drew her to his side. She felt strength flow into her and switched her gaze from her stepbrother's arrogant features to Lord Bude's face.

'Damn you for keeping me up so late, Fustian,' he said loudly. 'I have missed the dress rehearsal.'

Rosamund wondered if his annoyance was a pretence. She noted that he was not in costume and his ordinary clothes were rumpled as if he had slept in them.

'Why have you brought this man here, Lord

Bude?' demanded Lady Elizabeth. 'These rehear-sals are private.'

'I am also interested in your answer,' drawled Alex.

His lordship flushed. 'I beg pardon, Lady Elizabeth, but we played dice well into the night and Fustian would insist on accompanying me here.'

'That is because you were a little worse for drink, your lordship.' Edward's smiling dark eyes embraced the company, lingering on Rosamund. 'My dear Rosie, how lovely to see you. How pale you look. I have been concerned for you, my dear. I heard that you have married this—this foreigner,' he said disdainfully. 'Your father would not have approved. I really should have taken you in hand after he died.'

Rosamund felt the words of protest stick in her throat and then Alex squeezed her hand. 'Tell me, Edward, was it my stepmother who taught you which plants to use if you wished to be rid of someone, such as my father?'

Her stepbrother's smile vanished and he looked furious. 'How dare you besmirch my mother's good character! Here is another sign of your madness. You really are not safe to be let out alone. You should not have run off in that foolish way to marry a man who is a liar, a pirate and a spy.'

'Really, Master Fustian, you are a fool, as I told my goddaughter and her husband two nights ago, to insult my goddaughter and the Baron in such a way,' said Lady Elizabeth.

'Aye,' said Alex icily. 'You will pay for your insults and lack of gallantry towards my wife.'

'You had no right to marry her without my permission,' said Edward hotly.

'I did not need your permission,' said Rosamund, her voice quivering. 'If I needed anyone's, then it would be that of my brother, Harry, whose inheritance you and your mother stole.'

Edward stiffened. 'You really are crazed. Your brother Harry is dead.'

'You know very well that is untrue. As a boy Harry was abducted and smuggled aboard a ship.'

'Where is your proof?' he snapped.

'Six months ago my father caught sight of him in London and thought he recognised him. He spoke of this to my husband and what happens next? Alex is attacked and left for dead and my brother vanishes. I have no doubt you were responsible for these deeds.'

'Is that what your husband told you and you

believed him?' said Edward pityingly. 'You should have listened to Sister Birgetta. She would have told you the truth—that your husband was jealous of any man who looked at his lover, Ingrid Wrangel. I know the mariner whom you refer to and I'll admit that he bears a certain likeness to your brother, Harry, but he is not Harry. Both he and Ingrid disappeared around the same time.'

Rosamund paled. 'I don't believe you. My husband has been searching for Harry and that is why he wished to see my father at Appleby Manor, not knowing that he was already dead.'

Edward shook his head. 'The Baron deceived you. He looks for this other man so that he can kill him, just like he killed his lover.'

The next moment Alex had Edward by the throat and was lifting him off the ground. 'It is you that is a deceiver and are crazed. Ingrid and Sister Birgetta are one and the same. Admit it!'

'You will die for this,' croaked Edward.

'I don't think you are in a position to issue threats,' said Rosamund jubilantly. 'We know things about you and—' She stopped abruptly.

Lady Elizabeth tapped Alex's arm and gave him a warning look. 'Release him.'

Alex opened his hand and Edward dropped to

the floor. 'Proof! Where is your proof?' he gasped, rubbing his throat. 'Unless you produce Harry, you have none. You will regret this, Baron!' He stumbled from the chamber.

His parting words were greeted by silence. Alex and Rosamund realised they were the focus of the attention of the dancers who had lingered in the doorway.

'Are you really a spy, Baron?' asked one of the ladies.

Alex's mouth curled up at the corners below the mask. 'I am a wealthy man in my own country, so why should I risk my life as a spy?' He sounded amused. 'Besides, Lady Elizabeth will vouch for my good character.' He paused. 'I add only that my wife's stepbrother and stepmother have been stealing what was rightfully hers and that of her brother after their father died. Is it any wonder Master Fustian resents her having a husband who is going to delve into these matters?'

There were murmurs of agreement and then Lady Elizabeth clapped her hands. 'Come, my lords and ladies. We must go our separate ways. I have messages to send before we meet again.'

The company dispersed and Rosamund noticed that Lord Bude was amongst them. She turned a strained face towards her husband. 'What a terrible scene! Edward was determined to try to convince those here that we were in the wrong.'

Alex said grimly, 'I should not have lost my temper. He was right about us having no proof.'

'It is too late for regrets now,' said Lady Elizabeth.

Alex removed his mask and his expression was stern. 'Aye. We'll need to be even more on our guard than before. Unfortunately, I must leave you both for a while. I will return in time for the performance. If I am late, I will meet you in the antechamber outside the hall.' He reached for his cloak. 'You should be safe enough here in the palace. Just make certain you lock the door of the apartment. There is someone I must see.'

'Who is this person?' asked Rosamund.

'Your friend, Master Wood. I have need of him here.' He hurried away.

'Come, my dear,' said her godmother. 'We will return to the apartment and change out of our costumes and have some food and wine. There is still much I have to do—but what a scene, as you said. I only pray that your stepbrother did not guess what you were going to say and does not warn his fellow conspirators and they escape.'

Rosamund said guiltily, 'I hope so, too. I should have been more discreet.'

'It is difficult to show discretion in the heat of the moment, what with him accusing the Baron not only of dishonesty, but murder.'

'I did not believe it for a moment,' said Rosamund stoutly.

'I should think not,' said Lady Elizabeth. 'But it would be helpful if Harry returned in the next few days.'

Rosamund could not agree more. She desperately needed to see her brother—he was the only one who could prove that Edward's story was a complete fabrication.

They dined simply at midday on bread and smoked fish and a glass of wine and still Alex had not returned. Lady Elizabeth had written several messages and gave them to Rosamund to deliver. She wasted no time in doing so, but was delayed on several occasions by the recipients not being in their chambers and having to go in search of them. Several times she was stopped and asked by people mulling around in different parts of the palace and gardens about the altercation between her husband and stepbrother. She marvelled at how swiftly the news had spread and was expecting when she returned to the apartment to discover that the King wished to speak to them.

But when she unlocked the door of the apartment it was to find her godmother sitting all alone, having already changed into her costume. She appeared to be dozing in a chair. Rosamund asked if she was feeling well. She mumbled a reply, but seemed a little groggy. 'Are you certain you can perform the dance, Godmother?' she asked.

Again the reply was indistinct, but Lady Elizabeth managed to heave herself to her feet. Rosamund turned to enter hers and Alex's bedchamber to put on her own costume. She heard a smothered giggle, then felt a blow to the back of the head and crumpled to the floor.

Alex arrived at the antechamber, out of breath with running from the stables to reach there in time. He could hear the musicians playing the introductory music and was aware of an uneasy murmur from the masked dancers. He looked about him for Rosamund and Lady Elizabeth; realising they were not there, he was filled with a sense of foreboding. Their late arrival would have been unusual if this had been just a rehearsal, but to perform before the royal family, their honoured guests and the whole court, meant something must have gone wrong. 'I'll go and see what has delayed them,' he said.

He was about to leave the antechamber when two black-and-silver clad figures entered the room. He noticed that Lady Elizabeth's wig was askew, but felt a rush of relief at their appearance. She signalled to the other dancers to go on ahead and beckoned Alex over to her. He smiled at the woman by her side. She fluttered her fingers at him as she passed him by. Only then did he realise that she was too tall for his wife; besides, Rosamund had never made such a gesture to him.

He sprang forward and dragged the veil from her head to reveal blonde hair. Ingrid! He should never have left Rosamund and felt heartsick, wondering what Fustian had done to her.

Ingrid wrenched herself out of his grasp and then he heard a woman call, 'Beware! Behind you, Baron!'

Alex turned and would have received the full force of the knife in his chest if Lady Elizabeth's maid had not rushed forward and gripped his assailant's arm with both hands and rested her whole weight on it.

The other dancers had stopped in their tracks at the sound of Hannah's voice and were now witnesses to the altercation happening before them as Alex grappled with the figure who at first glance had appeared to be Lady Elizabeth. The red wig had slipped and Alex was curious to know the identity of his attacker. Brown eyes widened in alarm behind the mask and then suddenly a strangled gasp issued from the painted lips and the eyes widened in shock.

Alex felt his body go slack in his grasp and blood welled between his fingers as he lowered him to the floor. Only then did he see the knife sticking out of his attacker's back. He glanced over at Ingrid, who had backed away towards the door. Had she killed him? If so, for what reason? Alex had been convinced she would like to see him dead. He bent over the man on the floor and removed the mask.

To his amazement the dead man was not Edward Fustian, but a complete stranger. Alex glanced around him. 'Does anyone recognise this man?'

'He's Master William Fustian,' said Hannah. 'Joshua and I came just in time to prevent his brother from carrying off the Baroness. I left the two men fighting. She told me I must go like the wind and warn you.'

'Thank you, Hannah,' said Alex, presuming that his wife was unharmed if she was able to give orders. But he must return to Lady Elizabeth's apartment to make certain and help Joshua in his struggle with Edward. But first—

He gazed about him for Ingrid, but she was no longer there and he realised she must have slipped out of the antechamber whilst he was distracted. But before he could make a move a courtier appeared. 'The King wants to know what is the delay,' he said.

'Master Edward Fustian's brother tried to kill the Baron,' said Lord Bude, 'but he in turn was killed in the struggle. I saw what happened with my own eyes.' He pointed a finger. 'See! He dressed up as Lady Elizabeth.'

The troupe gazed down at the sprawling figure on the floor and one of the ladies shuddered and another asked, 'Where is the real Lady Elizabeth?'

Hannah said, 'Baron, we must go! I had no time to see what had happened to my lady and she might be hurt.'

'What are we going to do about the dance?' asked one of the lords.

'You will have to perform without us,' said Alex.

'But that means there will only be six of us,' said a lady in dismay.

'Just do your best,' he said impatiently. 'I am sure the King and Queen will understand once they know what has happened. You must tell the Earl of Derby what took place and that I will wait upon him after I have discovered what has happening to Lady Elizabeth.' He hurried from the antechamber, followed by Hannah.

As the door of the apartment came into sight Alex could see Joshua holding a struggling Ingrid captive. 'Where's Edward Fustian?' demanded Alex.

'I am sorry, Baron, but he escaped,' said Joshua, 'but Mistress Rosamund is safe, if a little dizzy from a blow on the head.'

Alex swore beneath his breath. 'Bring her into the apartment.' He entered the chamber and at first could see no sign of his wife and then he noticed her over by an armoire. 'What are you doing?' he said more sharply than he meant and hurried over to her. 'You should be resting.'

'I believe Godmother is in here,' replied Rosamund, steadying herself by resting a hand on the side of the armoire.

Alex gazed into her face and was relieved to see that she appeared to be little the worse for her ordeal. Then, hearing a low moan coming from the armoire, he unlocked the door and flung it open.

'Praise St Jude that you have come,' wheezed a bald Lady Elizabeth, stretching out a trembling hand. 'I thought I was going to die in here.'

Alex helped her out. She was unsteady on her feet and he half-carried the old lady over to a chair and ordered Hannah to find a blanket to wrap around her shivering form. She hurried to do his bidding and he returned to Rosamund and swung her up into his arms and carried her over to the settle. Only when he had seen to her comfort did he deign to give Ingrid some attention.

'Lock her in the armoire, Joshua,' he said tersely, 'until I have time to question her.'

Ingrid spewed forth a string of words in her own tongue, which caused him to respond with a short sharp sentence that silenced her. Then he faced Lady Elizabeth and Rosamund. 'What happened to William?' asked Rosamund before he could speak.

'He's dead.'

Rosamund stared at him in disbelief. 'Did you kill him?'

'No,' replied Alex, kneeling in front of her and chafing her hand. 'Are you sure you are all right?'

'Aye. I don't think I was unconscious for long.' Her fingers clung to his and she added, 'If you did not kill William, then who did?'

'I am not sure if it was Ingrid,' he replied.

Rosamund was baffled. 'But why?'

'What happened about the dance?' ask Lady Elizabeth fretfully.

'It is taking place now, so you are not to worry,' said Hannah.

'I should have been there,' she said, tears rolling down her cheeks. 'I want my potion,' she added.

Alex turned to Joshua, who had bundled Ingrid into the armoire. 'Edward must not be allowed to escape.' He held out his hand for the armoire key and pocketed it. 'Go and tell the captain of the King's guard what has taken place and ask him to organise a search.'

Joshua nodded and hurried out.

Chapter Fifteen

Rosamund said, 'I am so glad that Joshua and Hannah arrived when they did.'

'I beg pardon,' said Alex, frowning. 'I should never have left you.'

'I am not blaming you for what happened,' said Rosamund sincerely. 'You were not to know that he managed to get a key to the door.'

'Even so, I should not have been away so long, but I convinced myself that you would be safe in here with the door locked.'

'Begging your pardon, Baron,' said Hannah, 'but it was one of Master Fustian's men who is to blame. I was fetching something for her ladyship when I was grabbed from behind and mishandled disgracefully and my key was taken from me. He locked me in a cupboard, but I yelled and yelled and eventually Joshua came along and let me out.'

'We have much for which to thank that young man. Unlike that young madam in the armoire,' said Lady Elizabeth, rolling her eyes. 'Can't someone stop her from caterwauling? She should be locked in a dungeon and the key thrown away.'

'I will speak to her and see what she has to say,' said Alex, taking the key from his pocket. 'Hannah, make her ladyship's potion and fetch us some food and wine, if you please?'

'Aye, Baron.' Hannah went to do his bidding.

Rosamund turned her attention on her husband as he opened the door of the armoire. Ingrid fell into his arms and clung to him. Instantly Rosamund sprang to her feet, enraged. But before she could ask Ingrid to unhand her husband, Alex disentangled himself and held Ingrid at arm's length.

'You will behave yourself,' he said sternly.

'Alex, how can you speak to me in such a way?' she said in a silky voice. 'I saved your life.'

'How did you do that?' he asked, frowning down at her.

'I killed him for you.' Ingrid bent her head and rubbed her cheek against his arm.

'Stop that,' he ordered, releasing her abruptly. 'You have admitted to murder and you could be strung on a gibbet and hung by your neck until you are dead.'

Ingrid gasped and put a hand to her throat. 'You would not let them do this to me? You once loved me, Alex, and I loved you in return. If it had not been for Harry—'

'So you say, but I no longer love you, Ingrid, that's if it was love I ever felt for you,' said Alex frankly. 'Right now I am more interested in what you have to tell me about Edward Fustian's plans.'

Her expression altered and she said sulkily, 'We are no longer lovers and he does not take me into his confidence.'

He stared at her pitilessly. 'You must consider me a fool. You would not have had access to the dance costumes and arrived at the antechamber with Edward's brother if you were not party to his plans.'

Ingrid tilted her chin and said, 'You must release me and then I will tell you.'

Rosamund held her breath. Would Alex free Ingrid despite his having said that he had never loved her?

'I can make no promises,' said Alex, 'but if you know anything about the plot to ruin the peace pact between England and Scotland, then it is possible that the King might agree to putting you in the care of the nuns at Syon House.'

Ingrid's shoulders slumped. 'I would rather tell

you how Harry deceived me that day you both disappeared. He said that he would meet me, but did not come. Later I received a message saying that he had gone away to leave the way open for you and I to marry.'

Alex did not know if she was telling the truth or not. He swore beneath his breath. 'I can see we are not going to get anywhere until you get this off your chest. Do you know where he went?'

'I thought he had returned to fighting pirates in the northern seas, but recently I met a girl, half-Irish, half-Scottish, who believed differently,' said Ingrid.

Rosamund drew closer to them and watched her intently. 'What was her name and what did she know about Harry?' she asked.

Ingrid spared her a scornful look and addressed Alex. 'She would not reveal any information despite the fact that I followed Edward's mother's instructions to persuade her.'

Rosamund drew in her breath sharply.

Alex glanced at her and their eyes met and he said softly, 'She will pay for her wickedness.'

Rosamund nodded and returned to the settle. Alex faced Ingrid once more. 'What is this girl's name?'

'Bridget McDonald. Her father is a sea captain and kin to Edward. These McDonalds proliferate,' she muttered. 'There are several of them involved in a plot to destroy the King of Scotland.'

Now we are coming to the heart of it, thought Alex.

'And how are they to do that?' asked Lady Elizabeth, suddenly seeming to come to life.

Ingrid glanced at her. 'What is this information worth to you?'

Elizabeth's mouth tightened. 'And what is your neck worth to you, madam? You will answer me!'

A muscle in Ingrid's throat convulsed and she swallowed. 'They believe the best way to do this is by waylaying the new Queen of Scotland's entourage once it has crossed the border. They will kill her before she can give James children of mixed English and Scottish blood, so joining the two royal houses together. They will also steal what they can and murder the rest of her entourage.'

Alex sent an admiring look Rosamund's way.

'This Bridget,' said Rosamund. 'Will we find her at my stepbrother's house in London?'

Ingrid nodded. 'I think she will thank me when she knows I have killed William. His mother and her uncle were arranging a match between them in the hope of getting their hands on the fortune they believe her father has hidden away.'

'Thank you, Ingrid,' said Alex.

He turned to Rosamund and Lady Elizabeth. 'I will leave for London immediately.'

'Take me with you,' said Ingrid. 'I can help you. They trust me.'

'But do we trust you?' said Rosamund in a honeyed voice. 'I think not.'

She glanced at her husband to see what he thought of what Ingrid had said, but he had left the room for their bedchamber. He reappeared a few moments later dressed for riding.

'You will release me before you go?' asked Ingrid eagerly.

'Certainly not,' said Lady Elizabeth with a sniff.

Ingrid cursed her, but was silenced by a banging on the door. A voice shouted that it was the Earl of Derby and they must open up. Lady Elizabeth told Alex to let him in. This he did, stepping aside to allow the elderly Earl and two guardsmen into the chamber.

'I hope you can give me a thorough explanation about what is going on, Beth?' The earl's rheumy eyes gazed into her face before looking at the others in the room. 'I have to inform you that so far Master Fustian has not been found, but the search goes on.'

'A word in your ear, my lord, if you please?' said Alex.

'And you are?'

'Baron Dalsland.'

'Ahhh!'

There followed a whispered conversation, after which the guards were ordered to take the prisoner away and lock her up. Ingrid struggled and told Alex that he was an ungrateful dog and that she would put a curse on him.

'It is very difficult trying to keep that woman quiet,' said Lady Elizabeth. 'Perhaps she should have her tongue ripped out.'

'Godmother!' Rosamund could not help but be shocked by the remark, despite her own antipathy towards Ingrid.

'That would be a foolishness, Beth, if we want to discover if she has any more information that would help us.' The Earl sat down and asked Lady Elizabeth to tell him her story.

She began her tale and, as Rosamund listened, she grew hopeful that she and Alex would be heeded when they recited their part in the events that had taken place. It came to her turn and she had began to relate what had happened when her voice suddenly faltered.

'What is it, my dear?' asked Lady Elizabeth.

'I was just thinking how close we all came to death.'

Alex broke in that point. 'My wife is extremely upset by all that has happened, my lord. I would take her away from the palace back to London immediately.'

'She has done well so far,' said Earl Derby, his brows bristling. 'And the King will most likely want to hear your story himself, Baron. You cannot leave just yet.'

'Aye, but—' began Alex.

Lady Elizabeth placed a hand on the Earl's arm. 'Have pity, Thomas, my poor goddaughter is confused and worn out with all that has taken place. She is with child and it would be terrible indeed if she were to lose the babe due to the deeds of murderous, thieving traitors. Besides, I am ill and I would have my goddaughter accompany me home by barge as soon as possible.'

'Is this true, Baroness, that you are with child?' asked the Earl.

How could Rosamund deny it? She would be seen to be accusing her godmother of lying.

'Of course it is true,' said Alex.

The Earl smiled. 'My best wishes to you both. I will speak to Henry and no doubt he will agree to allow the Baron and Baroness to leave with you in the morning, Elizabeth. Well done, all of you. I am certain it won't be long before we have Master Fustian under lock and key.'

The door closed behind him.

Rosamund looked at Alex and saw that he was looking frustrated. 'What is it?' she asked.

'I must leave now if I am to arrive in London before news reaches your stepmother that William is dead and that Edward faces ruin.'

'But you cannot,' said Rosamund, going over to him. 'You heard what the Earl of Derby said.'

'I know, but if she hears the news before I get there, then she and her kinsman and possibly Edward could take Bridget McDonald and go into hiding. I must leave now,' he said firmly. 'She is the only one who might be able to tell us where Harry is.'

'I understand that, but you would leave me behind?' said Rosamund with a sinking heart.

His face was grave. 'It will not be an easy journey and I will not risk your safety.'

'We have ridden together through the darkness before.'

'But not when you were with child,' he said, against her ear.

'It is not true that I am with child,' she whispered. 'I told you, I have never lain with another man.'

'No. But you have lain with your husband. You could now be carrying our child. You must keep him or her safe. God willing I will see you when you arrive in London tomorrow.'

His hand was on the door when Lady Elizabeth said, 'You take a risk, Baron, disobeying Derby. What if the King sends for you this evening?'

'I am certain you and Rosamund will be able to vouch for my good intentions,' said Alex.

He was through the door when Rosamund called, 'Wait! You would travel alone? What if Edward has escaped the palace with some of his men and they waylay you?'

Alex did not hesitate. 'I should imagine his men have already been put under guard. But I will not go alone. If it makes you happier, I will take Joshua with me, with your permission, Lady Elizabeth?'

'Of course.' Her chest wheezed as she sighed. 'You are quite mad, Baron, just like your grandfather. I was extremely fond of him, you know? May God be with you.'

Alex smiled, blew a kiss at his wife and closed the door behind him.

Lady Elizabeth exchanged glances with her

goddaughter. 'I think it is going to be a long night, my dear.'

Rosamund did not deny it.

It seemed an age before Hannah, accompanied by a couple of servingwomen, brought food and drink. There was a suppressed air of excitement about the maid. But it was not until the food was set on a table and the servingwomen had left that they were to be told her news.

'You will never guess, my lady, what has happened,' said Hannah.

'I am in no mood for guessing games.' Lady Elizabeth yawned. 'I am sleepy, so do not delay, Hannah.'

The maid hastened to tell her tale. 'Apparently, the King sent for one of the Scottish knights, but he could not be found, this despite a search of the palace being made. It is said that the King was angry about that, but he was even more so when it was reported that the woman the Baron questioned has also disappeared.' Her eyes widened with excitement. 'Rumor has it that she was a nun in disguise, but the truth is that she is a witch. They are saying she cast a spell over the guards and flew over the walls on a broomstick.'

Lady Elizabeth made an angry noise. 'Nonsense! Even if the woman were possessed of magic powers, where would she get a broomstick?'

'Easy enough to pick up one of them, my lady,' said Hannah roundly.

'I do not believe it. Someone must have helped her to escape.'

Hannah stiffened. 'I'll say no more, my lady, except that he and she cannot be found anywhere.'

Lady Elizabeth waved her away and, affronted, the maid walked stiff-legged from the room.

'Flying broomsticks,' muttered Lady Elizabeth, reaching for a chicken leg.

'I have heard that belladonna mixed with certain spices and oil can give one the feeling of flying,' said Rosamund in a careful voice. 'A supposed witch could have some mandrake ointment to hand. It can kill if not used with caution.'

'What are you saying, my dear?' Lady Elizabeth glanced across at her. 'You are not eating.'

'I seem to have lost my appetite.' She was thinking a terrible thought about Alex adopting a Scottish accent and helping his erstwhile lover to escape. Surely it was madness to even harbour such a notion? This was what love did to one. It filled a person with such anxiety concerning the loss of the object of that love.

'I am rather of the mind that the Scottish knight could be Sir Andrew Kennedy. Maybe he freed her, or perhaps it was Master Fustian? We do not know.'

'I have thought of someone else who might have helped her,' said Rosamund. 'Lord Bude. Perhaps he is able to adopt an excellent Scottish accent. If it is him, then maybe they will flee the country.'

'It has not been proved that Lord Bude has committed any error yet,' said Lady Elizabeth. 'This is purely conjecture, my dear. If our Scottish knight is a Kennedy, then he will not be concerned about the Ingrid woman. He will head for the border. If it is Fustian, he would be wiser to avoid London. Myself, I believe the Ingrid woman seduced one of the guards to let her go. Now, eat some of this excellent chicken and then it is bed for us if we are to return to London in the morning.'

Rosamund could see the sense in Lady Elizabeth's words. Much better to believe Edward would head north to Appleby and then on to Scotland. She helped herself to chicken and ham and forced herself to eat. If she was already carrying Alex's child, then it must be fed. The coming night would seem long, but dawn would come and hopefully bring with it a bright tomorrow.

* * *

The following morning, after a brief conversation with the Earl of Derby and the King, Lady Elizabeth and Rosamund were allowed to leave for London. A mist hung over the river and Rosamund was glad of her warm cloak as she boarded the barge. All her doubts and fears had resurfaced as she woke from a nightmare of her husband having played her false. Fortunately, the tide was with them, and by midday they had passed the Palace of Westminster. Soon she would know if dreams had any substance, but, God willing, Alex would be at her godmother's mansion to welcome them with good news.

Believing there was no time to delay, a weary Alex left Joshua at Lady Elizabeth's mansion to tend to their horses. His mount had thrown a shoe and this had slowed them down, so that they had arrived in London much later than hoped. As Alex made his way through the foggy streets of London to Cheapside, he could only hope that Walther had ensured a watch was still being kept on Fustian's house. On reaching the area, Alex did not immediately approach the house, but looked about him for Walther or one of his men. There were few people about, but he had not been standing on the corner for long when Walther approached him.

'I did not expect to see you back in London so soon,' said Walther in their own tongue.

Alex explained what had taken place the evening before and his friend let out a low whistle. 'I have been here several hours and have seen no sign of Master Fustian or of anyone going in or out. But I do know that Mistress Fustian left yesterday afternoon with her two daughters.'

'So Bridget McDonald could still be inside with her uncle and Lady Appleby,' said Alex. 'You will stay here and continue to keep watch. I will try to gain entry. Have you someone watching the back of the house?'

Walther nodded. 'If you need a helping hand, there will be more than two of us as I am expecting another man to take over my watch.'

Alex thanked him and then crossed the street and knocked on the door. A voice from within enquired who was there.

'I have news from Richmond and wish to speak to Mistress Fustian,' he answered.

The door opened and immediately he recognised the woman whom Mistress Fustian had addressed as Lady Monica. She had green eyes that slanted like that of a cat and wrinkles at the corners of her mouth. She was dressed in a russet woollen gown and her hair was concealed beneath a veil. Anger threatened to overcome him, faced as he was with the woman who had caused Rosamund so much suffering. It was with difficulty that he managed to rein in his temper and adopt a vague expression. 'You are not Mistress Fustian.'

'No. She has gone away for a few days to stay with her sister. I am Lady Appleby, the mother of Master Fustian. What is it you want?'

Immediately Alex adopted a grave look. 'In any other circumstances I would have been delighted to make your acquaintance, Lady Appleby. As I said, I am newly come from Richmond.'

Her eyes narrowed. 'What do you mean in *any other* circumstances? What news do you have of my sons? Hasn't the King granted Edward his wish? Is he not to be Lord Mayor of London?'

'It is doubtful. Perhaps I may be permitted to come inside to give you my news. You might wish to sit down.'

Lady Appleby looked thoroughly alarmed and seized his sleeve. 'No. Say what you have to say now! Has someone else gained the King's favour?'

Alex brushed her hand from his sleeve. 'Your son is dead.'

The colour drained from Monica Appleby's face and a keening cry left her lips. Then she grabbed his arm and demanded, 'Which son?'

'Your younger son, William.'

Her relief was apparent. 'Why did you not say so first, upsetting me the way you did? What of my son Edward? Is he safe? Why has he not brought me news concerning William's death?'

'Did I hear someone say that William is dead?' asked a voice that held a Scottish lilt.

Alex looked beyond Lady Appleby to the young woman a few feet behind her. 'Aye, mistress. Master William Fustian is dead.'

'You are certain of this?' she demanded.

'Aye.' He estimated her to be sixteen or seventeen summers. She wore a plain brown gown and wisps of auburn hair had escaped her headdress and curled about her heart-shaped face. 'I saw him die, myself. There can be no mistake.'

'This obviously means that the wedding will not take place,' she said, beaming at him.

'Be quiet, Bridget! Have you no sense of what

is fitting?' said Lady Appleby in a cold voice. 'Return to your bedchamber immediately.'

Bridget made no move to do as she was told, but instead said, 'Who are you, sir, so that I know whom to thank for this news?'

'I am Baron Dalsland,' he replied, amazed by her self-possession.

Lady Appleby started back. 'Get in, girl! Go fetch your uncle.'

'I would rather not,' said Bridget.

Lady Appleby brought up her hand and smacked the girl's face. Alex moved swiftly and seized her wrist. 'Do not do that again,' he warned.

'What's going on?' demanded a man's voice in a thick Scottish accent.

Immediately, Bridget ducked beneath Alex's arm and made her escape.

'Now see what you have done,' cried Lady Appleby. 'Unhand me at once, you swine!'

'You heard the lady,' growled the Scotsman, advancing on Alex.

Alex shoved Lady Appleby towards the man, whom he presumed to be her McDonald lover, and turned swiftly on his heel and went after the girl.

He caught a brief glimpse of Walther's surprised face and then it vanished in the mist. He ran on and became aware of the sound of thudding feet to his rear and presumed that McDonald was giving chase. Alex put on a spurt and soon the sounds of pursuit receded into the distance, but in that short time he had lost sight of Bridget McDonald. He came to a sudden halt in front of St Paul's Cathedral.

Could she have gone inside? He did not hesitate, but plunged into its interior, only to find that a mass was taking place and he had no choice but to adopt an attitude of worship whilst out of the corner of his eye, he tried to search the congregation for Bridget. But with so many heads bent in prayer he had an almost impossible task. He could only wait until the service ended and then he hurried to the entrance in the hope of finding the girl on her way out.

Alex stood there, watching all those that left the cathedral, but he could not see her. His expression was grim as he accepted that his reunion with Rosamund would be blighted by the news that he had been within an arm's length of Bridget McDonald, only to lose her.

Chapter Sixteen

'If all had gone well, then surely he should have been here by now,' said Rosamund, trying to remain calm as she planted another stitch in a tear in the hem of her blue gown. She could not bear to lose Alex now when there was a real chance of happiness ahead for them.

Lady Elizabeth said, 'The Baron is no fool. He is not going to walk into a trap. You heard what Joshua said about them arriving in London later than hoped. No doubt the Baron will walk through that door any moment now.'

The words were scarcely out of her mouth when the door opened and Alex entered the parlour. Rosamund's heart leapt in her breast and her relief was so intense that she felt dizzy.

He said without preamble, 'I have bad news. In my haste I lost her and now have no notion of her whereabouts.' He removed his hat and ran a hand through his tawny mane of hair and then went over to the fire and stood gazing into its flames.

'We are talking about Bridget McDonald?' asked Rosamund.

He lifted his head and stared at Rosamund. 'Who else would I mean?'

'No one else,' she said hastily, banishing the unworthy and foolish thought about Ingrid.

He sensed she was not being completely honest with him. 'If you were thinking about your stepmother, then she is still at Fustian's house with McDonald.'

'What happened?' asked Lady Elizabeth.

He told them and both looked relieved. 'At least Bridget McDonald is alive and no longer their prisoner,' said Rosamund, touching Alex's arm. 'You must not blame yourself for what happened. You could not have foreseen her escaping the way she did—also, the weather was against you.'

He smiled wryly. 'That is true, but it might not be easy to find her again.'

'She definitely seems a resourceful girl,' said Rosamund.

'We can organise a search,' said Lady Elizabeth, her eyes brightening. 'Sooner or later the mist will lift and, with the help of my men and your friend Walther and your other accomplices, we will find her.'

Alex warned, 'We are not going to be the only ones searching for her, so we must act swiftly.'

'Do you not think it possible that my stepmother and McDonald will decide to cut their losses and leave the city?' asked Rosamund, presuming he referred to them. 'The news of William's death must have given them some indication that Edward's plans have gone awry.'

'Aye, but it's possible they may linger, hoping for word from him,' said Alex.

'You will never guess what happened after you left,' said Lady Elizabeth, a mischievous glint in her eye.

Alex contained his impatience. 'Tell me,' he said politely.

'Sir Andrew Kennedy and that impudent madam you questioned both vanished from the palace.'

Alex's eyebrows shot up. 'What do you mean— vanished?'

Rosamund bent her head and toyed with the amber-and-silver ring on her finger. 'Someone released Ingrid and, although a search was made, just like Edward, she was not found.'

He stared down at her bent head and wondered if she had allowed herself to doubt him and, despite his words to the contrary, still believed that Ingrid had some power over him. Soon he was going to have to convince his wife without a measure of a doubt that she meant much more to him than Ingrid had ever done.

'Of course! Rumours were flying around that she was a witch and they had flown over the walls on a broomstick,' said Lady Elizabeth. 'I, myself, firmly believe that Sir Andrew and this—this so-called witch will ride for the Scottish border.'

'Whereas I was convinced she would come to London,' said Rosamund, glancing up at him.

'Why?' asked Alex bluntly. 'Do you not deem it possible that Edward could have freed her and set out north for Appleby Manor and from there head for the border?'

'Aye, that could be a possibility,' said Rosamund, 'but I cannot accept it. I do not believe Edward would abandon his mother. There is a bond between them that I now consider quite unhealthy.'

'Rosamund thinks that Lord Bude could have freed Ingrid,' said Lady Elizabeth breathlessly.

Alex slanted a smile at Rosamund. 'Now that is a more likely scenario for me. But let us not be distracted from our purpose—finding Harry, and Bridget McDonald is our key to doing so.'

'You do not deem she might return to Fustian's house?' asked Lady Elizabeth.

'I greatly doubt it, despite her having no cloak or gloves to keep her warm in this freezing fog,' said Alex. 'But if she were to attempt to sneak into the house by a back door, then she will be seen. A watch is being kept in case Lady Appleby and McDonald consider making a run for it.' He looked at Rosamund. 'I was repelled by the way she accepted the news of her younger son's death. It was as if it only mattered to her that Edward lived, so no doubt you are right in your estimation that he will come to London.'

Lady Elizabeth leaned forward and hugged her knees. 'You are presuming that he has not been captured. My kinsman, Derby, is bound to send word to me in the next day or two—that is, if he does not come himself. I will inform him of what you say.'

Alex nodded. 'I must change my garments and I need some refreshments before I go out again.' He left the parlour without a backward glance.

Rosamund wished he had asked her to go upstairs with him. They could have talked in private, but he obviously believed he had no time to waste and considered that she had no part to play in the search for Bridget McDonald. It was possible that he was correct in his presumption, but she resented being expected to just meekly stay in the background with her godmother.

Rosamund stood up. 'Will I ask a servant to bring food and wine here for the Baron?'

'Certainly, my dear. Then we must discuss what is to be done when this young woman is found. It is possible that she will be reluctant to divulge to us the whereabouts of your brother if her own father—who is a McDonald, don't forget—and treasure are involved.'

As Rosamund arranged for refreshments for Alex, she considered her godmother's words. She could see the sense in her reasoning, but deemed there was little point in discussing it before Bridget was found. She would rather be involved in the search.

'I wonder what she was wearing when she escaped and whether she had any coin with her,' said Rosamund, picking up her sewing again.

'Ask the Baron,' said her godmother.

'I will,' she murmured.

Alex did not waste much time in eating and drinking, and talked not at all but to answer

Rosamund's question concerning Bridget McDonald.

'She wore only a brown homespun gown and a plain headdress. I doubt that she would have any coin with her. Can you see your stepmother and the uncle providing her with money?'

Rosamund could not, but if Bridget was as resourceful as she estimated, then it was possible she might have had the wits to obtain pennies from somewhere and sown them into the hem of a gown. Surely she would have given some thought to escaping during her captivity?

When Alex took his leave of Rosamund, he warned her against going beyond the perimeter walls of her godmother's mansion. 'If your stepbrother does reach London, then he will be determined to have his revenge on us. I hope to return before nightfall,' he added, 'but if it so happens that I deem it necessary to follow McDonald and Lady Appleby, then I will do so. If they can lead us to your stepbrother, all the better. This might mean my being absent for a day or more.'

'You will take care,' she said, unable to conceal her concern.

His face softened and he touched her cheek with

a gentle hand. 'Trust me, Rosamund. I do care about our future.'

She felt tears prick the back of her eyes and nodded wordlessly before pressing her lips against his palm. He kissed her and then, with a nod in Lady Elizabeth's direction, hurried from the parlour.

Rosamund spent a few moments composing herself before facing her godmother again. 'I have been thinking that instead of worrying about what to do once Bridget McDonald is your guest, perhaps we should play our part in trying to solve the puzzling question of where she could be hiding.'

'Certainly,' wheezed Lady Elizabeth. 'We have a young woman of some sixteen summers with no cloak or gloves to keep her warm.'

'She might have a little money.' Rosamund divulged her thoughts about coin to Lady Elizabeth. 'We do not know if she has any friends in the city. It is possible that Edward's wife, Marion, would have befriended her as she was staying in her house, but we know from what the Baron told us that Marion has taken her daughters to stay with her sister.'

'Are we to presume that the girl arrived in London on horseback or by ship?' asked Lady Elizabeth.

'Horseback, if she travelled here from Appleby

Manor.' Rosamund paused to consider her poor, misled but unpleasant younger stepbrother, who had been intended for Bridget's husband and prayed God would have mercy on his soul. On a more cheerful note, she thought that at least when Harry did return to reclaim his inheritance he would not have William to contend with and he would certainly appreciate it if their stepmother and Edward were also out of contention. She felt an old familiar chill thinking of them, but then thought of Alex and determinedly did not give way to that paralysing fear of them.

'Is her father not a pirate?' asked Lady Elizabeth.

Rosamund nodded. 'Although, perhaps it is best if we do not use that term when speaking to Mistress McDonald about him, but it does mean that he must have a ship.'

'Would he risk sailing into London?'

'That we cannot know, but it is possible that father and daughter would have means of getting in touch with each other if it was needful.'

'I am convinced, Rosamund, that would be difficult. Ships can be blown off course and end up God only knows where,' said Lady Elizabeth.

'Aye, that is true. But if I were Bridget

McDonald, I might be tempted to haunt the quay-sides and taverns were mariners abound and make enquiries concerning my father's ship.'

Lady Elizabeth shook her head. 'It would not be seemly for a young woman of her age to do so and it would also be dangerous. No, Rosamund, if she is a young woman of sense, then she will seek aid from those who have her well-being at heart.'

Immediately, Rosamund felt deflated. Who could Bridget McDonald turn to if she had no friends in London? Again she considered what she would do if she was in the Scottish girl's shoes and came up with an answer—one that she decided to keep to herself.

To her relief, Alex did return to the house several hours later. Over supper he informed them that a man had arrived on horseback and entered Fustian's house. He had remained inside and after a short while a wagon had drawn up at the front door and several items had been loaded onto it, including a large trunk. It had departed, taking with it the first man, whom Alex and Walther had presumed to be a messenger. A couple of men had been despatched to follow the wagon whilst Alex remained on watch so that Walther could slip home and have a meal and rest. He had returned to relieve Alex, so he could get some sleep after what had been an extremely long day.

Rosamund had planned to talk to her husband about some of her thoughts concerning Bridget McDonald once they had retired to their bedchamber. As it was, her hopes were not realised; no sooner had Alex's head touched the pillow than he fell into a deep sleep. She spent a restless night, only to drop off just before dawn.

When eventually she awoke, it was to find that she was alone in the bed. She performed her *toilette* swiftly, dressed and hurried downstairs, only to discover that Alex had already left the house.

Frustrated by his lack of communication, she was tempted to follow him, but she remembered what happened last time she had gone out alone behind the perimeter walls and changed her mind. As it was, that proved to be the sensible course; no sooner had Rosamund and Lady Elizabeth finished breakfast than they had a visitor in the elderly person of the Earl of Derby.

Her ladyship welcomed him warmly and Rosamund would have excused herself if he had not waved her to a chair. 'Sit down, my dear. I hope you are both well and recovered from the attack on your persons?'

'Indeed, we have, Thomas,' answered Lady Elizabeth. 'What news do you have from Richmond? Have you caught those villains yet?'

He grimaced. 'I am not here to talk of them, Beth, I bring other tidings. But I will tell you, while I remember, that Kennedy's reason for leaving so precipitously was due to news that his son is dangerously ill and his wife requested his presence at the bedside,' he said drily. 'As for the Fustian fellow, there has been no sighting of him, but his barge was seen being rowed away yesterday just after noon. It was out of sight before anyone thought to report the incident.'

'Now that is interesting,' said Lady Elizabeth. 'Have you discovered yet if it has tied up here in London?'

'The matter is being looked into, but I expect naught to come of it. The Fustian fellow is not going to hang around waiting to be arrested.'

'Well, I can tell you, Thomas, that the Baron has not been slow in visiting Fustian's home and is having a watch kept on the building,' said Lady Elizabeth, 'but so far he has not shown up.'

Derby nodded sagely. 'I tell you, ladies, that the

Baron is wasting his time. Fustian will be heading for the border. I must be on my way.' He rose to his feet. 'Oh, the other news I had for you. It is the Queen. She is at her apartments in the Tower for her confinement. We are all praying that she will be safely delivered of a son.'

'I, too, will pray for her,' said Lady Elizabeth. 'I suppose this means that the celebrations have come to an end and your Scottish visitors are preparing to depart for their northern lands?'

'Aye. But Margaret will not be accompanying them. She awaits news of her mother and the child.'

Lady Elizabeth looked relieved and went with him to the front door, leaving Rosamund sitting by the fire. She wondered what Alex would say when he heard the latest tidings from Richmond.

Rosamund did not have long to wait as he arrived back at the house in time for the midday meal. He greeted her with a smile and asked when they were alone whether she was feeling any aftereffects from the blow on her head.

'It aches a little, but otherwise I am well,' she answered, warmed by his solicitude.

'Good.' He took her hand and nursed it in his

own. 'I beg your forgiveness for having spent so little time with you since returning to London.'

Rosamund assured him that she understood why he was so occupied. 'But while you were out we had a visit from the Earl of Derby. He told us news that will be of interest to you.'

His expression sharpened. 'Tell me!'

'Edward's barge was seen being rowed away yesterday afternoon. No one thought to report it immediately because the Queen was making her departure to the Tower for her lying-in.'

Alex's eyes gleamed with satisfaction. 'This is indeed good news. The wagon that left Fustian's house yesterday was taken to a warehouse close to a wharf the other side of London Bridge. It would not surprise me if today we were to discover Fustian's barge tied up at a quayside close by.'

'You think you will find Edward there?'

'Possibly,' he answered, 'but it could be that we only find his mother and McDonald. It is likely that Fustian sent the message yesterday and no doubt they have passed on the news to him that not only has Bridget McDonald escaped their charge, but that they've had a visit from the Baron Dalsland.'

'But where would they go in a barge? Surely it

is not made for sea travel? They would need a real sailing ship for such a journey.'

'That is true, but I deem that it is most likely their intention to leave London by sea,' said Alex, 'despite the risk of serious storms at this time of year.'

'But you will be paying a visit to the barge?' said Rosamund.

'Certainly, but you need not fear that I am fool enough to walk into a trap of Fustian's making again. He would have to use exceptional bait to lure me this time. So do not disobey me, Rosamund, and remain within these walls,' he said strongly.

Rosamund grimaced. 'I did so want to visit St Paul's to pray for the Queen's safe delivery. I had even thought that I might see Bridget McDonald there. Surely she will want to pray for deliverance from her enemies and the safe return of her father.'

For a moment Alex was silent, and then he said, 'I will escort you there. I can understand your frustration in having to stay here when you are anxious to discover if she really does know Harry's whereabouts.'

'Indeed!' Rosamund's face lit up. 'I will go and fetch my cloak.'

As she fastened the ties on the plain brown cloak, one of the ties came loose. Knowing that she had no time to sew it back on, she took Harry's silver brooch and used that to pin it together. Then she joined her husband and hurried from the house.

For a while they walked in silence and then Rosamund said hesitantly, 'A thought has occurred to me, regarding your search for Bridget McDonald.'

Alex gazed into her rosy face. 'I am listening,' he said gravely.

'If she were to have even a single penny on her person, she would be able to purchase some used clothes. I am thinking of male garb. Dressed as a youth, she would be able to enter taverns and saunter along the quayside without too much fear of being spotted. She could ask questions of mariners as to whether they have seen her father's ship in a far-flung port—or even a harbour in these islands of ours.'

Alex stilled. 'Now why did I not consider her taking such measures?'

Rosamund smiled. 'Because you have never been a woman in desperate need.'

'There is that, of course,' he said drily. 'I will speak to Walther and ask him if Maud has had an auburn-haired Scottish lass for a customer.'

'Perhaps it would be best if you did that immediately,' said Rosamund. 'I will go to St Paul's alone.'

'No,' said Alex firmly.

'Then I will not go! There is no time to waste.'

'I will escort you back to the house and then visit Maud myself, and if her answer is as you suggest, then I will scour the taverns and the waterfront,' he said, his eyes alight with determination.

Rosamund opened her mouth to ask, *could she not come with him?,* but already he was dragging her by the hand through the crowded streets.

There came a moment when Rosamund's arm was tugged from Alex's and she lost contact with him. She looked for him and became aware that she was the focus of a pair of curious hazel eyes. The hooded figure drew closer and briefly touched the brooch at her throat. Instantly Rosamund covered the silver cross of Thor's hammer.

'That is a rare gift,' said the youth.

'It belongs to my brother,' responded Rosamund.

The youth backed off as Alex appeared, looking anxious. 'What happened to you? I feared that Fustian had—'

'I'm safe,' she reassured him, 'although, a moment ago, I thought I was in danger of having Harry's brooch stolen.'

'You were not hurt? Who did this?'

Rosamund turned to where she had last seen the youth, but he was no longer there. Alex wasted no time escorting her back to Lady Elizabeth's mansion. He did not linger, but left immediately. Rosamund retired to her bedchamber, for she wanted to be alone so she could ponder on the events of that day and spend some time in prayer. Then she lay on her bed and fell asleep.

On waking, Rosamund swilled her face with cold water and then wandered over to the window and gazed out, hoping to catch sight of Alex approaching the house. There was no sign of him, but she stayed there, watching and hoping. Suddenly she saw movement close to the perimeter wall. Instantly, her heart seemed to climb into her throat and she drew back behind the curtain. Her pulse was racing because she feared that, despite all Alex's determination to protect her from her stepbrother, Edward could reach her even here and steal her away from her husband.

She peered around the curtain, but there was no sign of anyone. Were her eyes playing tricks on her? Then, as she watched, a figure appeared from out of the trees. She was relieved to see that it was much too small and slight to be her stepbrother. It moved cautiously away from the trees and then suddenly stopped and dived into the shrubbery. Could it be a burglar out to steal Lady Elizabeth's jewellery?

Anger and curiosity overcame Rosamund's fear and she left her bedchamber. Outside the door in the passageway there was a chest. Just as she had hoped, there was a lighted lantern and several unlit candles on top of it. She lit a candle and went downstairs. All was quiet, except for voices and clattering coming from the kitchen. She slid silently past it and out of a door at the far end. There was only the slightest breeze, but it blew out the candle.

She stood a moment, letting her eyes become accustomed to the starlight and then she made for the trees close to the perimeter wall. She had not gone far when, sensing someone behind her, she turned. The blow caught her on the side of her face. A rag was stuffed into her mouth and a sack pulled over her head. She was heaved on to someone's shoulder and carried away.

Chapter Seventeen

Rosamund woke. Her head throbbed and her eyelids fluttered open on to pitch darkness. Panic spiralled inside her and she kicked out, only to discover that she was enclosed in the confines of some coarse material. Only one person could have done this to her and that must be Edward. She clawed at the sacking in an attempt to find a break in the fabric so she could pick at it and make a hole.

'Keep still, Rosie,' said a hated familiar voice. 'You are wasting your time.'

'Where are you taking me?' Her heart thudded in her chest and she hugged herself in an attempt to stop herself from trembling.

'Wouldn't you like to know? If you stay quiet and listen, then you might be able to deduce where you are,' said Edward.

Wherever I am, I am in danger from you! she thought. Nevertheless, she remained still and listened. Gradually, she became aware of rocking and the muffled sound of what she presumed were oars propelling them through water.

'Hazard a guess,' he said.

'You are taking me to your barge,' she said breathlessly.

'Now that is a good guess, but wrong.' He laughed and the noise terrified her because it was so similar to the sound that haunted her nightmares.

Rosamund told herself that she must not show fear. 'I don't believe you. My husband will soon realise it is you who has abducted me and then you'll be sorry.'

'Not if he's dead he won't,' said Edward. 'He destroyed all my plans and this time he won't be coming back from the dead.' She felt as if ice encased her heart and her mouth went dry and she was unable to speak. 'Lost your tongue?' asked Edward with another of those insane giggles.

'I wish Ingrid had killed you instead of William,' she managed to say.

'What do you mean, Ingrid killed him? It was the Baron who did so.' There was no laughter in his voice this time.

Rosamund smiled in the darkness. 'Is that what she told you?'

He was silent for a long time and she wished she knew what he was thinking. No doubt he was plotting something evil to happen to Ingrid now.

'No matter,' he said abruptly. 'The Baron really has proved himself a nuisance. I tried to get rid of him once before, but, just like Harry, he refused to die. I wish I knew where your brother is, but irritatingly I don't. He sailed away, not knowing his father had recognised him, leaving a farewell note to the Baron, saying he did not want to lose his friendship because of Ingrid. Your fool of a father came to me and told me he had seen a man he believed to be Harry. He had no idea that Mother was behind his disappearance, but had this notion that someone had rescued Harry from the river where he had received a bang on the head and lost his memory.'

'So you decided you had to get rid of Father?'

'What else could I do? He was going to give all that would have come to me to Harry. I couldn't have that now, could I?'

She heard the sound of liquid splashing about and then of swallowing. Was he drinking and getting soundly drunk?

'Of course, I still hoped that Harry's ship would founder somewhere and he'd end up at the bottom of the sea, but I couldn't guarantee that happening. Also, your father told me that he'd spoken to the Baron, so he had to be silenced, as well. He still needs silencing, because Harry might just return. I regret I'll have to close your mouth for good, too. But first we will enjoy ourselves together, Rosie. At least I will find great pleasure in our times together. You might not. What do you say?'

She remained silent.

'Perhaps it's best you save your voice for screaming. I do believe we're here.'

Rosamund fought her fear, wondering where *here* was—no doubt she would soon find out. Wherever it was, she was determined to fight Edward to her last breath, even as she prayed that somehow Alex would find her.

She heard another man's voice and the next moment she was lifted and dragged over something hard. She suspected it was wood. When she heard the creak of ropes and was emptied out of the sack as if she was a hunk of meat, the smell of the sea came to her on the breeze. She looked up and saw a mast with a furled sail and stars twinkling in a midnight-blue sky. *He was going to take her out to sea!* Then waves of fear swept over her and she almost gave up hope of Alex ever finding her.

'Take the boat over to the barge where Ranald McDonald and my mother will be waiting. I expect you to return within the hour with the news that the Baron is dead.'

Rosamund struggled upright, having no intention of being forced to go where she did not want to. Almost immediately she collapsed on to the deck because her feet were so cold that they could not hold her. She cursed Edward.

'Devil take you, Rosie, do you have to swear? Remember you are a Baroness, and show some dignity.' Edward seized her by her hair and dragged her along the deck. She fought all the way, gritting her teeth as she dug her fingernails into the planking. He lifted her head and thrust his face into hers. 'When are you going to learn it does not pay for you to resist me?'

'Is it not time you learnt that my wife is always going to resist your evil intent?' said the voice that Rosamund had begun to believe she might never hear again.

The curse died on Edward's lips as Alex plucked him by the back of his cloak and heaved him upright. He spun him round and smashed his fist into Edward's face. The strength from the blow sent Edward skidding across the deck.

Rosamund heard the hiss of her stepbrother's breath escaping as he crashed into the side of the ship. She let out a yell of pure joy. Alex bent over her and lifted her upright. Her fingers clutched his doublet and her lips found his and they kissed briefly but passionately. Then he set her aside and faced Edward, who had managed to struggle to his feet.

Rosamund caught the glint of starlight on the blade in his hand and cried out, 'Beware, Alex, he is armed.'

'Aye, love,' he murmured, before moving gracefully as a dancer towards their enemy.

She wanted to join in the fight and clenched her fists and looked about her for a weapon, but could see none. The men warily circled each other and now she could see that Alex had his own blade. Then they were grappling with each other and moments later one of the weapons came sliding along the deck towards her. She bent and picked it up and realised it was Harry's short-sword. How had it come here? Alex must have had it. A despairing cry escaped her and she ran across the deck. As she reached the two men, she heard a gurgling sound and then one staggered back and collapsed at her feet.

Fear clutched her heart, but it lasted only a moment because she realised that the man before her on his knees was her stepbrother. There was an expression of disbelief on his face as his fingers clung to the hilt of the dagger in his chest. She did not hesitate, but placed a foot on his shoulder and pushed him over on to his back.

'At last you have paid for the death of my father,' she said.

Edward made a strangled sound and then his eyes glazed over.

Rosamund looked up and saw Alex standing close by and she dropped Harry's short-sword and threw herself into her husband's arms. 'How did you find me?' she whispered against his shoulder.

'You were seen being carried off,' he replied, hugging her close.

'By Joshua?'

'No! He was with me. Besides, if he had seen what happened, then he would have confronted Fustian and his fellow conspirator. Your saviour was much smaller and she used her wits to the best advantage.'

'She?'

Alex held Rosamund a little away from him so he could see her face. 'Aye. I suppose I will have to become accustomed to having a clever wife around.'

A voice came out of the shadows. 'Baron Dalsland, have you forgotten about me?'

He did not reply, but Rosamund stared at the slight figure standing there. 'Who are you?' she asked, even though she sensed that they had already met.

'Bridget McDonald.' She came forward. 'I never knew Black Harry had a sister until a few hours ago.'

'You're that youth who admired Harry's brooch!' Rosamund held out a hand to her.

Bridget clasped it firmly and smiled ruefully. 'Indeed I am. You can have no idea how I felt when I saw you wearing the cross of Thor's hammer. The last time I saw it was when Black Harry and my father set sail for the New World.'

Rosamund gasped. 'My brother's aim was to cross the Great Ocean? I don't want to believe it. It is such a dangerous journey to make.'

'Oh, it's true enough,' said Bridget, her eyes glinting. 'I wanted to go with them, but Black Harry put his foot down and said he wouldn't allow it.'

'What did your father say?' asked Rosamund, fascinated by this insight into her brother's life.

Bridget said indignantly, 'When I would have argued with your brother, my father took me aside and said, "You don't mess about with Black Harry. He knows what is right for you!" I was furious because in the past I sailed with my father many times and I resented your brother parting us.'

'How long is it since you last saw them?' asked Rosamund.

Before Bridget could reply, Alex drew his wife close to him once more. 'The rest would be better told indoors. You will catch a chill if we linger here any longer.'

Rosamund stayed him with a hand to his chest and looked up into his rugged face. 'During all the days I spent on horseback with you, did I ever catch a chill?' she demanded. 'I need to know the rest about Harry now—' She looked at Bridget. 'But first, am I correct in presuming that you were the figure I saw in the garden earlier?'

Bridget nodded. 'I followed you home. Of course, I had recognised the Baron, but I was not sure whether I could trust him. To cut a long story short, I have since decided that I can trust you both,' she added with aplomb.

'I deem I can tell my wife the rest of your story later, Mistress McDonald,' said Alex firmly.

'Despite her protestations, I find standing on this deck exceeding chilly. Let's away to Lady Elizabeth's and a warm fire and a hot drink.'

This time neither of the women argued with him. Rosamund picked up her brother's short-sword and thrust it through her girdle. Alex spoke to one of his accomplices and left him to deal with Edward's body. Then he helped the two women into a boat and rowed them across the river. On the way, he told Rosamund how he, Joshua and Walther and several other accomplices had raided Edward's barge and discovered not only Lady Appleby and her kinsman aboard the vessel, but also Lord Bude and Ingrid.

'Bude and Ingrid were willing to talk for the price of their freedom,' he said.

'You mean you let them go?' asked Rosamund, astonished.

Alex said gruffly, 'They left empty-handed.'

'What do you mean, empty-handed?'

'Lady Elizabeth has not yet realised it, but a burglary took place at her mansion whilst we were at Richmond. It was Bude who provided the gang of thieves with the information concerning the layout of her house and the kind of valuables she owned. Fortunately she had taken her most precious jewels with her to Richmond, but amongst the booty I found Harry's short-sword. I thought you'd be happy to have it returned to you.'

'That was exceedingly generous of you,' said Rosamund, smiling now. 'I almost had an apoplexy when it came sliding across the deck to me. I thought Edward had stabbed you.'

He shook his head at her in reproof. 'You should really learn to trust me more.'

'I do now,' she said with a twinkle.

He grinned. 'Good. When I allowed Bude and Ingrid to escape, I believed at the time that I had no choice if I was to discover where Fustian was taking you. As it was, Mistress McDonald had seen you being abducted and had followed as best she could. But she had no boat, so she decided to seek me out.'

'But how did she find you so quickly?'

'It was pure chance or fate, call it what you will,' said Alex. 'Walther spotted Bridget, recognised the youth's clothes that you had worn when he first set eyes on you and realised that Maud must have sold them to her. He told Joshua, who swiftly had the message relayed to me. So all's well that ends well.'

Rosamund wondered whether he felt he owed

Ingrid a kind gesture for misjudging her six months ago. It was probably best if she, herself, put the Danish woman out of her thoughts and concentrated instead on thinking about what she and Alex would have to say to each other once they were alone.

When they arrived back at Lady Elizabeth's mansion, it was to learn that her ladyship had retired for the night. Rosamund took it upon herself to direct one of the servants to prepare a bedchamber for Bridget. Over cups of mulled wine the young Scottish woman told the rest of her story.

'It was six months ago since *Thor's Hammer* set sail. My father had lost his own ship in a battle with Irish pirates, along with his treasure. Fortunately, we escaped with our lives. Still, when he met Black Harry and they recalled the days they had spent together in Harry's youth, Father declared himself ripe for an adventure that would regain him his lost fortune, but honestly this time. So they set sail and I have not heard from them since.'

'But they could be dead,' burst out Rosamund.

The corners of Bridget's mouth drooped and her shoulders slumped. 'I know,' she said forlornly.

'Yet my instincts tell me that they are still alive. Besides, what I knew of Christopher Columbus's voyage across the great ocean to the New Indies convinced me that they should be on their way home by now. Working on that supposition, I decided to make enquiries amongst the mariners to be found in the taverns and boats down by the river. Anyway, when I saw you wearing Black Harry's amulet, or one I thought similar to it, I went in search again of a mariner who told me that he had seen *Thor's Hammer* in the harbour of Ilha da Madeira.'

'Where is that?' asked Rosamund, her hope of finding her brother renewed.

'It is an island off the coast of Africa and I am determined to go there,' said Bridget firmly. 'Somehow I will find the money and a captain who will take me there.'

'God grant you your wish,' said Rosamund, glancing up at her husband with a question in her eyes.

Alex knew what she was asking of him, but decided that the hour was too late to discuss the matter now. He dragged her up from the settle. 'Let us go to bed. You have been through a frightening time and need your rest.'

Bridget also rose. 'Thank you for your kindness in listening to me. I would also like to go to bed now.'

'I'll have a servant show you up,' said Rosamund. 'I would do so myself, but I do not know where all the rooms are here.'

Bridget smiled. 'It is of no importance. God grant you a good night's sleep.'

When Alex and Rosamund reached their bed-chamber, he drew her towards him. After the shock of nearly losing her, he wanted her in his arms again. He had not expected that in such a short space of time she would have become so vitally important to his well-being. He kissed her with mounting ardour and she responded with an eagerness that inflamed his senses. He tore at her clothes with impatient fingers and in no time at all she was naked. Only then did he pause to look with blazing eyes at the smooth contours of her body, the skin of which appeared molten gold in the firelight.

'You are beautiful,' he breathed.

'Am I?' Her voice was just a husky thread.

'Are you? You still need to ask me that? My God, Rosamund. Accept my word, for I speak the truth,' he said fiercely. 'I could not bear to lose you.'

Alex began to unfasten his shirt and then

suddenly she was on her knees on the bed up close to him. She brushed aside his hands and took over the task. She eased off his shirt and together they removed his woollen vest. She could feel his stomach quivering as she touched the hard muscles. But she hesitated when her hand rested a moment on the fastenings of his hose.

'Too much, too soon, to expect you to—touch me—there,' he croaked.

She lifted her gaze and stared into his face and such a desire to please him welled up inside her. 'You saved me from Edward's foul attentions. If it would give you pleasure, my husband, may I continue?'

'Aye to both questions, wife,' he answered in a throaty whisper.

She seized his face between her hands and kissed him hard. Then she unfastened his hose and peeled them down the long corded muscles of his shanks and calves and dropped them beside his shirt. It would have been impossible for her to ignore his manhood, but she only had enough courage to touch it once lightly with a fingertip. That was enough for Alex. He flung her on the bed and kissed every delicious curve and sensitive spot of her body before taking her in a storm of passion. Afterwards Rosamund lay in a relaxed state curled up against her husband's back and almost immediately she fell asleep.

When they woke it was morning and they could hear the patter of rain on the window. Alex got up and drew the curtain and looked outside. It was a dreary day. He smiled at Rosamund. 'Shall we go back to bed?'

Rosamund held out her arms and he went into them.

Later, whilst they were having breakfast with her godmother and Bridget, they told Lady Elizabeth all that had taken place yesterday. Alex also returned to her the iron box that they had found on the barge. It might not have contained her most expensive jewellery, but there were still many items of value in it. She was delighted to see it and immediately decided to send for her lawyer.

'No doubt you will need a man of good sense to deal with your stepmother's lawyer,' said Elizabeth. 'Now your stepbrothers are dead, Rosamund, and we have some notion of Harry's whereabouts, then matters can be put into motion to see that the business and property they claimed illegally is made over to him.'

Alex agreed, but added, 'Harry has yet to be found and so preparations must be made for a couple of ships to make the journey to Ilha da Madeira to discover if *Thor's Hammer* is still there. It would make sense to talk some more with the mariner who gave the information to Bridget.'

Bridget leaned forward across the table. 'I beseech you, Baron, that you will allow me to travel on one of these ships?'

Alex said seriously, 'I will give your request much consideration, Mistress McDonald. It will take a little while before they can be made ready for such a long voyage. Besides, it would be best to wait until the storms of winter are over before setting sail.'

'But what if Black Harry's ship was to leave Ilha da Madeira before then?' cried Bridget.

Alex said, 'Harry is too good a sailor to risk setting out in such inclement weather, although it is possible that he might set sail for Sweden or England as my ships head in the opposite direction. It makes sense to wait at least until April to see if he returns. If he does not do so, then my ships will set sail at the beginning of May. God

willing they reach their destination—if it is discovered that *Thor's Hammer* had already departed
before they arrived there, then surely someone on
that island will know Harry's destination.'

'It seems a long time to wait,' said Bridget,
frowning.

'I know,' said Alex, 'but it is just as difficult for
Rosamund to contain her impatience. Even so,
you must both do so.'

Rosamund said, 'What Alex says is true, Bridget.'

'In the meantime you must stay here, Mistress
McDonald,' said Lady Elizabeth.

Bridget's relief was apparent. 'That is kind of
you, Lady Elizabeth. I admit to not having come
to a decision about what I was to do before setting
sail. Thank you.' She turned to Alex. 'What will
happen to my uncle and Lady Monica?'

'They will be brought to trial for treason and attempted murder,' he said.

'As is just,' she murmured.

'What of Bude and Ingrid?' asked Rosamund.
'I presume you had them followed, Alex?'

He nodded. 'Aye. I am now of the opinion that
they will either take refuge at Bude's place in the
country if they decide to stay together, or, if
they decide to separate, then it is possible that

Ingrid will seek sanctuary at Syon House and Bude might go north of the border.' He rose to his feet. 'In the meantime, if you will excuse my wife and me, Lady Elizabeth…' he inclined his leonine head in her direction '…Mistress McDonald, there are matters we need to discuss,' he said.

'Of course, of course,' said Lady Elizabeth. 'There is still much I would hear from Mistress McDonald about her father and I would know why Harry is called *Black Harry*.'

'I have no idea,' sighed Bridget. 'It would be interesting to have that explained.'

Alex tugged on Rosamund's hand. 'Come, let us go,' he said in a low voice.

She went with him. 'Are we to speak of lawyers, business and property for Harry's sake?' she teased.

He smiled. 'Hopefully Edward has not bled the company dry, but I am certain we will be able to turn it around again if that is so. But rather what is on my mind is that I need to visit my father and report to him my findings at the Palace of Richmond.'

'May I come with you?'

'I was not planning on going without you. I would like your opinion of my father.'

'One of the Earls of Douglas, is he?' she asked, raising an eyebrow.

Alex smiled. 'I said you were clever.'

She chuckled. 'Perhaps he'll give you the opportunity to get to know him better this time. What do you think about us living in your Scottish house until Harry reappears?'

'I am glad you can speak so positively of Harry's return. If it would make you happy then of course we will spend some time in the Scottish house. My father did tell me that he and my mother spent many happy hours there.'

'Perhaps you will find a sense of your mother's presence in that place,' said Rosamund.

'That thought never occurred to me.' He sounded surprised.

'Then think of it now,' said Rosamund.

He drew her towards him. 'I will. Perhaps my father will fill in the gaps of my knowledge of her that my grandparents couldn't.'

They were comfortably silent for a while. Then he said, 'How long ago it seems since we met.'

'Yet it is less than a month ago,' she murmured, raising her head and gazing at him. 'This time when we set out on our travels I will not run away from you.'

His eyes twinkled. 'I would only bring you back if you did. I am never going to let you go now you are mine. I love you, Rosamund.'

Rosamund was extremely glad to hear those words. 'And I love you.'

They kissed, and for a while there was naught else in their heads but the desire to show the other just how much they loved. Their lives had changed so much within this past month and now they had a future together. Yet, although Alex had completed the task that his father had asked of him and he had found the love of his life, he had not completed his self-appointed task of finding Harry.

As if his wife could read his thoughts, Rosamund suddenly said, 'Harry must be found. I want him to feel as loved as we both do.'

'Aye,' said Alex, remembering that Harry had sailed away in the belief that he was leaving the way open for Alex to be happy. He had achieved what he had set out to do, but not in the way he had intended. Still, if it had not been for Harry's noble gesture, Alex would never have gone in search of him and found Rosamund. He felt a surge of happiness, but mingling with that emotion was the longing to see his dearest friend. There was so much he had to tell him and he determined to waste no time setting in motion all that was needed to find him.

Epilogue

'Are you sure about this, Godmother?' asked Rosamund worriedly for the umpteenth time.

'As sure as one can be of anything in life, my dear,' wheezed Lady Elizabeth, tying a scarf over her hat so the sea breezes would not carry it away. 'Sea air is supposed to be good for one and Bridget must have a chaperon. I know the Baron has decided Joshua Wood is the right man to act as her protector on the journey and he has supplied her with a maid, but Bridget needs a woman of sense to prevent her from behaving in an unseemly fashion. You never heard some of the tales she told me when she sailed with her father.' The old lady rolled her eyes. 'He sounds an exciting rogue and I have rediscovered my taste for travel.'

Rosamund could not help but laugh. 'All right!

I accept that you have made the right decision. I only wish that Alex and I were going with you.'

Lady Elizabeth placed a hand on her goddaughter's belly. 'My dear, I expect you to take care of this proxy grandchild of mine and the Baron to take care of you. Hopefully by the time I return you will have been delivered safely and I can take him or her in my arms and my cup of happiness will runneth over.'

'I pray that it will be as you say.' Rosamund kissed the old woman warmly and determined to hold her tears at bay.

At that moment, Alex and Bridget approached. 'It is time to go, Rosamund, or the Master will miss the tide.'

Rosamund faced Bridget and thought that young woman looked both excited and scared. Impulsively Rosamund placed her arms about her and gave her a hug. Then she stepped back and her violet-blue eyes shone with tears. 'May our Lord and Saviour, His Holy Mother and all the saints be with you on this journey. I pray that your search will be successful and that you all will come home safely.' Her voice broke and her hand searched blindly for that of her husband's.

Alex gripped it tightly; although there was part of him that wanted the thrill of adventuring at sea and continuing the search for Harry, himself, the greater part of him knew that he belonged at Rosamund's side, that her safety and well-being and that of their child was the more important. He had entrusted the task of finding Harry to Bridget, Joshua and Lady Elizabeth and now he must trust them to succeed.

His arm went about his wife's shoulders and he assisted her down the gangplank. Then they both stood on the quayside, watching and waving until they could no longer see their friends clearly; only then did they both turn and, arm in arm, walk away.

* * * * *

HISTORICAL

Large Print

DEVILISH LORD, MYSTERIOUS MISS
Annie Burrows

The menacing Lord Matthison has the reputation of the
devil, but secretly still yearns for his one true love, lost seven
years ago. Cora Montague's body was never found, and
when he encounters a fragile-looking woman, the image
of his betrothed, Matthison is convinced Cora still lives.
But what should he do to claim her…?

TO KISS A COUNT
Amanda McCabe

Leaving Sicily, Count di Fabrizzi and her heart behind
her, Thalia Chase returns to England. She's shocked to see
him again in Bath – with a suspected thief! The Count's
dangerous mission doesn't leave room for beautiful Thalia.
But what is a gentleman to do when a lady is so insistent
on adventure, and so very passionate…?

THE EARL AND THE GOVERNESS
Sarah Elliott

Isabelle desperately needed the governess position William
Stanton, Earl of Lennox offered her. However, working for
the green-eyed Earl is more of a challenge than she expected!
When their passion explodes in a bone-melting kiss, Isabelle
knows she must leave. But the Earl has other plans for
his innocent governess…

MILLS & BOON®

HISTORICAL

Large Print

COMPROMISED MISS
Anne O'Brien

Despite being unconscious at the time, Lucius has been accused of compromising a lady! Now he must marry Miss Harriette Lydyard. The Earl of Venmore is lethally attractive, and Harriette knows she should refuse him. But her reputation is in tatters – she must make a pact with this disreputable, dangerous devil of a man!

THE WAYWARD GOVERNESS
Joanna Fulford

Claire Davenport flees to Yorkshire, where enigmatic Marcus, Viscount Destermere, employs her as a governess. Revenge has all but consumed Marcus until Claire enters his life. She is irresistible – but forbidden fruit. Then their secrets threaten them both and Marcus realises he cannot let happiness slip through his fingers again…

RUNAWAY LADY, CONQUERING LORD
Carol Townend

Lady Emma of Fulford is a fallen woman and desperate to escape the brutish father of her son. She begs honourable Sir Richard of Asculf for help – and offers the only thing she has…herself. Sir Richard is only human, and Lady Emma tempts him. Can this conquering knight tame his runaway lady and stop her running for good?

MILLS & BOON